BLOOD QUEEN

SIERRA ROWAN

AUTHOR'S NOTE

If you would like content guidance, please see the author's website at sierrarowan.com.

1

WREN

The world was bright.

I blinked, looking around in confusion. A white sky hung above me, no definition to it to give me any sense of depth. The ground beneath my feet was soft and obscured by swirling fog, all of it glowing like moonlight. I couldn't feel heat or cold.

Or pain.

I spun in place, my eyes darting everywhere. Was I dead? Was this what vampire heaven looked like?

"I'm sorry."

At the voice behind me, I turned back quickly.

Tauluria stood only a short distance from me. The vampire princess I'd been in a past life was surrounded by light, her dark hair stirring as the clouds swirled around her. Leather armor covered her body—the outfit she'd had on when she died—but it glistened like it was touched with starlight.

"What is this?" I asked.

A sorrowful smile lifted the corners of Tau's lips, such resignation in the expression that it made me want to cry. She reached out, placing her fingertips just above my heart. "It's ending the same as before." Grief filled her eyes. "He wins."

"—get your asses in here. She's waking up."

I opened my eyes. I was on my back, nothing but concrete and metal all around.

Instantly, fear shot through me. Oh, God, I was a prisoner of the rabids again. They had me in that same tiny closet, and any moment, they'd turn their speakers on and try to drive me mad.

I shot upright, and the world spun.

Hands took my shoulders.

I shrieked, only to fall with a strangled sound as pain caught up to me, lancing through my chest like someone had stabbed me with a stake of pure fire. My vision swirled in a kaleidoscope of agony, turning everything wavy and fragmented like I was looking through carnival glass.

But there had been something...

Blurred images played through my mind too fast to catch. A street. We'd been fighting rabids. And then...

Amalie. She'd thrown something at me that looked like... like a *spear*.

Gasping and blinking to try to make my vision clear, I looked toward my shoulder, seeking the source of the pain.

My eyes focused on my skin and then went wide. Between my collarbone and my left breast, an explosion of pitch-black ink stained my skin, stark above the hem of my white tank top. The core of it was a circle, scabbed over and yet dark as night where the spear had stabbed me. The darkness radiated away from it like a starburst, the black ink twisting and becoming thinner the farther it extended from the center.

Like whatever the hell this was, it was *in* me, tracing my veins.

My breath came in ragged gasps, and I tried to sit up again.

The hands pushed me back before I made it very far. "Don't move," a rough, rasping voice said.

My eyes flashed to the side and found Liam.

Relief flooded through me. This wasn't like before. Maybe I was trapped in a cell, and even if I wouldn't wish that on anyone, I also wanted to sob because I wasn't alone.

"Wren."

I blinked, my vision still swirly but slowly bringing more details into focus. Asher stepped closer and crouched down beside me, taking my other hand.

Trembling, I gripped him hard. "A-are we..." My voice was thready. "Did they catch us?"

God, it was painful to speak. To *breathe*. What the hell was wrong with me?

From the worried look the men shared, some of my confusion must have made it onto my face. "You've been hurt," Asher told me.

I swallowed hard, trying to find more of my voice. "W-what happened?"

Liam threw Asher another glance and then slid his hands around my shoulders, gently lifting me. More of the room came into view, and a shudder racked me at the sight. The space was larger than I'd originally thought, though it wasn't exactly massive. A concrete box maybe thirty feet across and just half that distance wide, it looked like a storeroom of some kind, if the metal shelving against the walls was any indication. A rough pile of clothes and blankets formed my bed, most of them with the price tags still attached. Gideon stood near a gray metal door, and he was watching me with an expression I couldn't hope to read. Closed off, but with a strange tinge of... Was that worry?

Had to be for Liam and Asher. God knew the guy thought I was some kind of Amalie puppet just waiting to enslave them again. But my heart still ached at the sight of him. Even if he despised me, God, he still looked awful. His face and arms were covered in cuts like someone had used him as a testing dummy for their favorite knives. His eye patch was gone, leaving only the scarred skin and deflated socket where his other eye had once been.

But it wasn't like he'd appreciate my sympathy. Hell, he'd almost certainly be an asshole about it, and I definitely didn't need that right now. The world was fucked up enough without him being a jerk.

Saying nothing about his wounds, I looked away, only to freeze when I spotted Ulysses.

Far beyond the others, the fourth Sentinel had his back against the far wall of this concrete room like he'd tried to get as far away from me as possible, and he was watching me with a strange intensity to his gaze, like he was waiting for me to explode. But at the sight of him, more memories returned. The street in St. Louis. We *had* been fighting rabids—Asher, Liam, and I. We'd come to the city looking for Gideon and Ulysses, since they'd both been captured by Amalie and that ancient vampire, Urlfeige. At Amalie's order, Ulysses had attacked me, throwing me down and lunging at me like he was going to tear my throat out.

Except...

I scanned the room, shaking. "A-are we still in St. Louis? Did they catch us? Why..."

Before I could even finish the question, I ran out of breath, like I'd been starved of blood to the point that I could barely take in any air.

Asher was already shaking his head. "No, we got away. We're still in the city, though."

There was something strained in his voice. And at the words, Ulysses closed his eyes briefly and turned his face aside.

The coldness that'd been there when he was Amalie's prisoner was entirely gone.

Now he looked pained.

My heart began pounding faster. The beat was thready, barely more than a flinch in my chest, but by God, it still sped up as adrenaline made a second appearance. "Then what's going on? Why are we—"

I cut off as the floor suddenly quivered. A distant boom accompanied the shaking.

Shrieks and howls followed the reverberation, so distant they were as faint as whispers.

A trembling breath escaped me. "Oh, God."

Liam's grip tightened on me, as if to pull my attention back to him and away from the sounds.

My eyes darted over the four men. "How..." I swallowed again. It was getting easier to speak, though I didn't exactly sound healthy. "How bad is it?"

For a moment, none of the Sentinels spoke. "As far as Lazarus can tell," Asher admitted finally, "the whole city. Any vampire for miles around went rabid."

My shaking grew worse, and my gaze dropped to the black mark on my chest. Now that I wasn't moving, it just felt numb, but not like it was cold or deadened. Like it was gone. Like something had been taken.

Drained.

And I knew why.

This was my fault. I'd come to save Ulysses and Gideon, determined to free my Sentinels from Urlfeige's and Amalie's grasps. But I'd known Urlfeige had twisted my past life connection to the dormants into a weapon. Any of them who even *looked* at me got turned into rabid vampire killing machines. And when he knew Amalie and I were in the same area, he could do so much more, turning whole cities.

His vampires had wanted to take that connection from me. Drain it out and hand it all to Amalie. So if *whatever* the hell this mark was had let them do that...

How many dormants had been in St. Louis? Hundreds? Thousands? All of them just regular folk who happened to be vampires.

At least until I came to town.

Nausea tried to climb my throat. My best friend, Brayden, had been in St. Louis. Was he still alive? And what about my family? Last I heard, they'd fled all the way to California, but what if they'd doubled back for some reason?

God, why had I come here? I should have stayed away like Asher and Liam originally wanted.

Liam made a comforting sound, as if our connection let him pick up on how I was spiraling. Swallowing hard, I tried to calm down. But then my brow twitched lower, the rest of Asher's words playing back in my head. "Lazarus told you that?" I asked them all, confused. "How come you all don't know?"

Asher's mouth tightened, as if he was trying to weigh how much to say. My weak breathing sped up to join my heartbeat.

"The GSS have cut off communication with the outside world. Cell towers are down. Landlines and Wi-Fi too. Anything beyond local TV and radio stations are cut off somehow, and local ones aren't broadcasting—or if they are, it's only government announcements to stay inside. They're claiming a dirty bomb went off in the city. The cell phones Friday gave us let us reach Lazarus and keep in touch with your family, but—"

"Friday?" Confusion hit me again. I thought the elderly demon had been killed when Amalie used my memories to find and destroy the manor safe house.

Asher gripped my hand tighter. "She survived. Barnaby too. Amalie kept them alive as prisoners, and Gideon got them out when he escaped."

I could read between those lines—and remember what Amalie had been like when I was her in a past life, too.

She'd tortured those old, kindly demons. No question.

I cleared my throat, trying to stay focused. "You said you talked to my parents, though?"

Asher nodded. "They're okay. Still on the West Coast. And Friday and Barnaby have gone to Gateway City. It's underground, not far from here, and it's heavily defended." He hesitated. "It's also home to the Consortium."

I shuddered. I didn't know much about that group, but my shifter friend Ollie had told me they were basically the United-Nations-meets-Parliament of the supernatural world.

They'd also put a price on my head.

"The demons have their ways of getting into places, so they've gone to convince the Consortium to call off the proverbial dogs." Asher grimaced. "We have to get the bounty hunters off our backs if we're going to stand a chance of keeping you safe once we're outside St. Louis. Rabids are bad enough."

"And only a fool fights a war on two fronts if it can be avoided," Gideon added.

"But regardless," Asher finished. "Urlfeige hasn't attacked there yet. The demons and your friends should be okay."

I managed a smile, touched he remembered and cared. Ollie and her girlfriend Emma had been headed to meet their families in Gateway City, in an effort to get away from the vampires who'd destroyed our small town. The idea Urlfeige would attack there...

I made myself keep breathing. Asher said the city was heavily defended. Maybe that would be enough.

Liam drew me a little bit closer, tightening his hold around my shoulders. Nearby, I saw Gideon's brow lower, that same unreadable look on his face. But this time I could guess why, at least a bit. Last time I saw him, Liam had still been uncomfortable with touching me or vice versa.

We'd all changed since then.

"Where are we?" I asked.

Asher's jaw worked around. "Back of a shop, a few miles north of where we found Ulysses and Gideon. We've been hiding out here for the past few days. No one's tried to come by." Unspoken was the implication that maybe the people who would have come were dead. "The GSS have the town surrounded, and vampires have the rest on lockdown."

"And the people? The ones who live here?"

By the wall, Ulysses closed his eyes, looking away. No one answered for a long moment, and then Asher said quietly, "Some might have gone out."

Chills rolled through me. I could hear the implication, and it made me feel sick. So many innocent people trapped in a city suddenly gone mad.

I drew another shaky breath, trying to stuff the guilt down with all the rest of my horror. I had no idea how we'd fix this, but dammit, we would. We'd made it this far, after all.

Tau's words from my dream came back to me. *He wins.*

My nausea grew worse, and I shoved the memory down too. I couldn't deal with that right now, and maybe I wouldn't have to. Maybe Brayden would be okay. His mom and everyone else who lived here too. Maybe my family would stay safe in California, my friends would be all right in Gateway City, and as for the rest of this nightmare...

We'd fix it.

Somehow.

"So what's the plan?" I asked, trying to pour confidence into my voice no matter how much my body was shaking.

"We've been lying low until the rabids widen their search for you," Asher said. "The minute they do, we're getting you out of town. The rabids moved fast after you were hurt. The city was under siege almost immediately, and our escape routes were cut off. But hopefully, now that it's been a few days, they'll start to conclude you got away and begin expanding their search, which means there will be larger gaps to escape through their numbers undetected." A dark expression twisted his face briefly. "We need to get out of here, but we have to move carefully. We can't risk Amalie or Urlfeige finding you."

I looked away, guilt fighting to bash through my tight hold on it. "So... hiding and running again, eh?"

I tried to keep my tone light, but from the grim looks on their faces, I clearly failed.

"More or less, yes," Asher acknowledged.

I leaned my head against Liam's shoulder as he rubbed his hand up and down my arm, attempting to comfort me. I could feel Gideon's attention still on us. I didn't hold his gaze. Likely, he was still angry about my presence in their lives. Probably more so now, given that I was apparently also damning the world.

It was so... uncomfortable. I had all these memories of past lives where I'd known him. Hell, when I'd been Tau, I loved him and he loved me. I could remember times in that life when he held me, kissed me, and made love to me.

But it didn't matter. A past life didn't mean we'd be together now, and why should it? We were our own people, not puppets of some past existence. If anything, Amalie was proof that past lives were basically irrelevant. After all, she had been Tauluria, and she'd made the Sentinels' lives a living hell.

And I'd been her.

Shivers ran through me. Past lives meant nothing. I wasn't Amalie, she wasn't me, and neither of us were fully Tauluria. And even if my memories of life as Tau made this painful, Gideon and I were still barely more than strangers, and—in this life, at least—we probably always would be.

Since he hated me.

I shifted my shoulders, attempting to stop my thoughts from spiraling. "Guess we should see if we can get going then."

I glanced down, but I couldn't find the jacket I'd been wearing before waking up here, so I fished a zip-up hoodie from the pile of clothes that had been my bed. Technically— well, literally—I supposed it was stealing to take it, but I silently promised the shop owners I'd pay them back once we survived.

Tearing off the tag, I tried to shrug the hoodie on, only to tense as pain spiked through my chest again. Hissing between my teeth, I winced as I waited for the rush of agony to pass.

"We should wait," Gideon said to the others. "She's not ready."

I fought back the urge to tell him where to shove that opinion while Liam gently helped me slip the thing around my shoulders and zip it up. Gideon was always thinking me weak. Always thinking I was a problem—not to mention talking about me *again* like I wasn't even here. "The longer we stay in town, the more we're in danger too, right? What if there's an opening to escape now?"

"Moving slowly because you're injured would significantly increase the danger to all of us, including you." Gideon's voice was hard. "We can't continue feeding you our blood indefinitely to keep you alive." He gestured sharply at Asher and Liam as if to include them in the statement.

The heat in his tone made me want to snarl, but confused shock drove me to look away. They'd been feeding me when I was unconscious?

Even *Gideon*?

Why the hell would he do that? Moreover, given how thready my breath and heartbeat still were... how this mark was *still* here...

That much blood should have left me feeling like Wonder Woman.

God, how close had I been to dying?

"It's still a few hours until sunrise," Asher said evenly, cutting into my thoughts. "Whatever we do, we should wait until the sun comes up, if only to keep the rabids away. It doesn't solve the GSS problem, but it will make the speed of travel less of an—"

Shouts came from beyond the door.

Asher and Gideon moved like lightning. Launching to his feet, Asher raced for the door as Gideon yanked it wide, and in an instant, they were both gone.

More shouting followed. *Scared* shouting.

Oh, God.

Grunting with pain and attempting to ignore the way it made my vision swim, I shoved upright.

"Wren," Liam protested.

I braced myself on a nearby wall and staggered toward the door. Ulysses took a step closer like he wanted to intercept me, only to stop himself—which was fine with me. As I moved, my legs grew marginally steadier. Maybe I just needed to be on my feet to get my strength back. This could work. But when I reached the doorway, I froze.

The guys had said we were in a shop.

They hadn't mentioned that it'd been set on *fire*.

Beyond the charred wreckages of displays, Asher and Gideon stood near the entrance, just inside the shattered and melted remnants of the floor-to-ceiling windows that had fronted the store. Burned wires and metal dangled from the ceiling, scorch marks marred the walls, and the smell of smoke was heavy on the air.

"—one block west," Gideon was saying. "Heading this way. They— What the hell?" He glared over his shoulder at me and the others alike.

"Get her back," Asher ordered Liam.

Ignoring him, I shrugged off Liam's hand and continued toward the window. "What's going on?"

Asher's jaw muscles jumped, while Gideon just shook his head, muttering something I couldn't hear while he looked away.

Well, screw him. "Asher?"

"Humans down the street. Rabids may have already gotten their hands on them, but we can't be sure."

I waited, but neither man made a move toward the street. "And?"

"Go back to the storeroom, Wren." Asher's voice was resigned.

I gaped at them both, baffled. This wasn't like Asher. Liam or Ulysses either. Hell, even though he hated me, Gideon had still risked his life to keep me and others from being killed by rabids. "But we have to help them."

"And the minute those rabids see it's *us* doing the rescuing?" Gideon replied. "If a *single* rabid survives and escapes us, they will tell Amalie you're here and they will come for—"

"So, what? We just let those people die?"

Scowling, Gideon turned away to watch the street.

I stared at the others. "People can't die just to protect us, guys. *Definitely* not just to protect me."

Asher's face was grim. "If Amalie or Urlfeige get their hands on you, the gods only know how many more people will suffer. Those two did this with just *part* of whatever connection to the dormants is inside you. If they captured and drained you fully, you would die, and there'd be no telling how far they could extend their reach." His voice was solemn, but our connection was practically throbbing with how much pain the words caused him. "Keeping you safe is keeping countless others safe too. We cannot risk being seen. You understand that, right?"

I looked away, seething and anguished. Yeah, I got what he was saying, but I couldn't just let people *die*.

Another scream came from down the street, closer now.

My hand flexed before I even registered the impulse, summoning my sword from whatever realm it occupied when it wasn't in my grasp.

A sharp jolt of pain ripped into my shoulder and chest, burning like I'd been jabbed with a red-hot poker and radiating from the dark stain on my skin. Crumpling in on myself, I choked on a cry.

Asher grabbed me. I blinked fast, trying to make my eyes focus past the agony.

"Gods," Gideon growled furiously. "Could you stop risking yourself for five damn sec—"

A woman ran past, clutching a baby in her arms. She threw a frantic glance over her shoulder, only to catch sight of us hiding in the shadows of the store. Skidding on the gritty concrete, she looked between us and whatever was chasing her. "Help me! Please, you have to—"

Two rabids flew at her in shadow form, like smoke and darkness come to life and radiating a sense of wrongness that made my skin crawl. She screamed as one of them lunged at her child.

"Dammit!" Asher leapt through the shattered window. Shifting into his own shadow form, he slammed into the rabid, ripping through it. Whirling around, he caught the other one just as it shifted back in an effort to attack him, and the creature died screaming as it became ash.

The woman stared at us, shock and horror in her wide eyes as Asher flew back into the shelter of the destroyed store and returned to human form.

Doing my best to look nonthreatening, I held up my hands. "It's okay. We're not going to hurt you."

Screeches came from my left. I risked a swift peek beyond the melted glass window frame.

Rabids were racing down the street at us.

And from the way they were moving, I'd bet money they'd spotted Asher.

"Wonderful," Gideon snarled. He threw a furious look at Liam and gestured to me. "Get her out of sight!"

Not waiting to see if his order was obeyed, he and Asher raced right at the rabids.

2

GIDEON

I ran at the rabids, my knife appearing in my fist and Asher at my side. The woman with the infant stumbled back, gaping at us. More at me than Asher, and it wasn't hard to guess why. My missing eye was one thing. I still didn't have an eye patch for that. But it was the cuts covering my entire body —souvenirs of Amalie's torture—that made me look like a nightmare.

Too bad the rabids wouldn't think so.

The creatures howled as we charged toward them. Past the smoke and shadow, I could see a man on the ground. He was already bloody, courtesy of the vampires, and even as several of the rabids flew at us, the rest remained huddled around him.

They wouldn't let go of their dinner so easily.

In an instant, Asher shifted into shadow, flying at them. The transformation wasn't as alarming as it would've been a few days ago. Ulysses and I still hadn't regained our powers to shift into shadows, but for some reason Asher and Liam could.

We all had theories regarding that. Or, really, one theory. And she was currently back in that shop, likely still convinced I thought nothing of her.

Rather than knowing how deeply I regretted believing she was Amalie.

Or how I knew I could not make that up to her—at least not yet.

As Asher tore into the rabids ahead of him, I flipped my knife in my grip and sliced across the shadowed shape of the nearest creature, sending the snarling thing howling to its demise. Another charged at me, trying to wrap its smoke around my arm to pin me while its companion attempted to knock my knife from my grasp.

They clearly hadn't learned anything about fighting us from their brethren.

My knife vanished from my right hand only to reappear in my left, and I slashed the blade through both of them in swift succession.

The surviving creatures spread out, moving to surround us. Their prey still lay on the ground at the intersection, though now the man stared at us, his eyes wide in his bloodied face.

At my side, Asher shifted back quickly, displeasure radiating from him. It had been eating away at him, this choice between protecting Wren by staying hidden or helping the humans suffering in this city. Defending the innocent was practically the core of Asher's being, and he'd argued for days over finding *some* way to save the people dying all around us.

Yet I'd met the creature known as Urlfeige. I'd been his prisoner—and Amalie's—for weeks. Whatever Urlfeige may have been in our past lives—a vampire, a king, even a human being at one time—now he was a beast made of nothing but the blood of the innocent, and he sought to create a world where all of humanity was reduced to thralls, mindlessly craving our bite and having no will of their own. So no matter how horrific the choice was, I'd insisted we had to stay hidden, had to stay focused on the bigger picture of saving Wren and therefore the world from what Urlfeige would do if his people spotted any of us.

Because the cost of taking action was already coming due.

"I go left, you go right?" I murmured to Asher. He made a quiet sound of agreement, but his attention kept flicking to the man on the ground. We needed to get to him quickly. The scent of his blood was thick on the air—too much for the loss to be survivable if he didn't receive medical attention soon.

But between him and us stood fifteen rabids determined to make him into dinner before he bled out.

I adjusted my grip on my knife, and one of the rabids grinned. "Sentinel," the vampire chuckled. "She's looking for you."

The creatures lunged at us.

In midair, something struck them. I only saw a flash of candy pink before the shape erupted with water.

The rabids howled, stumbling as their flesh began to burn where the liquid had touched them.

My gaze flew from the vampires to the fragments of pink latex rubber on the ground.

Holy water... in *water balloons*?

Shouts rang out from nearby, and suddenly humans raced into the intersection wielding baseball bats, guns, and more balloons. While some of them opened fire on the rabids—their bullets not having much effect unless they struck the creatures' heads—others whipped balloon after balloon from their bags and flung them like they were hand grenades.

Rabids took to the air in all directions, racing away from the intersection.

Asher snarled a curse, tensing like he was half a second from taking off after them. But even if he chased down the ones escaping to the west, that still left all the other directions he couldn't account for.

And I was trapped in this form, useless to help him.

I ground my teeth, fighting back a snarl of my own. The rabids would rush to alert Amalie and Urlfeige to our presence. This was *precisely* why we'd stayed hidden.

"Get eyes on those things!" shouted a ruddy-faced man wielding a nail-studded baseball bat. "Keep watch in case they circle back!"

Three of the humans moved to do as he said, while two others raced toward the man on the ground, first aid equipment in their hands. Still others watched us, guns in their grip. Unless those were specially made GSS bullets, though, there was little chance they'd do us significant harm.

"They're like the others!" the man on the ground cried, pointing a shaking hand at Asher. "That one turned into a smoke-thing like they did!"

Ungrateful bastard.

"Stay back," one of the humans ordered us. A young man who looked barely into his twenties, he wore a leather jacket with the collar zipped up around his throat. While the other humans around him had guns or water balloons, he held a knife long enough to be a machete in his fist.

Smart. The former would slow down anything attempting to bite him, and if swung hard enough, the latter would possibly take someone's head—a blow that would kill even a rabid if they didn't shift form first.

Either he was lucky in his choices or he knew about vampires.

At his words, though, a flash of absolute panic caught my attention, originating from my link to Wren and the others. I threw a look back to see her staggering toward us as fast as her unsteady legs would allow. Liam was beside her, trying to hold her back and keep her upright at the same time. He wasn't having much success stopping her, given how she was pushing him away. Short of physically picking her up and carrying her back into the store, there didn't appear to be any way to keep her from continuing on.

Damn that beautiful, stubborn woman. What the hell was she *thinking*, continuing to risk herself like this?

The humans stalked toward us, only a few of those cursed water balloons still in their grip. They'd hurt like hell if they touched us, but in Wren's weakened state, the gods only knew what they would do to her.

"Shit," Asher muttered. He shifted position slightly, bringing his shoulder closer to mine in an effort to block their view of her. "Back up."

I nodded, retreating. We couldn't hurt the humans. Wren would never forgive us.

But if they tried to attack her...

The kid took a step toward us. "Don't you try anything, you—"

"Brayden!" Wren shouted.

The young man pulled up short, blinking in shock. "*Wren*?" Instantly, he whirled, holding up his hands toward the humans. "Don't shoot!"

Glancing at each other, the humans cautiously eased their grips on their guns, not lowering them entirely but not aiming at her either.

The guy started toward Wren, looking between her and us like he was trying to make sense of what he saw. "What the hell are you—"

His eyes went wide with horror. I started to throw a look over my shoulder to find whatever he saw, only to catch sight of him lifting his gun.

In an instant, the bullets cracked through the quiet of the destroyed city. Pain shot through my connection to Wren and the other Sentinels. Horror ricocheting through me, I spun.

Beyond Wren and Liam, Ulysses staggered as the shots took him in the chest.

"No!" Wren cried, whirling and stumbling toward him.

Asher and Liam didn't hesitate. Shifting instantly, Asher grabbed the closest human who was raising their gun while Liam snagged the young man and slammed him straight into a wall. Pinning him there, Liam shifted back, his fangs bared and pure murder in his gaze.

All hell broke loose.

Humans sprayed bullets at us while balloons of holy water flew at me and my fellow Sentinels alike. I ducked and raced for the nearest human, disarming them swiftly. Taking to the air, Liam hoisted the boy several floors up and pinned him again as holy water struck the brick wall below him uselessly. Across the street, Asher ripped a gun from a man's grasp and then threw him aside before twisting out of the way of another balloon and snagging the next closest human, stripping them of their weapon too.

"Stop! Please!" Wren begged. "Liam, don't hurt him!"

I threw a glance back to find her plastered to the ground, Ulysses covering her despite his wounds. Bullets shredded the air around them.

Dammit.

I caught a woman's wild swing of her baseball bat, my hand stopping the weapon in midair. Staggering with her halted momentum, the woman stared at me, her brown eyes widening with terror.

Ripping the bat from her grasp and tossing it to the sidewalk, I glared at her. "Stop this. We aren't your—"

A balloon struck the wall nearby, splattering me with holy water.

I roared with pain, my face and arm burning as if they'd been splashed by acid. Through the haze of agony, I saw a man raising his arm to throw another.

Asher slammed into him, whipping the guy around and

then using him as a shield, his hand on the man's throat. "Stop or he dies!" he snarled at the other humans.

There wasn't a chance in hell Asher would make good on the threat, but the humans didn't know that. They hesitated, their gazes darting around as if unsure what to do.

"Tell your people to lower their weapons," Liam rasped.

The young man's eyes went wide at the sound of his voice.

"Brayden, please," Wren begged.

The guy's gaze darted to her and then narrowed with confusion when he saw how Ulysses was shielding her. "St-stand down," he called. "Just... everybody stand down."

Wary looks passed among the humans.

"*Now*," Asher snarled.

Guns and water balloons lowered all around the intersection.

Cautiously, Ulysses rose to his feet, his face tight from the pain of being shot. Bloodlessly pale, Wren climbed upright as well, casting a confused glance to Ulysses when he immediately backed away from her.

But I could see her shaking from here.

Something of my fury at that sight must have shown on my face, as it caused a woman nearby to whimper in terror. I fought to control my expression. The gods knew we didn't need to prompt the humans to attack all over again. But Wren shouldn't be out here. She'd come *so* close to death from that damned spear in her chest, and the wound wasn't healing correctly. Not to mention it looked like hell, as if pure darkness had erupted in her skin. The thing had to be poison—and quite possibly a curse as well.

"Liam." Wren cleared her throat, and her voice steadied. "Please bring Brayden down here. *Safely.*"

Liam's low growl filtered out onto the air, but after a moment, he sank toward the ground again. The wild look hadn't left his eyes, and it was obvious why. The guy could have hit Wren with those bullets.

It was only because she'd asked him to spare the guy that he was still alive.

"Let her go," the young man snarled at Liam. "She's not your dinner."

I revised my assessment. It was a *miracle* he still lived.

"It's okay, Brayden." Wren held out a hand as if to calm the young man before turning her attention to the other humans. Her chest rose and fell in shallow gasps, and my gut twisted at the sight. We'd given her so much blood just trying to keep her alive, yet even with all that, she was still barely breathing. "Please. I-I know what you've seen. Him, yeah?" She nodded her head toward Ulysses. "Those videos online?"

The humans were silent, but their expressions told the story well enough. While I'd been a prisoner of Amalie and Urlfeige, Ulysses had been their puppet.

And the things he'd been forced to do in that time chilled us all—not that he'd speak of them now.

"It's not what you think," Wren continued. "He's not like that anymore, and it wasn't his choice to do that stuff in the first place." A pleading expression took up residence on her face. "We're not your enemies, okay? I swear, we're not like the others, so please just—"

A hoarse sound left the young man. I looked back to find him staring in horror at Wren, and the reason clicked a heartbeat later.

She'd said *we.*

"You fuckers!" he shouted at Liam and the rest of us. "You fucking *turned* her? You—"

"Brayden!" Wren tried to walk toward him, but her legs weren't steady enough. Ulysses caught her as she stumbled.

The sight only galvanized the young man. In Liam's grip, he struggled to break free, going nowhere. All around us, the humans brought their weapons up again. Asher shifted position fast, moving to put himself between them and Wren.

"They didn't!" Wren shouted. "Dammit, Brayden, please! They saved me!"

The young man froze, visibly shaking with fury.

Wren's chest rose and fell in tiny, rapid gasps. "They saved me, okay? And they're helping me. I swear to you, none of us here are like those others. So *please stop.*"

For a moment, she and Brayden stared at each other. There was history in that look. Years of it, I'd wager.

Who was this guy to her?

"Weapons down." Brayden directed the order at the humans, though he didn't take his eyes from Wren. "All of you."

The man who'd swung a bat at Asher made an incredulous sound. "Like hell. These things ripped my neighbor apart! If you think I'm going to—"

"Calvin, *weapons down.*" Brayden jerked his head toward us. "Apparently, there's more than one kind."

The man stared at him like he'd grown tentacles.

"Come on, Calvin," a woman with dark hair, light brown skin, and military garb said. "Let's hear them out."

Jaw muscles jumping, the guy held up his hands and stepped back.

"Gideon, you okay?" Wren called.

Something warm took up residence in my chest that she'd care for my welfare after how I'd treated her ever since we met. "Fine."

My skin still stung, belying the words. I'd have burns there, at least for a time, though feeding would make them heal faster.

Not that there was blood available these days. Well, unless Wren would consent to—

I shoved the thought away before distracting desire could grab hold of me. It wouldn't happen, and not just because she was injured. Compassion was one thing. But granting me access to her blood was too intimate. She would never wish for that with *me*.

And I'd recover, regardless. That was enough.

"What's going on, Wren?" Brayden asked her, an intensity to his words that suggested he wasn't nearly as calm about all this as he was attempting to appear.

She drew a shallow breath and stepped closer to him. Cautiously, Ulysses released her and backed away again, his expression as torn about her as it had been for the past several days. The gods knew he cared about her. That was obvious to anyone. But he also hadn't come close to touching her in days. He never explained why, but even now he looked nervous that he had somehow hurt her.

Wren didn't appear to notice. Wetting her lips, she answered her friend. "It's a long story. But we want to stop this. That's why we tried to help them." She nodded to where the human woman still stood with her infant clutched in her arms, back in the shelter of the store we'd used as a hideout for the past few days. "But those others, the rabids. They're hunting us. So we need to get—" She winced, faltering.

Ulysses was back at her side in an instant, keeping her upright and saying something to her in a voice so low, I couldn't hear. From his expression, I suspected it was a request she stop and let us get her somewhere to rest.

I wasn't surprised when she shook her head.

Stubborn. And why did that make me want to scoff like her obstinance was endearing? Of course it wasn't.

Except for how it rather was.

"Gideon," Ulysses called to me, his face tight.

Moving carefully so as not to prompt the humans into any potentially fatal stupidity, I crossed to his side. Taking Wren's arm, I held her upright while Ulysses retreated.

Wren gave us both a confused look.

"What's wrong?" Brayden took a step toward her. Liam moved to block him, not laying a finger on the young man but not letting him pass either.

"It's nothing." Wren waved a hand dismissively. "We just—"

Shrieks rose in the distance.

"Shit." Calvin shifted his weight from one foot to the other as if attempting to determine in which direction to run. "We've got more incoming."

"Time to go," Ulysses said to me and the other Sentinels.

Asher and Liam backed away from the humans, not letting them out of their sight. Where the hell we could take Wren I had no idea, but staying in the open was out of the question.

"Where are you going?" Brayden asked her.

Wren shook her head. "I don't know. I'm sorry. We can't be found by them."

Among the humans behind him, several threw each other a brief glance.

"Did they really help you?" the woman in military garb called to the lady with an infant.

The human nodded.

Immediately, the military woman turned to Brayden. "We should bring these vampire folks with us."

Calvin sputtered.

"Sorry," Asher said, not remotely sounding it. "But we need more than water balloons to protect Wren."

Brayden took a step toward us. "We have that."

My brow twitched down.

"Come with us," the guy continued to Wren. "Please. We have a secure place where you can hide. None of those things can get in."

Wren cast a hopeful glance at the rest of us.

Asher shook his head. "We can't risk—"

The shrieks came again, closer.

"Fuck," Ulysses muttered. Circling far wide of Wren, he

started toward the humans. At my incredulous look, he said, "You got a better option?"

I stared. "They *shot* you."

He flicked his gaze to me and away, something grim in his expression. But he kept moving.

"Come on." Brayden motioned for us to follow him around the turn of the intersection. "We can get out of sight this way."

I met Asher's eyes, and Liam's too, and not one of us looked pleased with this development.

But Amalie might be coming.

"Dammit," I muttered. "Let's go."

3

AMALIE

It had been *entirely* too long since last I'd watched a city burn.

I'd missed it.

I walked down the center of the broad concrete street, breathing deep the scent of smoke on the air. The sky was orange from the flames currently devouring buildings on the city blocks all around. Even from here, when the wind shifted just right, I could hear the screams.

No humans were burning, of course. That would have been a waste. No, these were the howls and cries of the captured. Of those fleeing for their lives.

Of the prey.

Shadows twisted through my skin, stronger with every passing day. My father had given me the power of the empty realms, and now that strength fed from the destruction around me, absorbing the fear and pain from the very air. With that energy, I'd caused much of the destruction currently terrorizing the humans fleeing throughout this city, and I'd leveled a curse at that annoying imposter girl. Even now, I could feel it slowly sucking the life from her, pouring more power into me. On some level, the fact she still lived at all was surprising.

But regardless, she wouldn't last.

I smiled at the structures around me. This world and the people in it thought they had come so far in the centuries since last I'd walked the earth. I marveled at the beauty of their creations, to be sure. Cold, soulless towers stretching into the skies, all of them made of steel and stone that had never been alive. And yet still they fell. Still they burned. It didn't matter what humans tried to do. Ultimately, I could still tear it down.

Shadows raced across the orange-painted sky, and my smile grew. This was the way it should have been all along. All of our kind, returned to their true natures. The world, burning at my feet. One of the greatest frustrations of my past existence was that I'd been unable to grant this gift myself. Any vampire I turned centuries ago had only become like the ones now called "dormants"—essentially human, with all the useless morals and ethics and *consciences* that entailed, rather than a pure creation ready to feed upon anything foolish enough to cross its path.

It would have been so much easier if I could have granted this gift.

Especially to my Sentinels.

Frustration twisted through me, pulling my gaze from the sky. They wouldn't be gone forever, my possessions. True, days had passed and my servants had yet to find them. But that was only a testimony to my pets' skills, and their luck as well—the latter of which would run out.

Debris crunched behind me, announcing a new arrival. I turned, mildly interested to see if a human was trying to attack me. I wouldn't have minded the snack. But it was only a vampire shifting back to human form, approaching me with a look of obsequiousness.

"Yes?"

"Good news, Mistress." Worry cracked past his subservience. "Maybe good news."

That was hardly encouraging. Neither was the fact he had not yet continued. "*And*?"

"We spotted the Sentinels."

I grinned. "Do you have them?"

The vampire took a step backward as he shook his head. "Our attack was routed by an unexpected development. Humans with weapons that can hurt us."

My brow arched, contempt rising in me. These creatures may be restored to their proper form, but they would never be my brave Sentinels. "You fled because they *hurt* you?"

The man had the decency to blanch, though it hardly meant I forgave him. "Killed, Mistress," he corrected quickly. "Killed. Without reinforcements, we would not have been able to capture the Sentinels as you wish."

Useless fools.

"Then where were they?"

"Several miles from here." The rabid pointed. "They're fleeing with the humans."

"And are there others following to see where they go?"

He took another step backward as if that would save him from me. "We were unable to, Mistress. The Sentinels were—"

I stalked toward him, and he scrambled in retreat.

"We think we know where they're headed," he blurted. "We saw the direction, and humans can't travel far on foot without being spotted. And the girl—"

I stopped. "What about the girl?"

"She's hurt. She could barely stand up."

Ah, well, there *was* that, then. A smile pulled at my lips. "Good."

Nervously, the man attempted a smile in return, only to flinch back when mine fell. The idiot was hardly forgiven.

Whirling around, I strode back down the street. "Come. You will tell us exactly where they were headed."

His footsteps took a heartbeat before they crunched after me on the debris-strewn road, the sound laced with his reluctance and fear.

But he followed, and thus, for the moment, he could live.

I'd take my time dealing with his disappointing decisions later.

Two twists of the road later, I walked through shattered glass doors and into the vast gallery of an open marketplace, complete with stores on multiple levels overhead. Decorative trees stood throughout the area, as if to let humans make believe they remained outdoors, and white marble tile glistened with gold flecks beneath my feet. At the center, a vast pool waited, only about a foot deep but with a fountain in the shape of leaping mermaids at its heart.

Of course, now blood filled the pool and gushed from the shells held by each mermaid. The marble underfoot was speckled with the same. But the additions were an improvement.

As any of the humans who'd been chosen for turning rather than food would undoubtedly agree.

I rounded the fountain, and a figure on the opposite side came into view. Gone was the vat of blood and the mist that had once housed his presence. Now, he stood and walked and could even speak like the vampire he'd once been. His skin was a thin barrier, translucent and offering no disguise over the red blood coursing and pumping inside him. He was a nightmare come to life, speaking with the deep voice of a self-contained god who knew precisely how unbridled his power over life and death was. He already possessed a face and hands and a body.

But no eyes.

And oh, how the humans cowered and screamed and ran

whenever they saw him—especially since he was the *last* thing they ever saw.

Standing before the sprawled figures of a dozen nearly dead humans, he surveyed the bleeding bodies with the air of a connoisseur.

"That one," he said to the rabid cowering at his side, pointing. "Those three. And that one over there."

At his gestures, the rabids around him hurried to retrieve the indicated bodies, while the other vampires set to removing the others. The selected humans would be fed enough vampire blood to turn them. The rest would be drained by the newly turned vampires currently recovering in one of the many stores in this massive marketplace. A candle shop, I thought it was. Or maybe they'd moved on to the one filled with shoes.

"How goes the search?" my father asked me.

I turned back to him, dismissing the bodies as they were dragged away. "The vampires are making progress. They have a direction now."

"And the girl?"

I kept my face still. He thought he needed her, so showing my pleasure over the fact she was hurting would hardly go over well. But she'd die soon. The continued irritation of her existence was only temporary. "She's with them."

I could feel his satisfaction, like the warmth of the sun. "Then prepare the next stage of the curse," he said. "Drain her. Take it all."

Relief washed away my irritation, and I grinned. "Consider it done."

4

WREN

Everything hurt, but I wasn't going to let that take away from my elation at the fact that Brayden was alive.

Holding on to Gideon, I made myself keep walking down the street after Brayden. It'd only been a few weeks—barely any time, really, in normal life—but my friend had changed. It wasn't just the clothes, though yeah, those were... different. My whole life, Brayden had been the fashionable one of the two of us. *Dress as well as you'd like your ghost to look,* he used to joke. But the polo shirts and slacks I knew he liked were long gone, and in their place he wore a leather jacket with a collar protectively up around his neck, black cargo pants, and thick boots.

Post-apocalyptic chic.

The outfit was understandable, given the hell around us, but it spoke to a level of preparedness that left me confused. Brayden wasn't *whatever* this was. He was a quiet, loyal guy who'd spent his childhood obsessed with musical composers the way other kids fixated on the careers of actors and actresses. We'd been inseparable growing up, sharing a love for everything from cartoons and triple-decker sundaes to books and history—albeit the latter was entirely through the lens of music, on his end. He'd been born to play, I used to tell him, and the songs he wrote were some of the most beautiful things I'd ever heard. But he'd been there for me when I broke my arm falling off my bike and when a bully in fifth grade had put hot glue in my hair. I'd been there when his parents split and when he cried after finding out his first boyfriend had only asked him out as a joke. We'd been *normal.*

Now dirt smudged his cheek, and his ordinarily smooth hair was wild like he hadn't bothered to tame it. He even had a gun gripped in his hand, and he moved like he knew to watch the shadows, knew how to aim if a rabid appeared, all of it.

How the hell had he been ready for this? It'd only been a few days since St. Louis went to hell.

Chills crept through me. Surely he wasn't...

I shoved the thought down. My other close friends had turned out to be shifters. The odds that, on top of that, my best friend since kindergarten was part of the GSS or something were... well, come on. My next stop would definitely be some kind of Vegas casino.

I shivered.

"Are you okay?" Gideon murmured.

I flinched with surprise, the question snapping me back to the present. *Gideon* wanted to know if I was okay? "Uh, yeah. Fine."

That Calvin guy turned from where he was walking ahead of us, throwing a dark glare back in our direction, and I bit my lip, not saying anything else. Brayden didn't take his attention from the street, while the other humans were a mix. Some seemed okay with us, not bothering to look our way as they kept a watch for threats. Others were bringing up the rear by walking uneasily in the vicinity of Asher and Ulysses, their hands gripping their weapons like they would use them on us at the first whisper of danger.

But no one was coming too close to me or Gideon, and it wasn't a huge leap to guess why. Yes, Gideon looked... well, terrifying, probably. And Liam was on the other side of me. Sure, he never said a word, but he radiated enough predatory malice to set the air on fire.

"What about you?" I asked quietly once Calvin turned away. Holy water had bloodied and blistered Gideon's other arm and the side of his face too, adding to the injuries everywhere on him that I could see. "Are you sure you're all right?"

He gave me a terse nod. "I'll be fine."

"Okay, but if you need to slow down—"

A low scoff left him. "Will that make you do the same?"

I looked away. Walking was a struggle. My legs were shaky. Hell, my entire *body* was shaky, and I was having trouble staying on my feet. I didn't really want to think about why, because I had no idea what to do about any of it.

So in the grand tradition of all uncomfortable things people didn't want to think about, I did my best to ignore it.

Softly, Gideon made an angry sound, and suddenly, Liam moved slightly ahead of me.

Brayden had turned around and was walking back toward us.

I exhaled, though I barely had enough breath to sigh. "I need to talk to him." I eased away from Gideon.

Unexpectedly, Gideon's arm tightened on me. "Here is sufficient." His tone brooked no argument. From anyone else, I'd say it was almost *protective.*

Maybe it was meant for the other Sentinels, though. After all, Brayden had *shot* Ulysses.

I suppressed a grimace. "Okay."

Gideon's jaw muscles clenched, but after a moment he threw a glowering look toward my friend. "If you wish to speak, then speak."

Brayden didn't even glance at him. "Are you okay?" he asked me.

I nodded.

"Then what's this?" He twitched his chin toward the way Gideon was helping me stay upright. "What's wrong?"

I didn't know where to begin. "Long story."

I'd known him long enough to be able to read the confusion underneath the wary distrust of the Sentinels on his face. But we were surrounded by people with guns, so this didn't exactly feel like the best time to try to explain everything.

Not that I had a clue what to say anyway. God, I hadn't seen him since the hospital weeks ago, back when I didn't believe I was a vampire and I was still determined to pretend none of this was actually real.

And then I'd vanished out of my hospital room; my life had gone even more insane, and the next time I tried to find him, he'd been down in St. Louis at some classical music symposium. But rabids had torn apart Fort Briar not long after that, and then the GSS descended on the town, locking it down with stories of a chemical spill that meant everyone should stay away.

Wonder what they'd tell people about St. Louis. "Dirty bomb" seemed more complicated—not to mention more terrifying.

Brayden's eyes narrowed slightly, but he didn't press for more. Not yet anyway.

Ulysses made an uncomfortable sound, drawing my attention instantly. I looked back to see him straighten, the hints of residual pain fading from his expression as the bullets dropped from his wounds like he was some vampire version of Wolverine.

I blinked. Healing that fast was... damn.

Except it meant he'd probably fed recently, and given that we hadn't seen him in weeks...

Discomfort made me want to grimace, and I struggled to keep my face blank, not wanting to worry the other Sentinels, let alone any of the humans who currently appeared about a millisecond away from opening fire on us. But somehow, I just knew Ulysses hadn't been drinking bagged blood. Not given the recording we'd watched or how—back before he was free of Amalie—he'd regarded us like we were nothing but targets to destroy.

He noticed me looking at him and dropped his gaze away quickly.

"So, um…" I turned my attention back to Brayden. My friend's eyes were flashing back and forth between the Sentinel and the spent bullets currently lying on the road. "What about you? What's all this?"

Blinking fast, Brayden pulled his focus back to me. "Patrol duty. Top floor's rotation tonight."

"Top floor?"

"You'll see."

At Brayden's words, Calvin cast another dark look back at us. Wariness prickled through me. Whatever he said, that one didn't trust us an inch.

I just hoped he didn't try attacking us—for his sake and the sake of everyone around him.

"What are you doing in St. Louis?" Brayden asked me.

"Trying to stop this." I shrugged.

He glanced at the Sentinels again. "So that's what you do now? Go around with vampires to stop other vampires?"

Liam growled at the bitter edge in my friend's voice.

I winced. "I'm sorry I didn't call you. I couldn't."

"And Harper? Ollie and Emma?"

My wince deepened. Dammit, I guess we *were* doing this now. "I—"

"No one told me what the hell was going on, Wren. School shut down overnight, Fort Briar was suddenly off-limits, and as far as I knew, you all were dead. I've spent weeks trying to figure out what happened, and then vampires attacked this city, and now you're one of them, and—"

"She's been rather occupied with *survival*, boy," Gideon snapped. "Or would you care to know how many times this woman has nearly died trying to save others these past weeks?"

I faltered at the heat in Gideon's tone—and at his words. But getting into all that wouldn't help anything, especially when the other humans were looking more edgy by the second.

And God knew in Brayden's position, I'd be furious too. "It's okay," I told the Sentinels.

Gideon's jaw muscles jumped, and beyond him, Liam's eyes were shards of ice, but neither of them spoke again.

"I'm sorry," I continued to Brayden. "That... that must've been awful."

A tinge of embarrassment touched his expression, and his eyes darted to Gideon and Liam before returning to me. "No, I... I'm sorry. They're right. You're obviously hurt, and every-thing's fucked, and I shouldn't have..." His mouth tightened. "Sorry." Worry flickered through his eyes. "I'm glad you're not dead."

Gideon looked him up and down, not saying a word, while Liam glared, a touch of satisfaction in his expression.

"Same," I replied awkwardly. "For you, I mean."

Brayden tried for a smile. "So you're a vampire secret agent, then?"

I tensed all over again. "No. I'm just... caught up in it, same as you."

His eyes went between me and the others a second time, and I couldn't read his expression. My gut twisted. What I'd said felt like the truth but also a lie, and I couldn't separate out the reasons.

I took a breath, trying to focus. "There's an ancient vampire behind all this. Two, really. Him and a vampire queen who..." I grimaced. "It's complicated. But we're trying to stop them."

Even if I had zero clue how to do that.

I glanced at the buildings around us. Over the past few minutes, we'd left the commercial area and all its brick and marble behind. Now, a neighborhood surrounded us. Not a single house had a light on, and if not for the distant glow of fire somewhere in the city, the darkness would have been nearly impenetrable.

The area made the hairs on the back of my neck rise. It wasn't just the way each house was lifeless or the way the smoke on the air burned my nose. It was the feeling of stilled motion, of life brought to a screeching halt... and now it was just waiting. Somehow, I suspected not all the houses were empty, but from the busted-in doors and shattered windows, I knew several were. The scratch of our shoes on the road felt too loud in a quiet that should have held a whisper of traffic or the sound of dogs barking. But there was nothing. The heavy silence of places whose inhabitants had died or who were hiding and praying for a fast sunrise.

"Why'd they pick St. Louis?" one of the women nearby asked me, pain in her voice.

I shook my head. "I don't know." My eyes twitched to Ulysses. Did he have any idea? He hadn't said, but admittedly, I hadn't spent more than a short while with him—the time I was unconscious from Amalie's attack aside.

But if any of the other Sentinels knew, they weren't saying so.

"Why you?" Brayden asked.

I gave him a confused look.

"Why are you the one trying to stop it? And who are these guys? Were they just turned into vampires too?"

Liam's growl returned.

"No, they weren't," I said, a placating note in my voice,

mostly for the Sentinels. "And they're..." God, I couldn't think of another word. "Complicated. But they've saved my life... a lot. My family's lives too. They're pretty much why we made it out of Fort Briar."

Brayden didn't respond.

"The thing that did this to the vampires here in town, the thing that made them crazy like this? It did it in Fort Briar too."

"But not to you."

It wasn't a question. Not even a bit. And maybe the truth was obvious—I was standing here talking to him, after all. But his tone made it seem more pointed than that. "No."

"Why?"

I bit my lip.

"It's complicated?" he prompted dryly.

Gideon made an angry sound, and I threw a glance to him, silently begging him not to add fuel to this fire. God only knew why he even cared about Brayden being short with me. He'd been far colder all on his own since I met him. And even if he and I did share a faint link inside us—barely a shadow of what I had with Asher or Liam, and fainter even than what I had with Ulysses—I still couldn't make heads or tails of what was coming through that connection to him now. Anger, yeah, but in a weird way I couldn't sort out.

Maybe he was just irritated we might draw attention.

"Something like that," I answered Brayden.

In awkward silence, I kept walking. The houses around us were unchanged—dark, seemingly empty—but when we rounded a corner, another kind of structure came into view.

My feet slowed. Behind wrought-iron fencing, the sprawling brick building stood three stories high, with peaked roofs hinting at attics above and brick-filled windows at its base suggesting there was a basement too. Staggered short flights of cement stairs led from the sidewalk across the slope of a grassy lawn, all the way to the double doors of its entrance. Twin wings stretched off on either side of the central part of the structure, making the building easily span half a city block. The windows were tall, and at the crest of the rooftops, a pair of chimneys rose on either side.

My eyes narrowed. "Was this a—"

"A school." Brayden nodded. "At least, a long time ago. Now it's an apartment building."

There was something odd in his voice, but before I could ask, a woman up ahead unlatched the gate. Without looking back, she started toward the door, and the other humans followed, moving past us as if anxious to get inside.

I trailed them, eyeing everything. Formed of red brick with pale, decorative stone surrounding the arched entryway of the door, the building looked like it dated back to the nineteenth century. I could almost picture the schoolkids running across the yard under the watchful eyes of teachers in prim and proper dresses. The pale stone continued to the peak of the roof above, where a coat of arms was crafted of the same material, along with some words in Latin that I couldn't interpret. But the windows were covered from within, plastered thickly with paper and possibly cloth too. Not a single one gave a hint as to what was inside.

At the double doors, one of the women knocked a quick pattern on the yellow-painted metal. A moment passed, and then the latch clicked and the door moved back just enough for a teenage Black girl to peer out of the opening. Relief spread through her expression at the sight of the others, faltering into alarm when she spotted us.

Or, really, just the four men with me.

Which was fair, I supposed. I appeared more or less like the college student I'd been. Asher looked like an ice-cold soldier; Gideon was burned and had enough cuts to make it seem like he'd gone ten rounds against a Weedwacker, Liam radiated a guarantee of lethal violence, and Ulysses... well, maybe she recognized him from the recordings online.

"It's okay, Jasmine," Brayden called from the back of the group where we stood. "Let us in and then go tell your stepmom we're here, all right?"

She hesitated before pushing the door open, revealing a foyer flanked by twin staircases and a long hallway stretching back through the building. "Come on, come on," she whispered, motioning to the others, though she never took her dark brown eyes from us. Her countless braids were gathered back in a low ponytail, and like Brayden, she wore a leather jacket with the neck pulled up high as if to stop anyone from biting her. Tension lined every move she made as the other humans filed past her quickly. But when the Sentinels came near, the girl backed away from the door, and for the first time, I caught sight of the Bowie knife she'd been holding behind her, gripped in one fist.

And then Liam slammed to a halt, his eyes snapping over to Brayden as his arm flew out to stop me from coming any closer to the door. Gideon pulled me backward, gripping my arm hard.

Ulysses growled nearby. "You little fucker."

"Get her out of here," Asher snarled at Liam. "We'll follow."

"Wait, what?" I looked around to find whatever it was that had brought them to a stop. "Guys—"

"It's not what you think." Brayden directed the words at the Sentinels.

"Somebody tell me what the hell is going on," I demanded.

"Vampire warding," Asher said, not taking his eyes from my friend.

Brayden's mouth tightened, but he just walked toward the door. "It's not dangerous if I let you through."

"Yeah, right," Ulysses retorted.

"The symbols have additions to them." Gideon's eye narrowed as he studied the frame around the door.

I stared to lean closer, and Gideon's grip tightened, stopping me. But I could make out scratch marks in the stone, barely larger than a coin. A crosshatch here, a *V* or a *Z* there, interconnected but making so little sense, it'd be easy to mistake them for something a bored teenager had chipped out at some point.

"I modified them in case I..." Brayden looked uncomfortable. "In case there was a vampire that wasn't... you know, evil. But that's why they look like that. Can I show you?"

In the distance, shrieks rose in the direction we'd come from.

"Fuck," Ulysses muttered.

I shifted my weight nervously. "Come on, we need to get inside."

"I'll check," Liam said.

Alarm shot through me. "Wait, if it's dangerous, though, shouldn't we let Brayden—"

I cut off as Liam started toward the door. Anger and some measure of fear carried through the connection between me and all the Sentinels, making it even harder to breathe than it was already.

"What will this do to him if it doesn't work?" I asked.

No one replied.

"Guys. What will this do?" Silence again. "Liam, dammit—"

He gave me a look over his shoulder, equal parts iron and something I didn't want to think about.

Because it looked like goodbye.

I tried to go toward him, but Gideon's grip didn't budge, and I wanted to punch the stubborn bastard for holding me back. Brayden pressed his palm to the frame of the door and then reached out toward Liam. After a moment's consideration, Liam took his hand.

Brayden whispered something so low I couldn't hear the words.

"Your friend is a witch?" Gideon asked me, caution and incredulity mingling in his tone.

Brayden threw him a quick look before I could respond. "No, I just learned this from a witch on the internet."

"Zeus's balls," Ulysses muttered. "Internet spells. So there's no way to know if that person had the damndest clue what they were—"

Liam stepped through the doorway. Gideon tensed, his grip digging into my bicep.

Nothing happened.

"See?" Brayden said as if it'd been fine the whole time, but I knew him well enough to see the relief in his body language.

He hadn't been sure. Dear God.

The shrieking came again, even closer. I glanced back at the street to see a shadow race around the corner.

"Shit." Ulysses motioned quickly for us to get inside. "Go!"

One after the other, Brayden grabbed our hands, saying something under his breath quickly.

"In, in, in," Ulysses urged behind us.

We hurried through the entryway while the shadow bore down on us like a falcon diving toward its prey.

"Get back!" Asher shouted, shoving me behind him as the rabid charged right at the entryway.

The creature slammed to a stop as if hitting an invisible wall, and it screamed as it burst into flame. As I watched, its smoky shape crumbled into ash, falling like snow onto the stoop.

I let out a shaky breath, looking at the others. Damn. So *that's* what they'd been afraid of.

"Come on." Brayden's voice was slightly unsteady, and he cleared his throat. "Diana's going to want to talk to you."

Word traveled fast, and as we followed Brayden down the hall, more than a few people popped their heads out to stare at us.

And just as many fled, terrified.

I tried to keep a calm expression on my face. Tried to look nonthreatening too. But the four guys around me were anything but unassuming on a good day, and right now, they probably wouldn't have appeared any less deadly if they'd been holding kittens.

Yeah, trying not to scare anyone was definitely a losing battle.

I gave up and turned my focus to our surroundings, if only to avoid the people staring at me like I was a monster too. The building was a strange mix, where I could see the school it had been in some parts, and others were nothing but remodeled and made new. Sleek modern light fixtures hung from the ceiling; sound-deadening carpet covered the floors. But the doorframes were slightly too wide, and the halls were too. The ceilings were abnormally high, and the wood beams crossing them were weathered and worn like they'd come with the original structure. Something in the air still carried the weight of so many lives passing through here over the decades, and if I closed my eyes, I could almost hear the echoes of all the kids who'd hurried up and down the corridors, calling to their friends as they rushed to class.

Diana sat in a room that *must* have been the teacher's lounge.

She didn't say anything as we followed Brayden inside, merely nodded to Jasmine, who gave us all a nervous look before fleeing out of a door on the far side of the room. Never taking her eyes from us, Diana waited for us to approach. She sat in a boxy armchair the color of grass in springtime beside a fireplace with no flames inside, and she had her hands folded calmly in front of her atop a knife that matched the one Jasmine had held. From the faint lines around her eyes and mouth, I guessed she was probably in her fifties, but her black hair didn't have a trace of gray. She had high cheekbones and a sharp nose, and though her eyelashes were dark and thick enough to be the envy of mascara users everywhere, I couldn't see any makeup on her brown skin. She showed no hint of fear at the sight of me or the Sentinels flanking me. Instead, she seemed to be assessing us from the moment we stepped through the door.

"You brought five strangers here." A hint of accusation touched her flat tone.

Brayden shifted his weight as if putting himself between the woman and me. "Wren is a friend. And she says they can help us."

Diana's dark eyes slid to me. "Vampires."

Her tone hadn't changed.

Brayden winced. "They helped save some people a few blocks from here. Vampires were attacking them—other vampires, I mean."

"And apparently there are different kinds."

No matter how her words could have been made to sound like a question, they never did. Somewhere between a flat statement and an invitation for you to confirm her information, they made me want to squirm like I was back in elementary school facing the principal after getting into a fight on the playground.

"I take it you're in charge of this place," Asher said before I could answer.

Her expression didn't change a millimeter. "As much, I assume, as you're in charge of your companions."

Asher's eyes narrowed slightly.

She simply returned her attention to us all. "I was the leasing supervisor of this building before your kind delivered us all to hell. But now I'm supposed to believe you're not inter-ested in attacking us as the others did."

God, was this woman actually *capable* of asking a question? "Those were rabids. They're not like us." I hesitated. "Well, the original rabids aren't. It's complicated."

From the look on her face, it was obvious my fumbling words didn't help much.

"What's the deal with this place?" I nodded at the hall. "Do you all live here?"

For an uncomfortably long moment, she simply watched us. "You've studied vampires for some time." She turned to Brayden. "Is she why?"

An actual question. Damn. Except she hadn't answered mine.

Discomfort flashed over my friend's face. "Sort of."

"Because she'd been turned."

"Because of what happened in Fort Briar."

I turned to Brayden, confused. That was weeks ago, and the GSS had covered it up. "You were looking into vampires?"

He shrugged awkwardly. "I knew some of the people in those videos online. Mrs. Yang was my neighbor growing up. Mr. Patel taught night school. And the news wanted me to believe they just *decided* to attack people and pretend to be vampires?" His brow rose and fell. "So I started digging online for a better explanation... and maybe some way to help everybody."

"But you weren't a part of that," Diana continued to us.

With effort, I made myself stay focused. "We got away from what happened there."

I wasn't about to tell her it'd also happened partly because I'd been there in the first place.

"We've been trying to get them free of what's been going on." I nodded at Ulysses and Gideon. "And we want to help the ones who've been turned rabid."

"But not the humans."

My mouth moved, a protesting sound leaving me before any words could. God, this woman—

"Didn't this young man just tell you we saved several humans only a short while ago?" Gideon retorted.

"Perhaps you only did that to give us reason to allow you in here."

"Rabids would scarcely resort to subterfuge. If they wanted inside your building, they'd get in here."

She scoffed. "You've seen the sigils on the door. Believe me when I say that's not the extent of our defenses."

I shivered, my eyes darting to Brayden.

"I trust Wren," he said. "If she thinks they can help us…"

Diana's dark eyes flicked to him, and Brayden's face took on an insistent look that—just for a heartbeat—made her own hard expression falter.

My brow furrowed. What was that about?

Iron returned to her gaze. "If you wish to stay," she said to us, "then there will be a price."

Tension rocketed through my connection with the Sentinels.

"These 'rabids,' as you call them. They've taken prisoners. If you want to stay here, you will get them free."

I swallowed hard. "Who do they have?"

Brayden shifted his weight awkwardly. "My mom." His chin twitched toward Diana. "And her wife."

Oh, God.

A rough breath left me. I didn't know Diana, but suddenly I wondered how much of her tension was someone just trying to keep from panicking, especially when panic couldn't do any good. And meanwhile, the sheer thought of rabids having Brayden's mom was enough to make me wonder how the hell *he* wasn't freaking out. I sure as hell was. Evelyn Michaels had been a fixture throughout my childhood. As sweet as a sugar cookie in human form, she'd turned their house into a second home for me, and I'd been heartbroken when she moved from Fort Briar to St. Louis.

But the idea that *rabids* had her...

"Have your people tried to reach them?" Asher's voice wasn't cold anymore.

Diana scoffed. "There are traps throughout the city. Trip wires and bombs, along with scouts hiding everywhere, all to catch anyone attempting to escape. The vampires are highly organized, so whatever you say about some of them being forced to do this"—her eyes skipped to Ulysses and then back—"I believe they've been planning this for a while."

I wanted to move between her and Ulysses. But when it came to what she said, I wasn't sure she was wrong. I remembered Priscilla. Before that woman had sacrificed herself by letting Amalie take over her body, she'd said something similar. That the rabids weren't nearly as disorganized as the Sentinels and everyone else believed.

"What about the government?" Asher persisted.

"Oh, they claim they're attempting to get people out, but evacuating a large city isn't exactly a fast operation—and that's without your enemy attacking every night, sabotaging your routes, and biting and turning anyone they get their hands on."

"And the government evacuated the nicer neighborhoods first," Brayden added, a sickened tone in his voice. "Nobody knows when they'll be coming for us."

My stomach twisted.

Diana drew in a breath. "Our people have been stuck here for days. All communication with the outside world is cut off, leaving us only what we can hear from emergency broadcasts and what we learn from others. But we've also seen enough to know we're safer here than making a run for it."

I cast a questioning glance at Brayden when she didn't continue, her face twisted bitterly.

"Bodies," he said. "Neighbors who tried to escape. The 'rabids,' they, uh..." He swallowed. "They hang them from the buildings."

"Gods below..." Asher murmured.

My gaze darted to him and the others.

Their horrified expressions were clear. They hadn't known that part.

"The vampires have left the electricity running," Diana continued. "They seem to enjoy using the lights at night to more easily stalk their prey—otherwise known as *us*. We've blacked out the windows, and so far they haven't poisoned the water, though that might only be a matter of time. But given the current conditions, we don't have supplies to last beyond another week. Not if we want to feed everyone in the building."

I looked over at Asher and the others. "Can we help them?"

Gideon appeared grim. Liam seemed ready to hunt down more rabids right now. Meanwhile, Asher had an expression on his face I was coming to recognize. I'd bet he was already analyzing every possible scenario.

"Do you remember anything else?" he asked Ulysses. "Where they may have laid traps? What their movement patterns were? Anything."

Ulysses' face tightened, and he didn't meet Asher's eyes even as he nodded. "Yeah," he said, his voice quiet. "I can tell you what I know."

My heart hurt for him. There was a haunted air to him now, like he didn't want to be inside his own head.

I glanced back to find Diana and Brayden both watching us.

"Any other humans still in the area?" Asher asked.

"A few. Most retreated here after the vampires attacked their neighbors."

He nodded thoughtfully.

"What are you thinking?" I asked him.

"Any chance there are government people with the hostages?" he said to Diana rather than answer.

I gave him a confused look.

Diana's eyes narrowed. "Possibly."

He glanced at the Sentinels.

"So will you help us?" Diana pressed. "Or do we need to utilize those defenses against you?"

I looked back at her sharply. It didn't matter that she was facing five vampires. It didn't even matter that she was all alone in this room, minus Brayden. Her eyes were like fire and her expression iron, as if she wouldn't hesitate for a second to do just what she said, let alone doubt that she'd win.

God, never mind that her threat was horrible. I wanted to have *half* that much confidence when I got to her age—or whatever the equivalent would be for a vampire.

Asher turned back to her. "Yes, we'll help."

5

ULYSSES

The others were trusting me.

I wish I trusted myself that much.

In a metal chair that kept digging into my spine, I sat. It'd been hours since we first arrived. Hours since that guy, Brayden, shot me, only for us to narrowly escape a rabid attack with that same guy's help. Sunrise would be coming soon. None of us had left the room, though most of the humans we'd seen earlier had retreated to their apartments or wherever else they felt safe. But the next shift of humans had arrived, drifting in and out ostensibly for "business" with Diana.

From the way they barely took their eyes from us, I suspected they just wanted to ogle the vampires.

Asher had taken to the strategic aspects of this immediately, gathering information and surveying the maps Diana had with her like the soldier he'd once been. Gideon stood nearby, making suggestions based on his knowledge of the history of the city. The man was an encyclopedia—probably a thousand of them, really. He could recall everything from architectural details to construction materials based on whatever the hell he'd read over the years. Meanwhile, Liam hovered near Wren in the far corner of the room, watching all the humans like he'd fillet them in an instant if they came near her.

And she sat in an armchair, doing her damnedest not to admit that it was hard for her to even fucking stand up.

Guilt drove its toxic barbs into my anger. I looked away.

I'd tried to help with the planning early on, offering what I remembered from my time as Amalie's favorite puppet—not that I wanted to remember any of it. But none of the humans were comfortable with me around—which was entirely fair—and so after a while, I'd drifted back, attempting to remain beneath notice and waiting for when the Sentinels might need me again.

I kept myself from shifting position on the torture device masquerading as a chair. Any little movement I made startled the humans into staring at me and gripping their weapons. Sitting quietly seemed to make them calmer than standing, so here I sat. For their part, the Sentinels were still watching me from the corners of their eyes. I knew it wasn't about the gunshot wounds. We'd been shot plenty of times over the past few centuries. As long as it wasn't a headshot—fatal to just about anything—or the GSS's fancy cursed bullets, we got over it.

No, it was because of all the things I wouldn't talk about. Because of how I'd withdrawn from the connection between all of us as much as I could, walling myself away and essentially doing the mental equivalent of plugging my ears and closing my eyes. Sure, we'd all become pretty damn proficient at that back when Amalie first made us, connected us, and tortured us. Only way to keep what she'd done to us from torturing the other Sentinels too like she wanted. And yeah, retreating was still barely effective at best.

But that didn't stop me from trying.

I could only hope the other guys wouldn't push it. The gods knew I hadn't discussed *why* I was doing this with them. Things had been awkward as hell over the past few days as we waited and prayed for Wren to wake up.

But that was the problem right there.

A strangely comforting feeling filtered through the connection between me and the other Sentinels, but it wasn't coming from them. My eyes darted over to Wren. She was watching me, concern on her face.

I turned away fast.

The sensation remained.

I gritted my teeth, trying to block it too—for *her* sake, not that she'd know that.

The feeling changed, turning to a grim sense of resolve. I glanced back to spot her pushing to her feet, Liam bracing her. How the hell he had become okay with touching her was a question for another time. Right now, they were coming my way.

I tensed on the gods-awful chair, wondering if I should retreat physically too.

And gods, didn't I feel like a coward for even thinking that.

"Hey." She gave me a smile as she came closer, ignoring the way the humans stared at us both. "Can I talk to you?"

I hesitated. Why would she want to talk? It wouldn't result in anything good. Not ultimately.

My heart turned to lead. I wouldn't run from this. "Uh, yeah. Sure." I glanced around, but I had no idea where to go. Did she even *want* to go somewhere else? Maybe she'd want to stay where the others could watch over her at all times.

Wren took my hand.

Everything in me froze, the softness and warmth of her like a balm and agony at the same time. Sure, I'd held her after that spear nearly ran her through. And I'd risked keeping her beneath me when bullets were flying. But this was different.

Focus, idiot.

"Come on." She pulled me with her as she headed for the

hall. At her friend Brayden's confused look, she only said, "I need to talk to him for a minute. We'll be right back."

I could feel the eyes of damn near every human tracking us as we walked out of the room and down the hall. But she never looked their way, resolutely striding along.

Or trying to. Gods, I could feel her shaking even from this small exertion. Her breaths were barely more than tiny motions of her chest.

In spite of everything, I caved and drew her arm around mine. I needed to keep her safe from the humans and to help hold her steady. I wasn't a total asshole.

At the sight of a room with an open door, she veered left, bringing me with her. The space beyond the door had probably been some kind of entertainment room, if the television and couches were any indication. But no one was in there now.

Pausing by the door, she glanced at Liam. "Keep people out, please?"

She wanted to talk alone?

Gods, no. This was a bad plan. "Wren," I started. "You shouldn't—"

Her grip tightened on my arm, and she threw me an insistent look. How the hell she could still be so strong and determined after everything she'd gone through, I had no idea.

But it only made me more determined to protect her, if only from myself. "Let Liam stay, at least."

Her mouth tightened, and she glanced at the other man.

Liam's jaw muscles jumped as his eyes went from me to the hall. But after a heartbeat, he stepped back.

I gaped at him. "Man, you heard me. What—"

"Come on." Wren started into the room, leaving me the choice of following and supporting her or risking she'd collapse.

Incredulous, I followed.

She shut the door behind us and then sank down onto one

of the couches. Immediately, I backed away to the far end of the room.

Consternation crossed her face. "What is it, Ulysses?"

I searched for an answer. "I just don't want to make you nervous."

"Pretty sure I'm the one making you nervous."

I didn't contradict her. I didn't want to lie.

Her brow drew down. "That wasn't really you in those recordings. You know that, right?"

I didn't respond. Her face took on a perplexed expression, and she pushed to her feet again. I started back toward her, only to freeze as I felt her questing touch along the connection inside us, like someone reaching out in the dark, seeking contact.

It was unsettling. I'd never felt anything like this from the others. Nothing even close. But it made me try to shut her out even more. "Stop. Please."

She hesitated, the sensation fading. "I'm sorry. I shouldn't have—"

"It's not you."

She was silent, but I could tell from her expression she didn't fully believe me.

"I just..." Gods, I couldn't leave her feeling like this was her fault. "I don't want it near you."

"Don't want *what* near me?"

Tension quivered through me. "What they did."

"Are you still feeling something from Amalie and Urlfeige?" A hint of nervousness flashed over her face.

"No." I wetted my lips. "But I still did those things. Everything you guys saw. More. I appreciate you trying to say it wasn't me, but... I was there. That *thing* was inside my head. I know the others can pick up on it. And I know I'm getting something from you too, and I don't want you to have to feel any of this. Everything that happened before in my life was bad enough. But this…"

"Do you mean when you all were prisoners of Amalie? But… I saw that. You showed me that."

Ah, yes, my stellar moment of utterly failing to show her the care she deserved. Nothing like ripping open a woman's mind and pouring in your hell to show her you could be trusted.

Yet somehow, she'd forgiven me. More than that. We'd shared a bed, and she'd fed from me, and the reality of that still left me flabbergasted.

The least I could do was not fuck things up this time.

"No. Not what Amalie did to…" I shook my head. "It doesn't matter." Shifting my weight back, I added a little more distance between us. The hurt expression flashed across her face again.

Fuck.

I looked away, drawing a breath, even if that simple act filled me with self-hatred too. I knew what it meant for me to be able to breathe this deeply. I'd fed off somebody. Probably an innocent. Probably someone who'd screamed.

Nausea twisted up inside of me, just as it had every time over the past few days when I thought about the blood currently coursing through my veins.

"Ulysses." Wren took a step toward me.

"Please." I held up a hand to stop her. "Sit back down. Don't hurt yourself."

"I'm okay."

Like hell she was.

Frustration burned in my gut. Dammit, how did I do this? Keep her safe from what I'd become?

The answer sucked. But it might work.

"I think it's better if we keep our distance from each other." I made my voice cold, no matter how it made my skin crawl. Fuck, that was the last thing I wanted. But times had changed.

I needed to do right by her.

Her brow furrowed. "Huh?"

"We need distance. Getting close was a mistake."

"Wait, what?"

"You heard me. I want you to stay away from me. I don't want anything more to happen between us. So whatever you're doing here, just—"

She walked toward me, and the words that felt like slime in my mouth cut off. I faltered, torn. Reaching out for her again wouldn't help my case. Letting her fall would make me even more of a bastard than I was being already.

Quivering faintly, she stopped in front of me and gripped the back of a nearby sofa, using it to steady herself. I could smell her scent, as intoxicating as ever. A hint of smoke from the destruction outside, a touch of starch from the bed of random clothes she'd been lying on. But underneath it all was *her,* and everything in me craved wrapping myself around her and breathing that in deep.

"Did Asher and Liam tell you about what happened when we went to Eden's?"

I knew what she was talking about. I couldn't quite believe it, though. Thanks to Eden's magic, they'd had some kind of past life flashback to a time when all of us had been together, thousands of years ago.

Which was great and all, but it didn't make me one bit safer for her now. "That doesn't change the fact that I don't want you to—"

"Whatever happened in the past few weeks of *this* life, it doesn't change who you are or who you were. It wasn't you."

I turned away. "There's nothing to discuss here. I'm not interested in there being anything more between us, so—"

"I know you don't mean that."

There wasn't any pain or speculation in her voice. Just certainty, and it hurt.

Inside my mind, I tried to retreat farther from the connection between us, to the point where the tension of holding myself apart from it made my head throb.

"Does that help?"

My eyes darted back to her, confused.

"Shutting yourself away from us? Does it make what they did hurt less?"

That's why she thought I was doing this? For *me*? "I don't want that shit to touch *you*. It might hurt you."

"Ulysses." Her eyebrow rose above a wry expression. "You've seen my chest, right?"

I blinked, my eyes flicking downward. Her...

Right. The wound. Not the breasts I ached to kiss, caress, and lavish attention upon.

Focus, focus, focus.

"Yeah. And maybe I could make that worse." I pulled my gaze back up to meet her eyes. "I *attacked* you, Wren. I had them in my head and—"

"And then you helped me. You *saved* me. Liam told me what you did, getting me away from there. Ulysses, Amalie would have killed me if not for you."

"But if *any* of what they did in here makes that worse"—I drilled a fingertip against my skull—"then it'll be the same either way. She'll get to... she'll..."

Images of Amalie hurting Wren filled me with such rage, I couldn't speak.

"Ulysses—"

"No. She..." As if they were ghosts, the screams of the long dead echoed in my mind, tangling with the choking fear I'd hear Wren scream like that too. "I will *never* let her hurt you like them."

"Like who?"

I shook my head, trying to drive the ghosts back. Dammit, I needed to get away from her. "Liam!"

The door opened immediately, and my fellow Sentinel gave me a confused look.

"Help Wren back to the—"

"No." She threw an impatient glance back at Liam. "Give us another minute."

"Dammit, woman." I rocked with the urge to get farther from her, but she was between me and the way out of here.

"Another minute," she repeated to Liam, ignoring me.

His eyes flashed between us, but then he eased the door closed, retreating back into the hall.

Traitor. "Listen, Wren—"

"Like *who*?"

My teeth clenched, my muscles tight with the effort of holding hell back in my head. Ever since I'd come back to myself, the memories had been right there, dredged up by what Urlfeige had done and used to torture me for the gods only knew how long. And they hadn't left me alone for a moment since, fresh as an open wound despite being a thousand years old.

Her face took on a careful expression, like she was easing her way out on a thin branch. "Ulysses, are you talking about..." She wetted her lips. "About someone besides them?" She nodded her head back toward the door as if to indicate the Sentinels, never taking her eyes from me, and there was something so cautious in her gaze.

Quaking spread through my middle. "My family."

A tiny breath left her, and her expression took on a pained cast. "Ah."

My heart ached. She knew. Of course she did. Amalie had been in her mind.

"I'm safe, though," she said. "Amalie can't get to me. Not with you and the others—"

I couldn't help it. I retreated like the words burned.

"Ulysses—"

"That's just the problem. If I'm near you and if *anything* they did to me could somehow hurt you... Dammit, I *couldn't* stop her. Not then. So I have to now."

She started to shake her head, but I cut her off, the words pressing out of me like blood escaping a wound. "If you remember any of that—and I wish to the gods you didn't—then you know I fucking tried. I couldn't fight her, couldn't even fucking *beg* her enough to get her to stop. She slaughtered my entire village before she started in on my family, and she killed them all except for my little niece. And before she let her go, Amalie bent down and smiled at me while she told Calliope she was going to make me into a monster too."

Hatred twisted like a red-hot poker in my gut—for me or Amalie, I didn't know—because in addition to my dying family, now there was a kaleidoscope of strangers in my memory, all of them begging *me* to stop too. "And she did. It took her a thousand years, but she did."

Wren's lips parted, soundless. Her eyes were filled with anguish for me.

I couldn't stand the sight, especially when I didn't deserve an ounce of it. "So when I say I don't want this shit to touch you, please know it's because I care about you so fucking much. But she finally made me a monster just like her, and I can't risk—"

"No."

Her voice was soft, but it silenced mine all the same.

"She couldn't."

"Wren, she—"

"Do you remember when you grabbed my sword, back when Amalie ordered you to attack me?"

I faltered, not sure where she was going with this.

"I felt you. Inside, down below all that darkness they thought could erase you. You were still there. Still fighting. They poured all that hell into your mind, but they couldn't destroy you. Even with Amalie acting like she fucking *owned* you, even when you were standing right by her side, she and Urlfeige didn't have the power to wipe away who you are." She shook her head. "That *thing* was not you."

My mouth moved, but I couldn't begin to think what to say.

She smiled, the strain of standing evident in the tension around her eyes but not dimming the expression in the slightest. "You're the good man you've always been, Ulysses. Amalie and Urlfeige can't take that away."

The ache in my heart turned warm, but in this strange way that hurt. "How can you still want to be near me?"

She chuckled breathlessly. "If you knew how many times I wondered that about *you* after I had her in my head too..."

I blinked, taken aback. "You did? Gods, I'm so sorry I—"

"It's *okay*. We're not—"

Her legs went out from under her, sending her tumbling to the carpet.

"Wren!" I dropped to my knees, but she didn't respond. Across the room, the door crashed open, and Liam rushed toward us. "Get Asher and Gideon!" I shouted at him.

He tore out of the room.

I looked back down, my hands hovering over her, torn between the urge to grab her and the fear I'd make this worse if I did.

I'd been a fool. Even coming this close to her had probably made this happen.

Shaking, I retreated. Raw sounds escaped her throat, like gasping from someone running out of air. The color was draining from her skin, and her eyes were wide and unfocused, rolling in her sockets like she was having a seizure.

Oh, gods, this was starvation. I'd only seen it a few times—never this fast—and there was no *way* it should be happening to her after all the blood Asher, Liam, and Gideon had given her when she was unconscious, just to keep her alive.

Her rasping noises grew more desperate. More panicked. Quick as a snake, her fangs punched out, and she lunged across the distance between us and slammed them into my forearm.

I jerked back, but her hands gripped my arm like a vise. With painful severity, she dragged on my veins like they were all that stood between her and death.

There was nothing erotic about this. Nothing but terror, because if simply *touching* her had hurt her, what the hell would drinking my blood do?

"Wren." I tried to pry her away, and she snarled like a feral animal, not letting go. "Baby, please. You've got to stop. This will hurt you."

Footsteps pounded on the floor, and Gideon raced into the room, Asher and Liam in shadow form with him.

Brayden was on their heels.

Shifting back to human form quickly, Asher turned to Wren's friend. "Keep people out. Please."

Brayden stared across the room at me and Wren, but he nodded. "Yeah." He yanked the door shut.

Gideon and Liam were already crouching down beside me.

"What the hell is this, brother?" Gideon demanded.

I shook my head, still trying to break her hold. Her desperate suckling from my arm was beginning to slow—a good thing since my head was spinning. Gods, she shouldn't have been able to take that much blood that fast. But, hey, starvation was a funny thing.

I shook my head against the delirium. I felt like she was dragging on the very depths of me, drawing more than just my blood into her. My essence. My *soul*.

Which couldn't be good, for all the reasons I'd just told her and about a million more besides. "Somebody stop her," I gasped. "This... Don't want to hurt her..."

Asher slid his arms around her, while Liam positioned himself by her head.

"One, two…" Asher counted. "Three."

Liam shoved his fingers into her mouth, breaking her seal around the bite and hissing between his teeth as her fangs caught him instead. Quickly, Asher yanked her backward.

Gideon was there immediately, binding my wound with fabric torn from the gods knew where. I collapsed against the back of the couch, searching for Wren immediately.

Asher held her in his arms several feet away. A keening sound left her, but she wasn't trying to bite him. Instead, she curled in on herself, shaking.

"Is she…" My head spun. "Gods…"

Gideon sliced his wrist quickly. "Here."

I swallowed down a few gulps before sealing his wound. The other Sentinels and I rarely fed from one another—weakening each other wasn't smart—but desperate times or whatever.

The dizzy feelings faded. Drawing a brief breath, I looked back toward Asher and Wren.

She wasn't shaking as hard anymore. In fact, she was straightening in his arms, blinking like she was trying to focus.

But her eyes dropped immediately to her chest, and she yanked aside the collar of her hoodie, exposing the black mark on her skin.

The black mark that was significantly smaller than it had been.

I stared at her. "What…"

Her eyes rose to mine, a breathless sound escaping her. And all she said was, "Thank you."

6

WREN

"What the hell was that?" Asher demanded, holding me tight in his arms even as he looked between me and Ulysses both.

I didn't know what to tell him. One minute, I was light-headed but talking to Ulysses about the seriously horrific things that'd happened to him, and the next...

Ulysses sat up a little more against the back of the sofa. "It looked like you were starving to death, but at hyper-speed."

My hand rubbed at the black mark on my chest. "That's basically how it felt."

"And that?" Gideon prompted, nodding toward where I was rubbing my skin.

I shuddered. "It was like..." I searched for words. "Like something was dragging me into it. Taking *me* into it. My energy, my... whatever. Self. And I just... reacted." I glanced down at where Ulysses' arm was ravaged, soaking into the bandage with an injury too large to simply seal up. "I'm so sorry."

Ulysses hardly seemed to notice the wound. "But it's better now." He jerked his chin at my chest, directing the statement at that rather than his own injury. "Smaller." Before I could say anything, he continued. "But these guys fed you blood for days, and it never... I mean..."

Worry hovered around the edges of his words.

My brow twitched down, memories playing back. When I hit the floor, everything had gone strange in my head, like my control of myself as a rational person had started to slip into pure adrenaline and fear.

Shivers rolled through me. I'd just become an animal. A desperate, hungry animal who was an inch away from death and needed to survive. Needed to feed, no matter the cost.

But once I'd bitten him, that changed. "It was you." I looked back up at him. "And... and me. When you attacked me back on the street a few days ago, I felt like I was reaching through our connection to you. *Into* you with... I don't know, power or something?" I hesitated to say magic, because seriously? I wasn't a witch.

But in my past life, I'd been half angel.

I shoved that thought aside. "It was like our connection let me find you in there, under all that darkness and crap they put in your head. And now it felt like someone..." Shudders rolled through me again as the sensations clicked into place. "Like *Urlfeige* was trying to drain me and take whatever it was that let me do that. But when I bit you, the power I used was still inside you, so I took some of it back in." I gave a vaguely baffled shrug. "And that stopped him."

He stared at me.

Uncomfortable, I glanced back down at my chest. Though it still looked like an explosion of night under my skin, the scabbed wound was maybe half its original size, and the threads of black ink twisting into my veins were almost gone. "I think it was both of us. Whatever I used to help you the other day, and your connection to me. The combination stopped that and helped heal this a bit."

Ulysses' brow furrowed, expressions flickering across his face too fast to read. But then he glanced up at Asher, a question in his eyes.

"You think you're safe to be near him again?" Asher asked me.

I wetted my lips, searching inside myself for the answer. The starvation-level hunger that had overtaken me had hit so fast, I didn't know if I could trust it wouldn't return. But it kind of felt like whatever Ulysses had given me with his blood had closed off some of a connection that had been intended to kill me.

And now I was better. More stable. Stronger.

I nodded. "I think so."

Asher helped me across the carpet to where Ulysses sat with his back to the sofa. Immediately, Ulysses pulled me into his arms, holding me tight.

Tension seeped from my body as I melted against him, my eyes stinging. I was so grateful I hadn't killed him that I had no words. With one hand, he brushed my hair back from my face before pressing a kiss to the top of my head like he was reassuring himself I was still here too.

"We've got to fucking kill this bastard," Ulysses said to the others. "Now."

Liam nodded, total agreement on his face. His hand found mine, squeezing it tightly and not letting go.

I gripped him right back, still shivering. Implications rolled through my mind for what I'd just said, but I didn't feel like I needed to speak any more of it out loud. Everyone in this room knew what it meant that Urlfeige had tried to take more of *whatever* this was from me.

God... how many more vampires were going rabid out there right now?

"Helping these people is still the best way to guarantee we can stay in this place while we plan for how to stop him," Asher said. "Even if they aren't ideal, those spells on the doors and windows will keep the rabids out."

"But what if Urlfeige was able to determine where Wren is located based upon what he just attempted?" Gideon countered.

Asher looked away, his mouth tightening.

"We can't leave these people here for him to attack," I said. "And we can't leave their families to be... eaten. Or turned."

The others were quiet for a moment.

What about the GSS? Liam signed.

"What do you mean?" I asked.

Asher's jaw worked around. "If there *are* GSS agents being held with the other humans, and if we save them, we can keep a handle on them so that they'll have to evacuate these people too if they want to be rescued."

Liam's smile was savage.

"So... we're taking hostages?" I stared at them.

"Leverage for the sake of protecting everyone here."

I blinked at Asher. "That still means hostages."

"Forcing their hand might be the only thing that keeps the people here safe. We don't know what the GSS is doing with evacuees."

I felt sick. There was that. Slayers had tried to kill me just for being turned. They'd been willing to murder me and cover it up to my family. What were they doing now that an entire city was under siege?

"It's a risky strategy," Gideon warned. "They could fight back if we try to hold them here. Innocents could get hurt."

Displeasure crossed Asher's face, but it didn't take away the grim look in his eyes. "Got a better plan?"

Gideon grimaced. "And as for Wren?"

I fought back a scowl. My God, the man never tired of talking about me like I wasn't even here. "I come with you."

All their eyes snapped to me incredulously.

"*That* is definitely not an option," Gideon replied.

I barely kept myself from snarling at him.

"We can't risk the rabids getting their hands on you," Ulysses said.

"And if you split up and Amalie captures you?"

Asher scowled. "We're having this argument again? Last time, we were potentially facing both Ulysses *and* Gideon under Amalie's control. This time, we're not."

Ulysses shifted slightly as if uncomfortable being reminded of that.

"You're still going up against Urlfeige, Amalie, and God knows how many rabids," I pointed out.

"All the more reason for you to stay *here*."

I opened my mouth to argue, but clamped it back shut as the latch clicked and the door opened just a crack.

Brayden peered in. "Is she—" Relief flashed over his face at the sight of me. "Oh God, Wren. What the hell *was* that?"

Before the Sentinels could make any move to stop him, he slipped through the opening and shut the door at his back. "Are you—" He stopped, appearing to register more details.

Details like Ulysses holding me as if he'd never let go. Like Liam crouched near my side, still gripping my hand, all while Asher and Gideon stood near us like protective watchdogs.

I tensed, not sure what he'd think. Even if we hadn't meant to, we couldn't have made it clearer that we were more than mere allies if we'd written it in neon in midair.

Brayden blinked and then fastened his attention back on me like he was dismissing it all as irrelevant. "Are you okay?"

I nodded. "Yeah."

He crossed the room toward me, ignoring the way Gideon shifted his weight like he was preparing to lunge between us if he had to—as weird as it was to see that much protectiveness from *him*.

"What happened?" Brayden asked, glancing at the Sentinels to include them in the question.

I floundered, not sure what to say.

"The ones behind all this want to kill her too," Asher told him flatly.

At Brayden's alarmed expression, I reached up and pulled the collar of my hoodie aside again. His eyes grew wider at the inky explosion beneath my skin.

"They poisoned me. Ulysses just saved my life."

Brayden's mouth moved, and then he gave a slow nod like he was absorbing the information. His eyes went to Ulysses. "I-I'm glad he could."

Ulysses gave a small nod in return, an expression on his face like my friend had just said thank you and apologized for shooting him, all in the same short sentence.

Men.

I forced my attention back to the argument at hand. "If Urlfeige knows where we are, that's all the more reason we need to hurry and get these people out of here."

Brayden's alarm returned. "Wait, what about the ones the vampires have?"

"We were just talking about that," I answered. "We're going to go get them, and then—"

"*You're* going?" My best friend gaped at me like I was nuts. "He just said this thing nearly killed you, like, two minutes ago. And now you're going to bounce back up and rush to... what? Go Mortal Kombat on it?"

Ulysses gave a tiny snort.

"I'll be fine," I ground out.

Brayden scoffed. "Wren, I love your stubborn streak. I do. But you're on the *floor*. You going to tell me the chairs just weren't as comfortable?"

I knew the Sentinels were eyeing us both, but not one of them spoke up. I got the feeling they approved of *someone* arguing with me on this, even if it wasn't them. Scowling at them all, I pushed to my feet.

The room only wobbled a little bit.

"You're all going to be facing rabids," I said to the Sentinels, ignoring Brayden's exasperated look. "Splitting up is a bad idea."

"So is losing you for good this time," Asher replied quietly.

My stomach twisted.

At my side, Ulysses levered himself up too, using the sofa as a brace. "If we have two targets, we have two teams, yeah?"

Asher nodded. "Liam and I will go after the humans that the rabids are holding. Gideon, you stay with Ulysses and Wren, just in case."

I made a protesting sound.

"Liam and I can change form," Asher continued before I could speak. "For some reason, Ulysses and Gideon still can't. If we want to guard this place and have a chance at stealth when we reach where they're holding the hostages, this is the best way to divide our resources."

I stared at him. Sure, it was the best way, as long as you ignored one *small* detail. "That leaves just two of you going into that place. Two against what? Potentially hundreds of rabids? No, if we're splitting up, Gideon should still go with you. We've got the protections Brayden put up around here. Out there, it's just going to be you with nothing else."

The Sentinels shared a glance, and I couldn't hope to know what it was about.

But then Ulysses shook his head. "If that bastard or Amalie come here"—he gave me a solemn look—"and there's even a *chance* I can't stop them from taking me over again..." His eyes flicked to Gideon, who looked equally grim, and then back to me. "I don't want you to have to be the one who needs to..." His brow rose and fell.

I stared at him. "We're not *killing* you, Ulysses. That's not up for debate."

"Anything it takes, Wren," he said quietly. "If we protect you, we protect the world." His hand took mine. "And our world."

My chest ached, but not from any magical wound. Speechless, I squeezed his hand. I wanted to continue arguing with them on this, but not a single other person in the room looked like they were going to budge on the issue.

But God knew I couldn't risk them either.

Which meant if there was even a *chance* Ulysses was still in danger from those two and I could help stop them like I had before, I had to stay near him.

Dammit.

"Okay," I relented. "How much longer until sunrise?"

"About twenty minutes or so," Asher said.

So little time.

I drew myself up. "I guess we should get ready then."

The minutes flew by, and then Asher and Liam were gone.

And I didn't know what to do with myself.

"So you all really can go out in sunlight," Brayden said as the two Sentinels disappeared around the corner.

"Yeah."

"No others, though?"

"No." I hesitated. "Not without every inch of skin covered, anyway."

He blew out a breath and shut the door. "Well, I guess... now we wait, yeah?"

I managed a nod, but I was running out of the ability to answer questions.

"You need to show us all your current security measures," Gideon said in a voice that made it clear it wasn't a request.

Brayden eyed him for a moment before nodding.

"And somewhere for Wren to rest," Ulysses added.

"I'm *fine*." I gave him a flat look. "You're the one I... you know."

I couldn't bring myself to say "almost killed," despite how it was one hundred percent true.

But Ulysses didn't rise to the bait. Arching an eyebrow at my friend, he just waited.

Brayden nodded.

An exasperated noise left me. "Guys, I'm—"

Brayden gave me a pointed look. "You nearly died."

Awesome, now they were ganging up on me.

Again.

I turned away, scowling.

"Lead on," Gideon said to Brayden, nodding to the stairs.

Biting back further arguments since no one was listening anyway, I followed as we climbed to the second floor. The wide hallways continued up here, though overall it was quieter than the ground floor had been. The doors were spaced far apart, and I wondered how many had been covered over to make larger apartments out of the former classrooms. Brass numbers glistened on the wall next to them, under steel light fixtures that somehow evoked a schoolhouse feeling, even if I couldn't have explained why.

At apartment 207, Brayden paused. Knocking briefly, he waited another moment. "Just making sure no one else is in here." He turned the handle and headed inside.

The entryway emptied into a large living room with eggshell-white walls and a high ceiling crisscrossed with metal pipes in a way that was simultaneously industrial and chic. The arched windows were plastered over with paper and cloth, same as everywhere else, but they'd probably let in a lot of light back before rabids tore the city apart. When Brayden flicked on a switch, a pair of wooden lamps on end tables by the mint-green sofa clicked to life, revealing a room decorated with precisely arranged throw pillows, inspirational sayings on the walls, and open doorways leading to both a bedroom and bathroom, as well as an archway to the kitchen. Everything was set just so, not a single item out of place that I could see.

Brayden closed the door behind us. "The couple who lived here tried to get out right away when everything went to hell."

It didn't escape me how he spoke of the former residents in the past tense, and at my glance, he gave an uncomfortable shrug. "Bodies. They answer questions, I guess."

I swallowed hard at the reminder of what rabids were doing with their victims, and suddenly everything in the pristine apartment took on a different quality.

Like a mausoleum. One that was kinda, sorta my fault.

I shifted my weight, wanting more than anything to get out of here.

Moving past us, Gideon checked through the apartment swiftly and then returned. "Does anyone have keys to this place?"

"Just Diana. Manager and all that."

Gideon didn't look pleased.

"Maybe I should just help you keep watch," I suggested.

He gave me a dry look. "Put something in front of the door."

Exasperating, that's what he was. All of them, really.

"We'll be back to check on you in a bit," Ulysses said more gently.

Without another word, the three of them left, Gideon already quizzing Brayden on their defenses and the intricacies of the spell he'd learned from the internet. Only Ulysses managed to cast an apologetic look back before shutting the door.

I scowled at the polished wood. They were being ridiculous.

Yes, I'd collapsed. But we were in a war, I had a sword, and they'd locked me in a dead couple's apartment to... what? Sleep?

Nothing in me wanted to sleep. To stop Amalie and Urlfeige from ever hurting anyone ever again, hell yes. But take a nap?

I'd been unconscious for days.

Energy quivered through me. I couldn't stay still. Clenching my fist to keep from summoning my sword, I paced a circuit around the room. The exhaustion and weakness from earlier were gone entirely, and now my veins felt like they were pulsing with electricity. But I didn't think it was just Ulysses' blood causing this. No, my gut said it was whatever I took in *with* the blood that was thrumming through me now. My own energy, but... different and growing stronger the longer I had it back again.

Which made the fact I was stuck here *utterly* absurd.

I glared at the wood cutout on the wall telling me to Live, Laugh, Love as I paced another loop around the room. Had the couple gotten that chance? No. Would anyone as long as we were stuck here? Also fuck no.

And yet I was trapped here.

Damn lot of good it did the dead.

Or the dying.

I walked faster. And what about Asher and Liam? Had they reached their destination yet? It'd only been—I glanced at the clock and grimaced—okay, twelve minutes. But still.

Would I feel it if something happened to them? The connection was affected by distance, but I'd been able to pick up on Gideon and Ulysses even when they were trapped by Amalie.

I squeezed my eyes shut briefly, resisting the urge to reach out for them in my mind. After all, what if I caught them just as a rabid was attacking, and I broke their concentration?

What if I got them killed?

My fists clenched tighter, and I walked faster, sweeping a quick turn around the broad oak coffee table and past the mint-green sofa, concentrating with all my might on *not* reaching toward the two men who could be fighting off psychotic vampires right now.

A quiet knock came at the door.

I stopped, my body rocking with the urge to keep pacing while politeness insisted I should see who was there.

The door opened slightly. Ulysses stuck his head in, and his brow furrowed. "I thought you were going to put something in front of this."

I turned away and kept pacing. If a rabid got into this building, a bookcase in front of the entrance wouldn't stop a shadow from slipping through the gaps—and the guys should have realized that.

The bottom of the door whispered over the carpet as he pushed it open wider, and a *clunk* followed when he shut it again.

"So can I head back out there now?" I asked without turning around. "Or are you all going to check the security of the yard next?"

He paused, and I grimaced. I was being a jerk. I knew that.

Without another word, I started pacing again.

He just let me, saying nothing as I completed circuits of the room. But I could feel his attention on me, even if, when I glanced over, he was studying the covered windows or the cheerful decorations on the walls.

"Is this what you came back here for?" I snapped finally. "To watch me pace?"

His eyes flicked up to me. I scowled at the sheer fucking calmness of his expression, like he was more worried about me than the goddamn apocalypse going on outside these walls, and I spun away to continue circling the room. God, I felt like my veins were on fire, even if my chest was still numb.

What if this was Urlfeige? What if the energy was really just something he—

I shoved the thought aside, walking faster with the stupid Live, Laugh, Love exhortation flashing past over and over in brilliant testimony to how that hadn't fucking saved anyone from—

Ulysses' hands caught me. "Wren, stop."

I was shaking all over.

He rubbed his hands up and down my arms. "They're going to make it."

I shook my head. "But what if—"

"This is Asher and Liam we're talking about. Two of the scariest motherfuckers on the planet, especially when someone's putting an innocent in danger. They've got this."

My mouth moved. My body was still trembling. "I just..."

I tried to push past him. I needed to keep moving. To be doing *something*, if only to keep my traitorous brain from imagining all the ways this could continue to go wrong.

His grip tightened. "You're leaving burn marks in the carpet, baby. Maybe let's not torch the place, eh?"

I looked back.

Oh my God, he was right. The carpet smoldered where I'd been pacing. Wisps of smoke drifted up from it, fading slowly.

How fast had I been going?

Ulysses took my cheek, bringing my attention back around but not letting go as I looked up at him. He smiled gently. "They'll be back."

"You can't know that."

"I know them. I trust them." His fingers strayed back, brushing a strand of my hair behind my ear. "And honestly? I know you do too."

The ache in my chest grew worse. I closed my eyes.

"Come here."

He pulled me into his arms, and I squeezed my eyes shut

tighter as I rested my head against him. His hand rubbed up and down gently on my back, and slowly, my panic eased.

"Thank you," I whispered.

I could hear his smile in his voice when he answered. "Anytime."

Seconds slipped by. It was so... comforting, being held by him. Like coming home, really. We'd hardly known each other in this life for more than a few weeks, and yet in some strange way, I just felt like I fit here, wrapped in his arms.

But of the two of us, I was the only one who remembered what we'd been, and the feelings I could pick up on through the connection between us were muddled and hard to understand.

I pulled away enough that I could see his face. "I guess you probably need to get back or..."

His fingers brushed my cheek, and I swallowed hard, a different kind of longing stirring inside me at the gentle touch. "Do you want me to go?" he asked.

The confusing tangle of emotions I was picking up from him felt like a storm he was trying to hold inside. I couldn't read it.

But I wasn't going to lie. "No."

The storm shifted, turning to desire, and as his fingers on my cheek drew me closer, I couldn't have breathed if I'd tried.

His kiss stole the world away. My lips parted, letting him in, and as his hand moved, raking up through my hair, I slid my own around him, slipping beneath the edges of his jacket to where his shirt met his pants.

Dropping his hands from me for only a moment, he yanked off his jacket, fighting to keep his lips on mine while he tossed it aside. His shirt followed, breaking us apart for only a moment, and I grinned, my eyes roaming over the muscled planes of his chest as I reached down to pull off my own.

His hands came back, stilling mine. Heat in his eyes, his brow arched, a smile hovering around his lips.

My insides turned molten.

Slowly, that fire never leaving his gaze, he drew my hoodie and shirt away, moving carefully as if not wanting to cause me pain, but nothing hurt anymore. And then only my bra remained. His wicked smile grew as he stepped around me, his rough hands slipping over my middle, tracing across my skin like he was laying claim to every inch. When he'd completed a full circle, he unfastened my bra, drawing each strap down and letting the entire thing fall.

My heart raced as the tips of his fangs slipped down. "May I?" he asked softly.

I twitched my head in a nod. "Please."

His smile grew. His hands took my breasts, supporting them, caressing them, and my breathing stuttered. I was wet as hell for him, and my core throbbed, begging for more. Gently, he ran his thumbs over my nipples, satisfaction in his eyes when they tightened.

"Ulysses…"

He chuckled softly. "I've wanted your gorgeous breasts in my hands for so long, Wren. You have no idea." His fingers squeezed down. "And more than that."

Lowering his head, he lifted one of my breasts as he continued massaging the other. His fangs pierced the skin around my nipple.

I moaned, my back arching to bring me closer to him. The connection between us surged stronger, becoming a flood of my desire and his mirroring back and forth until it consumed me. I felt his breath hitch, his hands clenching down on me, and my eyes flew open.

For a moment, I was me but Tau as well, and suddenly I knew what was happening. Eden's spell that let Asher, Liam, and I see our past…

It'd reached Ulysses. Maybe Gideon too. But she'd used my blood in that spell, and until the others bit me...

The flash of memories faded, leaving only the rush of my Sentinel drinking from me. Of his tongue tracing my nipple with expert skill while he swallowed me down.

His free hand moved, supporting me when my head fell back and my eyes closed. I moaned again as he worked my nipple, the molten feeling in my core building higher and higher.

"Oh, God... Ulysses!"

I came hard, my knees going out from under me, but he was there, picking me up. Moving me until a soft surface pressed against my back. I opened my eyes to find he'd shifted us to the couch, and gratitude flickered through me. I didn't want to do this in the bed. Anywhere was awkward, but the bed felt especially wrong somehow, given what we knew about what happened to those people.

"Focus, baby," he urged me. "Unless you don't want to—"

I grabbed him, pulling him toward me and locking my lips on his. I needed him more than words could describe.

A smile teased at his mouth when he drew away again. "Yeah, one orgasm was definitely not enough for my woman."

Despite his words, I caught the flash of worry when called me his.

"I'm yours." I grinned. "And I love it when you call me baby."

His smile could have outshone the sun, but it had nothing on the heat in his gaze. With breathtaking speed, he had my pants and underwear off. His own followed, and then he was back, diving between my legs and sucking my clit into his mouth.

Crying out, I arched into him as he worked me with the masterful tongue he *clearly* knew exactly how to use. With one hand, he reached up along my body, gripping my breast and pinching my nipple between his fingers. Pleasure shot straight from my hardened nub down to my pussy, only growing stronger as the fingers of his other hand slipped into me, stroking me from the inside.

I saw stars as my orgasm blasted the world away again.

As my vision cleared, I stared at him while he straightened and wiped his mouth clean with his hand. But my attention strayed down almost immediately, finding his cock hard and ready.

My pussy throbbed. God, I craved him.

He grinned like he could see the desire in my eyes. "Oh, I'm not done with you yet."

Lifting one of my legs onto his shoulder in a swift motion, he climbed over me and impaled me with his thick cock.

I moaned, relishing the stretch of him filling me. "Please, yes."

A hungry sound left him. With one arm supporting him, he took my hands one by one, lifting them above my head and holding them there. "You're mine." He drove himself into me harder. "Ours."

I couldn't even think for the pleasure pounding through me. "Yes. Oh, God, yes."

"No one's taking you from us."

I shook my head, breathless. "Never." My clit throbbed beneath his strong thrusts, and I moaned louder.

"That's right, baby."

I tried to nod, but the effort was lost as the orgasm he was pounding out of me suddenly hit. I cried out his name, pleasure sweeping through me in a wave that took away the world. I was nothing but light. Pure passion, and God, I never wanted it to end. I could feel his thrusts grow faster, more desperate, and then his hot seed was filling me too.

Heaven, all of it.

My muscles went lax as the orgasm faded, and I smiled as

he rested on me for a moment too, his heavy weight holding me down on the couch. My hip ached from the angle my leg was at, but I didn't mind a bit.

Not when I had him here with me.

Shifting around, he released my wrists and then moved my leg away from his shoulder. Propping himself up on one arm, he watched me without a word.

"Just so you know..." I grinned, feeling devilish. "You can fuck me like that anytime."

He chuckled, but the amusement faded after a moment, becoming tinged by a mixture of wonder and pain. "Those memories..."

"I know."

His brow twitched down. "I just..." His gaze roamed over me. "Remembering that... Having you again..."

I took his cheek, my thumb straying back and forth across his skin. "I needed you too."

A shuddering breath left him, and after a moment, he nodded. His eyes rose to mine, a hint of his customary humor coming back into his gaze. "And I will happily fuck you like that whenever you like. You just say the word."

"Oh, yeah?" I licked my lips, and his eyes tracked the motion. "And what word is that?"

His chuckle made my skin pebble. "Oh, I don't know." He leaned in closer. "How about we see what dirty things I can make come out of that mouth of yours?"

His lips claimed mine before I could think of a response.

7

ASHER

The city was barely touched by sunrise—or at least what little sunrise could make it past the smoke. The streets were empty and eerily silent, without even stray animals slinking through the dawn. Amid the stench of burned plastic and plywood, the rot of death hung heavy on the air.

I breathed shallowly and snuck past another intersection. We were creeping along in the opposite direction from where we'd hidden with Wren. The river and the heart of downtown were still quite some distance away, but the damage was worse the closer to that area we came, and as the light increased, so too did the evidence of what the vampires had been doing.

If you lived for nearly a thousand years, you saw a lot of horrors. Things that made you question whether humanity was worth helping or wonder how the world could possibly recover.

And vampires were no different. After all, most of us had been human once.

I pulled my gaze from the bodies hanging from the rooftops of the squat brick buildings around us, having studied them only long enough to be reasonably sure the poor souls hadn't been made into ghouls on top of everything else. But this was Amalie's work, I knew. Even rabids were rarely *this* sadistic and cruel.

I was grateful Wren hadn't seen it.

How do we come back from this? Liam signed to me.

I shook my head. *I don't know,* I replied.

Carefully, we checked around another corner and then paused. Our destination lay directly ahead, a multistory edifice of white stone that towered over the surrounding structures. Most likely it'd been a bank or some kind of office building in its former life, but Brayden and the others told us it'd been sold and remodeled in the past few years.

Which meant the current layout was anyone's guess.

The lower-level windows and doors were boarded up now, though—probably as much to protect the rabids from the sunlight as anything. Meanwhile the windows higher up had been shattered, and swaths of soot marred the white walls. Given the building's height and the numerous vantage points to keep watch on the street, approaching unseen in human form would have been impossible.

Another reason why Liam and I were the best choice for this particular rescue mission.

I scowled. I understood Wren's point. More people would've been better—if they could've shifted, that is. But at the moment, that meant her, and there was no way in hell I was bringing her into the proverbial lion's den when she'd just escaped dying.

Again. For the gods-knew-how-manyeth time in a few fucking weeks.

Two figures walked from the alley beside the building, and my attention snapped back to the present. Dressed in black leather jackets and cargo pants, they sauntered along the sidewalk, guns slung over their shoulders and more at their waists. Their heads and hands were uncovered, and while they were too far away for me to make out their expressions clearly, their body language was utterly relaxed and unconcerned.

Mercenaries, Liam signed.

I nodded, wariness prickling through me. The humans hadn't mentioned the rabids having help, but maybe they just hadn't been able to tell as easily who was a vampire and who wasn't, at least at night.

Maybe.

But the Consortium had plenty of bounty hunters who'd been searching the area before everything went to hell.

I watched as the two figures sauntered around the corner and disappeared from view. It'd been more than a day since we heard from Friday and Barnaby, and while yes, the demons were formidable, they also had been heavily wounded by Amalie and Urlfeige.

Could the Consortium have hurt them?

I shoved the concerns aside. One problem at a time.

What now? Liam asked.

I stared at the building. If there were mercenaries out here, there damn well would be more inside. I couldn't see anything from the blackened holes of the windows higher on the wall, though, meaning we'd be essentially diving in blind. In the sunrise, the eastern face of the edifice was cast in shades of pink and gold. Blue and gray shadows still clung to the western side, though they were thinning by the second.

They'd expect us to attempt the darker side. Sunlight wouldn't kill us, but it was exhausting in our other form. And trying to enter at the ground level was the most obvious entry point of all.

We'd be fast.

I signed instructions briefly to Liam, who nodded.

We shifted into shadows and took off, weaving through the patches of darkness still holding out against the dawn and then racing up the western face of the building. Darting through a shattered window, we whipped to the side immediately in the hope of evading a trap.

Magic flared to life behind us, scorching the air where we'd been only a heartbeat before. Bullets followed, spraying the wall in our wake. We swerved, and I caught sight of the attackers. Four people crouched behind the cement pillars and wooden crates scattered through the large, open room. The empty space looked like it'd been under construction at some point and then abandoned, only to be turned into storage. But the people shooting at us didn't seem like a coordinated team. They didn't move in sync, and the way they glanced around before changing position seemed like they were checking the others wouldn't shoot them by accident in their attempts to hit us.

Good enough.

I darted left, then right, getting them riled, before lunging between two pillars.

Gunshots and screams followed.

Liam twisted through a gap between several crates only to emerge at high speed, the energy of his blade slashing into the mercenary who'd sheltered behind the wood boxes. The one remaining attacker turned tail to run, making a break for the door leading to the stairs.

I had the feeling he hadn't fought vampires before—and clearly neither Urlfeige nor Amalie had warned him or the others about what it meant. But why hide all the way up here if not to wait for us to...

Oh, hell.

Magic electrified the doorway to the stairs just as the man reached it, and his screams cut off in only a moment as he fell to the ground, his corpse smoking. A rabid girl sauntered into view, a guy behind her who had to be a witch, if only from the number of protective charms on chains and ribbons around his neck.

The rabid smirked, a trail of dried blood on her cheek and more in her tangled brown hair. The sense of wrongness that marked all rabids radiated from her, like an invisible corruption. But all the stains on her yellow sundress looked recent, and the fabric wasn't faded like it would have been if she'd been wearing it for a while.

Dormant, then, probably. At least until Urlfeige had come along and changed her.

I shifted back to human form, and nearby, Liam did as well, the same grimace of reluctance on his face as I knew had to be on mine. The dormants were victims too. We both knew that.

And if we wanted to get out of here alive, we might not be able to save this one.

The girl chuckled at us, grinning around her fangs. "She knew you'd come. The Mistress will be *so* thrilled when we tell her she was right."

"Nothing she likes hearing more," I agreed while Liam eased to the side, seeking an opening past the magic sealing us inside the room.

Or, really, the kill box. Clearly, the rabids hadn't given a shit if the mercenaries survived this. Only that their gunfire would let everyone downstairs know we'd arrived.

The vampire girl smirked and glanced back at the witch. He lifted his hands, chanting under his breath. Electricity gathered in the air like a lightning strike.

Fuck.

Liam moved fast, shifting to shadow and snagging the mercenary's corpse from the ground. Lunging forward, he drove the body into the barrier across the door.

Like a shield.

I shifted and surged after him. Magic flared to life around the body, crackling over the corpse and snarling like a thing alive. The rabid girl and the witch stumbled back, and his chants sped up. The charge in the air strengthened, building like a bomb near to going off.

The charred corpse broke through the barrier. Liam and I darted after it instantly.

A blast of magic crashed down on the room behind us like an electric fist punching the ground. The air shook with the impact, but we wasted no time for relief we were still alive. Slamming into the witch, I sent him into the wall while Liam grabbed the vampire and we both shifted back to human form.

"How many supernaturals in the building?" I demanded of the girl while I pinned the witch to the ground with my knife at his throat.

She snarled, thrashing in Liam's grip.

"You have an answer for me?" I continued to the witch.

He scowled.

My knife breached his skin. A thin line of blood trickled down his neck.

"Rabids in the basement," he spat. "Maybe ten. Feeding, most of them. She's the only one upstairs."

"And you? This bunch?" I jerked my head toward the room behind us. "You working for the Consortium or Urlfeige?"

The man grinned. "Nobody's working for those fools anymore. Not when the vampire king pays so well." His grin spread. "Careful, Sentinel..."

Alarm shot through my link to Liam, and instantly, I rolled to the side.

Scorch marks lashed the ground inches from where I'd been. Two more witches charged down the stairs toward us. Snarling a curse, Liam leapt away from the rabid and lunged at the witches just as one of them raised a hand.

Magic burned through the air, but the blast went wide as Liam crashed into them. The second witch grabbed for him, shouting a curse.

Bad move. Using their own momentum against them, he

flung the one witch into the other with enough force to send them over the banister on the opposite side of the stairway.

Their screams rang from the walls, fading as they fell.

Liam whirled, starting toward the rabid girl.

Turning into smoke, she dove over the railing too, fleeing.

"Dammit," Liam muttered, returning to human form.

I echoed the sentiment. She'd warn the others. Hell, the dead witches would be warning enough too.

The witch pinned beneath me snarled, rage in his eyes. "Now what, Sentin—"

I cracked my elbow sideways across his face, knocking him out. Shifting again quickly, Liam and I dove over the banister after the girl.

Fire doors and random safety warnings flashed past as we descended, but there wasn't any sign of the girl.

And didn't that mean our options sucked? Searching for the girl could waste precious seconds.

Plan B, I sent to Liam.

I raced all the way to the bottom of the stairwell, shifting back the moment we reached it. The gray metal door ahead had Basement printed across it in red letters and no sign of a lock. Glancing across the doorframe briefly, I checked for traps.

Nothing. At least, no visible ones.

Gods below, they just *had* to hire witches.

Easing the handle down, I braced myself and then yanked the door wide. Liam raced through, and I shifted quickly, following.

Rabids flew at us from around the corner.

They died fast, with barely time to make a sound.

Disgust for the situation burned in me, but I couldn't linger on it as we sped around the corner. Half a dozen more rabids were up ahead with brass bars behind them stretching from floor to ceiling. The space looked like it'd been a vault for money or important files.

Now it held human prisoners.

The rabids charged.

Cursing internally, I flew at them. They weren't fighters. They were less coordinated than the mercenaries upstairs. But even if I tried to grab them and pin them, they never stopped trying to kill me.

My side burned as a rabid sliced at it. My insides lurched as another tried to tear straight through me.

Urlfeige and Amalie would pay for this. I sacrificed everything to save the innocent once, in a village before I was turned. I didn't even remember its name, but the men were being conscripted into battle there too, their families slaughtered if they wouldn't fight, and I'd disobeyed orders trying to stop it.

The officers attempted to execute me for it. But before the noose could end me, Amalie came. She offered me the chance to save myself and the village alike, if only I'd join her.

I'd been such a fool. She'd killed them all afterward, laughing as I fought to break free and stop her. The innocent were her favorite victims.

Even these ones now.

Ash and dust fell like snow as I shifted back to human form. Amalie and that old bastard *had* to pay.

In the cage, the humans stared at us, and I held up my hands, attempting to appear nonthreatening despite what we'd just done. "My name is Asher. We're not going to hurt you. My friend and I are here to help."

"Bullshit," one of the humans spat.

Moans came from deeper in the cluster of nearly two dozen humans. Desperate, pleading sounds that cut off with shushing noises. I glanced at Liam. Fuck.

Blood thralls.

"We can help you," I said. "*All* of you. We're looking for Evelyn Michaels and Samira Kane. We're here because a guy named Brayden and a woman named Diana sent us. They have a safe place for you all, protected from the vampires."

At the final word, the moans grew louder, and dread crept over me. If we'd come too late to save the ones we came for...

"I'm Evelyn." A woman pushed to the front of the crowd. Her brown curls were peppered liberally with gray, and her pink blouse was torn on one shoulder. A bruise darkened her right cheek, but her brown eyes were bright as she looked between Liam and me. "Brayden's alive?"

At my nod, she threw a look over her shoulder, motioning for someone else to follow. "Samira."

A woman with dark-brown skin and gold braids followed, a far more cautious expression on her face. "How do we know you didn't just kill them?" Samira asked.

Her tone reminded me of her wife.

I racked my brain, but there only was one thing I could think to say. "Do you know of Brayden's friend, Wren?" I asked Evelyn.

Liam cast me a quick glance, clearly not liking what I just said. But the woman only gasped. "Is Wren *here*?"

"We're her friends." And a hell of a lot more than that, if most of us had a say. "We came down with her from Fort Briar. We're trying to stop this."

Brayden's mother cast another look at Samira, clearly urging her silently to trust us.

"I think we should go with them," said a woman with curly red hair, her eyes unblinking as she watched us from behind her enormous glasses. One of the lenses was cracked, and she had a dark bruise on her cheek, but she didn't look frightened when she stared at us. More like she'd been pushed so far, she'd left fear behind and now was just in survival mode.

"Yeah," an older man agreed. His white hair was disheveled,

and he wore a blue button-down shirt with one sleeve torn. He hovered near the redhead, his arms crossed tightly over his chest as if he was trying to appear sure of himself, though in his case, he only looked scared.

"They're *vampires*," another lady argued, staring at the rest like they'd lost their minds. "Look what happened to those three. You want that to be us?"

I peered through the crowd at her gesture, and several people pulled back, revealing two women and one man pinned to the ground by others. Clawing at their captors and straining their arms out to reach us, the trio appeared delirious, a sheen of sweat covering them and a glazed look to their eyes. Their necks bore unhealed bite marks, and their wrists did too, along with scratches whose origin I didn't need to question.

They'd clawed at their own skin, trying to make themselves bleed, if only to tempt the rabids to bite them again.

"We might be able to help them," I told the other humans. "If you let us."

Wary looks passed among the captives. I resisted the urge to snap at them. I couldn't be sure that rabid girl had been among the ones who attacked us. For all I knew, she was bringing Amalie back here right now.

"Let them try," Evelyn said.

The redhead with glasses nodded in firm agreement.

Cautiously, the humans eased away from the gate.

Liam strode forward immediately. Gripping the door right above the lock, he tugged hard.

The lock shattered. Yanking the door aside, he marched through the crowd of humans toward the thralls.

Cries escaped the trio, victorious and frantic all at the same time. I could feel the rage pounding through my connection to Liam. But if anyone could help them, it was him. None of us were as gifted at this as he was.

He placed a hand to the forehead of the woman nearest to

him. Dark-haired with light-brown skin, she looked maybe in her late twenties. Under his breath, he whispered to her, urging her to remember who she was. What she wanted in life.

To be free.

Around him, the other humans tensed, murmuring in surprise at the rasping sound of his voice, and fear flashed across several faces. I held back a grimace. All these centuries, and still that reaction never failed, no matter how unjustified it was.

The woman gasped, blinking fast. Liam pulled his hand away and turned, doing the same to the person beside her.

"V-Valerie?" the woman called, still blinking at her surroundings. "Roland?"

The lady with glasses pushed through the crowd, the white-haired guy on her heels. "We're here, Tammy. We're all getting out of this place."

A sob left the woman, and with a trembling hand, she pressed her hand to the scabbed wound on her neck. But her eyes turned to Liam, and she gave him a shaky smile. "I heard you in my head." She swallowed hard. "You made it stop."

Liam gave the woman a brief nod as he rose to his feet. On the ground, the last of the blood thralls blinked and looked around, coming back to himself.

Murmurs of uncertainty passed through the crowd, but Valerie straightened from beside the woman Liam had helped. "We should go with them."

The murmurs grew. I glanced at Liam. We were burning time. If more mercenaries arrived, or more rabids found a way in here that was shielded from the sun...

"The government could be coming at any time," Valerie persisted. "And if we're all in one place, it'll be easier to get evacuated."

And then there was that...

I kept my expression neutral, but from the way her eyes

darted over me, I got the suspicion the woman had caught my tension anyway.

Brayden's mom walked toward us. "I'm going," she said to the others. "I want to see my son."

Samira followed immediately. Valerie helped her friend to her feet, and together they headed for the gate too.

One by one, the humans followed.

With a grim look to Liam, I twitched my head toward the humans. Silently, he waited as I started up the stairs, a train of humans in my wake, and then fell in behind them all.

The foyer of the building was awash in sunlight when we left the basement stairwell, and not a single mercenary or rabid was anywhere to be seen. Keeping an eye to the shadows, I approached the glass double doors and checked them over for any signs of booby traps.

Nothing. The rabids had been pretty damn confident about their cages downstairs, apparently.

Or they'd welcomed someone trying to get inside to hide, if only to trap them.

Just in case, I motioned for the humans to hang back before cautiously easing the door open.

The smell of fires carried on the morning air pouring through the doorway, and the eerie silence that had clung to the city for days remained. Somewhere in all of this, people would be trying to make it to the GSS barricades, but in this part of town, they were long since gone.

I motioned for the humans to follow as I stepped outside. Startled murmurs rose when I didn't burst into flames in the sunlight, and an undercurrent of worry carried through the air.

I cast a quick glance back.

"You're the only ones who can do that," Valerie said.

It didn't sound like a question, and my eyes narrowed with curiosity.

"Right?" she pressed.

I gave a short nod.

She started out into the sunlight after me. Eyeing me like I might bite them, the other survivors followed, steering clear of me.

Liam shrugged his brow as he followed them out and let the door swing shut behind him. *So far, so good,* he signed.

"What'd he say?" one of the humans demanded.

"So far, so good," a woman replied. At my sharp glance, she gave a small shrug. "My son is Deaf."

"Should you really be letting us just stand around out here?" another woman at the back of the group demanded.

I held back a scowl and jerked my head for the survivors to follow. Even if the air was cool, the sun glared from the sidewalks and streets. If I'd felt like we were painfully exposed before, now we were bugs under the microscope of all the GSS satellites that were presumably trained on this place.

My skin crawled, and I walked faster, weaving through the streets as fast as the cluster of tired, hungry humans behind me could travel. The sooner we reached Wren and the others and I could confirm they were okay, the better I would feel.

At long last, we rounded the corner and the remodeled school came into view. In spite of myself, I sped up, striding farther ahead of the survivors across the last few dozen yards between me and the building. It looked intact, no sign of attack or damage anywhere I could see. Likewise, now that we were closer again, I could feel Wren and the others more strongly through our connection, and all of them seemed fine.

Thank the gods.

"When we get to the door," I said, turning to Evelyn. "It'd be best if you went in first and found Brayden, just in case the defenses against vampires mean he needs to let us in again, okay?"

She nodded. "Of course. Thank you both for—"

The *beep-blurp* of a siren cut her off. I slammed to a stop, scanning the neighborhood fast.

A caravan of vehicles turned the corner at the opposite end of the street, each of them painted black with Emergency Containment printed in yellow letters on the side. Soldiers wearing black tactical gear walked beside them, guns in hand, splitting off the moment they reached the corner to fan out through the neighborhood.

Oh, fuck. The GSS were here.

8

WREN

I returned to consciousness with the warm feeling of Ulysses' arms around me and the sense that, for a brief moment at least, this tiny pocket of the world was okay.

I sighed. I'd lost count of the orgasms that man had wrung from me, and God, how I'd loved each one. Somewhere in there, we'd even made sure he could shift again—regaining that ability by drinking from me, same as Liam and Asher had. I wasn't sure when we'd finally fallen asleep, but I knew what had woken me.

Asher and Liam were coming back.

I smiled. They were on edge but not in danger or pain, and that was all I could have asked for. And the edginess was understandable, given that they were out there in the city, steering clear of God knew what.

But it seemed like they'd be back soon.

Ulysses' hand stroked my hair, and warm tingles ran through me from the contact. "Good morning." He paused, glancing at the clock on the wall. "Or what's left of it."

I chuckled and nestled closer to him. "Good day?"

"Definitely." He tucked his arms around me tighter. Before

we fell asleep, he'd had me against everything from the walls to the floor. But at some point, we'd ended up on the couch again, spooned together with a throw blanket over the top of us, and now I didn't really feel like leaving. Not yet. It was still difficult, being in the apartment of someone who wasn't ever coming back, but I couldn't help but appreciate the privacy.

A sense of alarm swept through my connection to the others. Ulysses tensed beside me.

"What is that?" I asked him.

He shook his head. "Get dressed, yeah?"

I scrambled up, retrieving my clothes from the carpet and pulling them on quickly. A moment later, Gideon strode past the door, not waiting for anyone to tell him it was okay.

His gaze flashed between us, lingering on me for a heartbeat as I tugged my shirt and hoodie into place, and as always, I couldn't tell what the hell I was feeling from him.

Indignation flared in me, and I braced myself for some snide comment, but despite what he probably thought about what the two of us had obviously done, for once he kept his surly opinions to himself. "We have trouble."

"Rabids?" Ulysses replied.

"GSS."

Oh God.

Ulysses didn't wait for more, and I damn well didn't need to either. Shoving my feet into my shoes, I took off, chasing after the two men toward the stairs.

Residents were murmuring with excitement as we ran down the steps.

"—they finally came—"

"—I thought they were just going to leave us."

"Do you think they'll shoot us?"

"Don't be silly. They'll know we're human."

My heart thumped hard in my chest. Even if the humans were reassuring each other, I could still see tinges of fear on more than one face. No one knew what the government was planning. Not really. With all communications shut down, it was anyone's guess.

And fear filled in the gaps.

We reached the main hallway just as pounding came on the front door.

Gideon was past me in a heartbeat, while Ulysses kept me behind him. Diana strode up to the entryway and jerked her chin at Jasmine, who pulled the door aside.

"Mom!" Brayden ran for the door.

Humans poured into the entrance. I only recognized Evelyn. But Diana pushed through the crowd to embrace another woman, holding her tightly and murmuring something I couldn't hear. The cold edge she'd worn ever since we met her appeared totally gone, replaced with relief so clear, it was palpable even over the distance. At whatever she said, the other woman nodded, holding her every bit as closely. Around them, other people hurried to friends or family while still more milled around as if not sure what to do.

My eyes skipped across them all, searching.

Asher and Liam stood outside the door.

Alarm shot through me. They were trapped out there, and if the GSS were coming...

"Brayden!" I waved a hand frantically at my friend.

He looked from me to the doorway, and his eyes went wide. Weaving through the crowd, he maneuvered over to the door-frame and pressed his hand to wood, saying something quickly and extending his other hand through the entry.

Asher and Liam rushed inside.

"Where are the GSS?" Ulysses asked immediately.

"Just coming down the street. They'll be here any—"

The sound of loudspeakers cut him off. "We are a government-sanctioned rescue effort. Please come outside your homes and prepare to be evacuated."

"Not being particularly subtle about it, are they?" Gideon muttered.

None of the humans cared. Excitement and fear were electric in the air.

I bit my lip briefly. "Now what?"

"Is there a back way out of here?" Asher asked Brayden.

Brayden gave him a confused look, his eyes going toward the sound of the loudspeakers and back to us. "Are you in some kind of trouble with them?"

"The government tends to stake first, ask questions never." Ulysses' voice was hard.

"Can't risk them hurting her," Asher continued with a twitch of his head toward me.

I scowled. I wasn't entirely helpless, and the reality was, all of us were in danger, not only me. But the Sentinels were nothing if not protective.

I just *damn* well wouldn't let anything happen to them either.

Brayden nodded. "Yeah, this way."

We wove through the crowd, following him as he hurried down the hall. An exit sign glowed around the next turn, above a pair of double doors that emptied into what looked like a parking lot.

I cast a nervous look at my friend. "You should come with—"

"Dammit."

I glanced back to see Asher staring past the security glass of the door. A heartbeat later, an emergency vehicle pulled into the parking lot.

"Leave it to the GSS satellites to let them know all the humans were here," Ulysses growled.

"Us too, possibly," Gideon murmured.

"I'll distract them," Brayden offered.

I looked over at him in alarm. "What? No! You—"

"That won't be necessary."

I spun. A petite woman with large glasses and curly red hair walked toward us, calm assurance in her expression as much as her tone. Two others were with her—an older man with white hair that hung down to his collar, and a dark-haired woman with a savage bite mark scabbing over on the side of her neck.

Asher took my hand, pulling me away from them all. "And why is that?" His tone was cagey.

The redhead glanced at her companions briefly. "Because we can talk to them."

"Yeah." Ulysses scoffed. "They don't listen that well, so…"

"We work for them," the woman with the bite mark said.

The tension ratcheted higher all around me. Liam growled, and the two people with the redhead blanched, taking a step backward.

She didn't move.

"Is that so?" Gideon replied.

The redheaded woman didn't flinch at his icy tone. "We're archivists. And yes, we work for the GSS. I apologize for not telling—"

The humans retreated fast as Liam took a step toward them. "Please!" the dark-haired woman said, holding up her hands with terror in her wide eyes. "It's not what you think!"

"Liam." Asher's voice was cold. He never took his eyes off the people in front of him.

The other Sentinel stopped, but he stayed between us and the humans.

Nervously, the older man cleared his throat. "My name is Roland. This is Tammy." He bobbed his head toward the dark-haired woman. "You've met Valerie." A more awkward bob went to the redhead. "We were in a small private library north of here, examining their records of shifter migrations in the early 1300s, when, well, rabids broke in, killed most everyone, and took the rest of us as... snacks." He grimaced. "We didn't say anything because, um..."

Valerie turned to me. "We wanted to see for ourselves whether the rumors were true."

I shivered at the look in her eyes. "What rumors?"

"The ones that said you were still in town with the Sentinels."

So much for the guys' goal of secrecy.

"*And* the rumors that say you're Amalie's weakness," Valerie continued. "Urlfeige's too. But the rabids claimed she did something to you that means all of this will be over in a few days—and humanity is going to lose."

I resisted the urge to rub at the patch of numbness above my heart. It was smaller now. Better. But not gone.

"The rabids were real excited about it when they had us as prisoners," Roland explained. "We think if we could talk to the soldiers outside, we could arrange for you five to come with us to a research—"

"Like hell," Ulysses interrupted. "You try to research us or come *near* her, we end you."

Tammy blanched. "W-we don't mean to study. To help. We have records. Archives. We could—"

"We've heard." Ulysses glared.

"The director told you that," Roland said like he was filling in a blank, even if his voice shook a bit. "We heard about what happened with her. She was... ambitious. Shortsighted."

"An idiot?" Valerie added sharply, not seeming bothered by Ulysses' threats in the slightest. "You would think that the woman never read a single report our division sent her. Trying to make a deal with the Bloodwright?" She made a rude noise, as if she couldn't imagine anything more stupid. "We're not the director. And we research *books*, not people, so..." She shrugged.

I didn't know whether to admire her lack of fear of the Sentinels or be damn suspicious of it.

Roland made a placating noise. "We lost friends in the director's ill-advised attempt. And the GSS lost very good fighters who were only following orders."

"Valerie's telling you the truth," Tammy added, nodding like she was begging us to believe them. "We're not like Director Lacrette. We don't want to *control* the supernatural, just understand it."

"And we're *damn* well not interested in making bargains with ancient serial killers," Valerie added.

Asher gave them a wry look. "That doesn't mean we're going with you."

"We can *help* you," Valerie insisted. "We heard the rabids speaking, and our intel has given us some indication of what Amalie and her... *patron* are planning." The woman's eyes slid to me. "They're draining you, aren't they?"

I shivered, saying nothing.

"Please," Tammy interjected. "He saved me." She nodded toward Liam. "Both of you did. Let us repay you for that."

"We have countless records," Valerie said. "Archives. We'll give you access to all of them. Because if there's a way to stop this, it's in there."

"Offering us the sun, moon, and stars again, is it?" Ulysses retorted. "You GSS folk really don't know another tune, do you?"

"More like offering survival," Valerie snapped. "They're trying to take this world. Everything we know of that creature indicates that he is a megalomaniacal vampire with unspeakable power. Maybe he's a ghost or some resurrected spirit under it all, but regardless, he wants to turn every vampire in this world rabid and make humanity into dinner or chattel or both. Unless we do something, it's only a matter of time until we lose."

"You're telling us nothing of which we are not already aware," Gideon replied.

"And are you aware of where their army is gathering? Or of the forces he's collecting within the supernatural community? Those mercenaries weren't the only ones who decided it was more advantageous to side with him. He has thousands like that, moving into place across the country and potentially across the world. How much longer until they attempt to take Washington, DC, or Johannesburg, or New Delhi? You *know* they're going to spread this as far as they can."

We didn't respond, and an exasperated look crossed Valerie's face. "Then let us prove to you that we are not a threat." She glanced at Tammy and Roland, some unspoken demand in her eyes.

Tammy gave a quick, nervous nod. Without another word, Valerie spun and strode toward the door, Roland on her heels.

"What's she doing?" I demanded.

"Making sure it's safe for you." Tammy's voice was tense.

"And you?"

She hesitated. "Hostage. If you need it."

I stared at her.

"Gods below," Asher muttered.

Tammy gave him an anxious smile.

"Should you all, you know, stop them?" Brayden prompted, speaking up for the first time.

The Sentinels glanced at one another. They could easily move fast enough to intercept the humans. But none of the men replied for a long moment.

"I say we let them try," Gideon murmured.

"Last time we trusted them," Asher said, "they tried to turn us over to Amalie."

"And if they're not lying this time?"

Asher looked away.

I bit my lip. "It's that or hurt people, isn't it?"

The guys appeared grim.

"Then at this point, what else we can do?"

No one answered me, and I didn't want to bring up the rest of the issue. The obvious parts. We were surrounded. Gideon still couldn't fly or shift. And summoning my sword earlier had caused the curse to flare up, which meant I'd be stuck facing those soldiers without a weapon.

Our options weren't good.

One by one, grimaces crossed the guys' faces like they'd come to the same conclusion.

"What's the definition of insanity, again?" Ulysses muttered.

Asher sighed as Valerie and Roland disappeared out the door at the other end of the hall. "Pretty sure it's this."

9

LIAM

I was not a fan of this.

I watched Valerie and Roland walk out the door, bracing myself for them to shout for the GSS soldiers to come kill us all. I hadn't been there when the GSS director had double-crossed Asher, Ulysses, and Gideon by handing them over to Amalie, but I'd gathered later what happened—mostly by the fact the director and all of her soldiers were apparently very, *very* dead.

I wasn't exactly broken up about that.

But it went a long way toward saying the rest of the GSS could never be trusted again. The word of a few archivists hardly carried weight with me—and that was assuming they were even telling the truth about their identities in the first place. They'd lied before, after all. But the GSS had not been our friends throughout pretty much all of history. And now when things were at their most dire and their director had already betrayed us once, they came along and offered help for a second time?

We need a backup plan, I signed to the others.

Ulysses nodded. "Worst-case scenario, you take her and you get out of here, right?"

"No!" Wren glared at all of us. "God, you guys are so damn determined to keep sacrificing yourselves, and there's no way in hell I'm letting you do that. We all stick together, and we *all* survive."

I didn't even have to look at the others to know none of us had the heart to tell her how long the odds were on that. I remembered our past lives, and the way she'd died. I remembered all the years we'd spent with Amalie too. The fact we'd lasted this long was a bit of a miracle.

But then, Wren wouldn't want us to give up hope.

"If the rear exit is blocked, then what other options do we have?" Gideon asked Brayden.

Wren's friend shook his head. "Not sure. Diana might know something, though."

I glanced around, searching for the woman. She and her wife were nowhere to be seen. The crowd was thinning as well, more and more of the humans streaming out the front door in total trust the slayers wanted to rescue them.

Foolish, at a minimum, but then, I couldn't blame them for wanting to get the hell out of here. Which, of course, was what the government promised—as long as they hadn't been bitten. Or unless the ever-merciful slayers thought of some other reason they should be staked instead of set free.

Gods, I hated this.

The front door opened again, and Valerie and Roland returned, two soldiers striding after them. I could tell from their bearing they were not common grunts. They moved like they were used to the people around them obeying their commands, with a tension like they were ready at any moment to take action if the situation warranted it. The one on the left was younger, still probably in his thirties but nothing like the weathered face and graying hair of the one on the right. They headed straight for us, the crowd parting around them even as people called out questions.

The soldiers didn't take their eyes from us.

"You would be the Sentinels, then?" the younger one asked.

Asher nodded.

"I'm Captain Evans," he continued. "This is Major Marcent."

The major looked at Wren. "And I take it you would be the one everyone's searching for."

None of us changed position, but from the way the soldiers' eyes flicked across us, I knew they hadn't missed the way our tension grew. If they made a single move toward her...

Wren said nothing, but the major continued anyway. "The archivists have explained the situation. We are aware of what Director Lacrette tried, and we want you to know that many of the commanders in the military branch of the GSS never agreed with the policy of the administrative branch. But she had allies that made disobeying her commands impossible." He bobbed his head, a wry twist to his expression. "For better or worse, most of them are also dead now. The vampires have been busy, even before they took this city."

We didn't respond.

Major Marcent scoffed at the silence. "Regardless, gentlemen"—he bobbed his head to us and then to Wren—"ma'am, I'm sure you would agree that making a bargain with the lunatics intent on destroying the entire world by *giving* them the one person they need in order to succeed is an absurd strategy. Therefore, on behalf of the GSS military and research branches, I would like to extend an offer of safe passage and access to the archives so that you can assist us in undoing this clusterfuck. Agreed?"

My eyes slid to the other Sentinels. This wasn't good enough. *Nothing* was, at least where Wren's safety was concerned. Fighting our way out of here would have been bloody from the start, but now...

Asher studied the soldiers and then glanced at Wren, and I couldn't quite tell what was going through his head.

"Many of the vampires attacking everyone were not originally rabids," Asher said, his tone unreadable. "They're Urlfeige's victims too. Is an effort being made to help them in any way?"

The major's eyes narrowed. "Based on the archivists' information, our suspicion is that if any attempt were going to be successful, we would need you."

I glanced at Valerie, Tammy, and Roland. The soldiers were putting a lot of weight on the researchers' word. More than I would've expected, if they were nothing more than academics buried in some library somewhere.

Gideon seemed to think the same. "Who *are* you?" he asked the archivists.

Roland blinked. "We told you. We were archivists working in a small local library—"

"And the GSS military makes a habit of listening to researchers this much?" Ulysses interrupted, a wry note in his voice.

Roland's eyes skirted to Valerie and Tammy, but he didn't say anything.

Valerie sighed. "They do with the head of research for the Eastern division."

"So when you said you sent reports to Director Lacrette..." Asher prompted.

"I was coordinating research across the eastern portions of the United States and Canada in order to determine the level of threat that the Bloodwright presented." Valerie scowled. "The director didn't listen."

"And yet you were here, in a local library?" Gideon said.

"Well, before the rabids burned it to the ground, this particular library not only had records of shifter movements since the 1300s, it also had scraps of vampire lore dating back to the Babylonians. The owner was very rich, very eccentric, and something of a collector. He thought they were fairy tales."

Ulysses and I cast a brief glance at Gideon. Our bookish friend was doing a good job of keeping his expression neutral, no matter how he must be itching to explore whatever records survived.

And possibly get his hands around the throat of any rabid who'd taken part in destroying the rest.

"How do you intend to protect her?" Asher asked, nodding toward Wren without taking his eyes from the GSS.

"And them," Wren added, irritation in her voice as she jerked her head toward us.

The soldier's lips twitched. "Our archives are located not far from here, in a building surrounded by seventeen different layers of magical and physical protections. We also have fail-safe locks that will seal the building in the event of an attack. While we would not recommend being *inside* the building if those are activated due to the inability to escape for quite some time, they are very secure." He glanced around. "The defenses on this place are impressive. But compared to what we have at the archives, they're like defending your home with a toothpick. You and your friends will be safe," he finished, directing the words to Wren.

I glanced at the others. I wasn't sure what to make of this. On the one hand, we needed to keep her someplace safe, and the gods knew we needed information as well.

But what was it they said about things that looked too good to be true?

"If those rabids do know where we are..." Wren said to us.

I scowled. Staying here wasn't an option. The city was a fiery mess, and the vampires would be closing in now that Asher and I had broken the humans out of their little snack box. The border of vampire territory was too far to fly to in full daylight; at night we'd be facing rabids the entire time, and in either case we'd be in clear view of anyone with a weapon.

We were fucked.

"We stay with her at all times," Asher said to the soldiers and archivists. "You do not take samples of blood, hair, or tissue, and by *no* means do you perform any spells on her or us at all. If you do, *we* will not be held responsible for the consequences—your people will. You can consider our reputations the proof we will follow through on that. Understood?"

The soldier's hint of a smile returned, but he had a respectful look in his eyes. "Understood. And none of our people are food."

Distaste crossed Asher's face.

Ulysses made a noise of revulsion. "Yeah, buddy. Not an issue. We don't feed from unwilling parties, thanks."

Tammy's nervous look flickered into a smile at me at that, and I shifted my weight closer to Wren. The admiration in the woman's eyes made me uncomfortable. People rarely ever looked at me that way.

But the major only gave a brief nod. "In that case, shall we get the hell out of here?"

10

AMALIE

By only a few hours, I'd missed them. My Sentinels had been in this place.

And now they were gone... again.

Trailing my fingertips along the wall, I walked through the hallway of the building where the girl and my possessions had been hiding. Shadows from the empty realms twisted through my skin, feeding on the residual magic and energy of life lingering in this place. Someone had placed spells around the exterior—rather destructive ones. But they'd been rudimentary in their construction, and certainly no match for the power I commanded. It'd been the work of moments to tear them down.

Only to discover no one remained inside.

My gaze raked over the open doorway of a dwelling. *Apartments,* the vampires said they were called. Living spaces crammed one atop the other, though each of them was larger than any hovel humans had called home when last I'd walked the earth. The plaster in all of them was the color of an eggshell. Humans seemed to love that shade these days, as if never realizing they were subconsciously reflecting their own fragility.

And such fragility it was...

My lip twitched. My pets were in the company of humans now, having rescued some of them and then departing with still more. And it wouldn't matter. Delicate as eggshells, those humans were—slayers or not—and the vampires had held them for days, bleeding them, twisting them.

It would be enough.

I continued walking. This was only the beginning. What we had done would change the world. Even now, my father was using the power I'd taken from that little imposter and flooding it through vampires for miles around, returning them to their true natures. And too many humans had seen the results, too many for those ridiculous slayers to be able to hide it from the rest. Not in this wonderful new age of "cell phones" and "cameras." No, those devices would capture the images better than any painting and transport them across the globe over and over, no matter how the slayers tried to discredit the tales.

They'd succeeded in reducing my kind to myth and rumor once.

They would not succeed again.

A tingle ran up along my arm from where I touched the wall, and I paused. The whispers of the creatures from the empty realms grew louder in my head.

Ah.

My fingers splayed on the eggshell wall. Humans were such fools. As with so many places in the world, they'd paid no mind to the energies here, thinking they could cover them up as if those forces were as easily dismissed as fog in a breeze. But true power was not something that could be concealed.

The whispers grew louder. The barrier between worlds was so thin here; of course my pets and any magic users had been drawn to it. This place had been a school once, but before that, it had been a graveyard. Presumably the city leaders thought it too expensive to move the bodies when they began their construction, and thus they'd simply buried them beneath the new building.

But humans were forever burying their dead in places of power, as if unconsciously sensing the connection to the worlds beyond their own. And though they'd tried now to transform this place into a collection of spaces where strangers lived on top of one another like rats in boxes, it didn't matter.

The power was still here.

I closed my eyes, drawing on it as he'd shown me how to do. Dark energy seeped into me, bringing threads of the power that lay dormant beneath this place with it as it came. Here, the petty spell that tried to stop me. There, the taste of the one who crafted it... but not its creator. Merely the latest to use it, as if the spell had been bandied about like a trinket changing hands before landing in the possession of the one who'd placed it here.

Such lack of respect for magic.

The energy inside me twisted and thrashed, growing stronger the more of the emptiness I drew in, and my lips curled with pleasure. That barren expanse just beyond the surface of reality echoed with power, as if the wall beneath my fingertips was nothing more than a thin layer of tissue, so easily punctured as to allow the endless nothing through. My father had accepted its bargain once, allowing the creatures that lurked in that emptiness to craft him into the world's first vampire. But he'd broken free of their control, drawing on *them* instead.

Now so did I. Soon, even the defenses of the supernatural cities would be as nothing to us.

But first... the one who placed the spell. I had their scent now. A boy. An unusual one, though, perhaps because he played at casting magic he had no business—

"M'lady?"

I removed my fingertips from the plaster and turned. A witch woman stood near the stairs at the end of the hall, a scrying device clutched in both her hands.

"We think we found the room where the girl and the Sentinels were located."

I strode after her immediately, heading for the steps. That imposter bitch had fought back when the spell drained her, and somehow, she had been able to stop it from taking her fully.

I'd make her pay for that when I found her.

At an open door on the second level, the witch leading the way gestured to the apartment and then retreated. I ignored her as I walked inside, studying the living space before me. Like so many others, it was filled with trinkets and soft furnishings, though this one was nearly pristine. Only a blanket tossed haphazardly on the sofa was out of place.

My eyes lingered on it, the magic beneath my skin churning as it read the air. The girl had been here. At least one of my possessions too. Ulysses, I thought. That protective shell of joviality shielding an aching tangle of so many centuries of pain was unmistakable. Together, their energy was... volatile. Intense.

Erotic.

Rage stirred in me, and black smoke seeped from my skin to build around me in dark, tumbling clouds. He had... *They* had...

I whirled, the churning magic pulsing out of me in a rush to slam all the useless trinkets and cheaply made furniture into the walls. Plaster cracked. Wood shattered.

I strode from the room.

She would pay for what she'd done with my possession there. They all would. By the time I was finished with her, they'd beg me to let her die.

In the hall, several vampires cowered. Even the witch looked terrified.

"Find them," I snarled. "Tear apart every building. Every person. I don't care. They're not escaping again."

"Yes, Mistress." They ran for the stairs, hauling on their leather gear to protect them from the sun's touch as they went.

"And you—" I snagged the witch.

The woman tensed, her face tight with fear.

"Send word to my father. Tell him…" My hand tightened. The witch whimpered. "Tell him my pets took the bait. It's time for the next step."

The woman nodded and then ran for her life when I released her.

I walked after the woman, dragging my hand along the wall and leaving a trail of fire in my wake. This place would burn. All of it, taking every trace of their betrayal down with it.

First this building.

Then that imposter.

And then the world.

11

WREN

When I climbed from the back of the GSS's large transport truck, I couldn't help but look around in confusion. Beneath the gray sky, an empty gravel lot surrounded us and a plain building waited ahead, with some rotting trailer homes about fifty yards off.

And that was it. After weaving a path through St. Louis, evading booby traps set by the rabids and damage done by the same, this squat structure in the Middle of Nowhere, Illinois, was... anticlimactic to say the least.

"*These* are the archives?" I asked no one in particular.

Ulysses regarded one of the GSS soldiers dryly. "Not much to look at, are they? What happened? Budget cuts?"

Valerie raised an eyebrow. "Sometimes the best defense is being 'not much to look at.'"

"Well, then. Nailed it."

I took Ulysses' hand, squeezing it. I didn't need our connection to tell me he was struggling—or that they all were, really. Asher hadn't stopped watching the GSS soldiers like he was weighing which one would attack first, while Gideon had retreated into silence like he was cataloguing every detail in case he needed to target a weak point later. Liam had gone still in a way that was like the millisecond before lethal action—a motionlessness that crackled with destructive energy about to be unleashed.

And Ulysses' snark had an edge like a knife, cutting but possibly also meant to distract.

Just in case the others needed to strike.

But regardless, he wasn't wrong. The squat building looked like a cinderblock painted white and plopped onto the gravel lot, surrounded by a chain-link fence that had fallen down in several places. Scrub brush and half-dead grass covered the dry terrain beyond the gravel, and past the fence, the collection of run-down trailer homes was sagging into the earth. From their busted-in windows and collapsed walls, it was pretty obvious they were abandoned. Hell, the whole area looked like some kind of industrial ghost town.

Not exactly the safety the archivists had been promising, unless you counted the fact I couldn't even see a *door* on the building.

Swallowing nervously, I trailed Asher and the others toward the structure. If the GSS wanted someplace to trap us inside, this would be a good option. And it had sort of been my idea to come here, which meant if anything went wrong...

I shoved the trepidation down and stomped on it for good measure. We'd be okay. Yes, most of the humans from the apartment building weren't here. They'd had no interest in supernatural archives or continuing apocalyptic battles. They'd just wanted to get the hell away from St. Louis as fast as possible, so Major Marcent had ordered the captain and a dozen of his soldiers to accompany us here while he led the caravan of survivors to the closest barricade. But Brayden and his mother had stayed with us, and surely the GSS wouldn't try to kill the Sentinels and me with two humans around.

Though that didn't mean they wouldn't do something to

separate us. Or that they wouldn't see my friend and his mother as a threat too.

Ulysses jiggled my hand, and I glanced over at him, not bothering to hide my worry since I knew he'd pick up on it anyway.

He gave me a caring smile. I could feel his compassion pouring back to me, the link between us even stronger than it'd been before he fed from me. Was the connection like this between the others? It felt so strong, it was as if it filled the world. But they'd never described their link quite this way. Admittedly, they'd never described it much at *all*, but it seemed like mostly a general sense of whether the others were okay.

And for some reason, that made me sad. Only a few weeks ago, having other people in my mind like this would have seemed like a horrible invasion—not to mention as foreign as suddenly breathing underwater. But back then, I hadn't known what I was missing.

God, I wouldn't give this up for anything.

A strange trepidation suddenly gripped my chest. I looked around, alarmed. The hairs on my skin were rising, and shivers rolled through me like my muscles wanted to bolt my ass away from here *right* now.

My gaze flew to the others. "Are you all feeling this?"

Gideon nodded. "I take it you have demons on the payroll," he said to Valerie.

Valerie simply looked back with a smile. "Among other things."

Ulysses scoffed. "Awesome."

Shivers rolled through me. Right. The manor had loads of "get away" magic wrapped around it, too.

"*Demons?*" Brayden sputtered.

I threw a glance over my shoulder. He was bloodlessly pale, and his mother had a look on her face like she was a heartbeat from bolting.

"It's perfectly safe," Valerie assured us. "They know we're coming."

"And they couldn't dial down the warding?" Ulysses retorted.

"Believe me, this *is* 'dialed down,' as you say. No one has come within ten miles of this place in nearly three decades."

"Dear God…" Evelyn whispered.

"But it's not affecting you?" Brayden pressed. "Can you make it stop for us too?"

"Resistance to the deterrents only works for GSS personnel. My apologies." She turned and started walking again. "Just keep breathing."

Tammy winced at all of us. "Really sorry." She scurried after Valerie, Roland hurrying along beside her.

Ulysses muttered a curse under his breath and kept going.

The need to be anywhere but here got worse the closer we came to the building. The primordial parts of my brain were screaming for me to flee, while my gut was convinced I was walking off a cliff with every step.

I dug my nails into my palms, fighting the overwhelming compulsion to turn around and run like hell. At my side, Ulysses continued snarling curses under his breath, while Liam's eyes glinted with icy rage.

Evelyn whimpered behind me, terror in the sound, and I managed to look back long enough to see how pale she'd gotten. "Dammit, when does this end?" I snarled at Valerie. They couldn't have just turned this *off*?

"Right here." Valerie walked up to the chipped white wall and calmly pressed her hand to a spot on the painted cement that looked no different than any other. A glowing palm print remained when she took her hand away. A *thunk* came from the wall, and then a door swung open as if carved straight from the cement itself.

"This way," she said, heading inside.

The Sentinels didn't budge, so I rooted my feet to the gravel, fighting the way my body wanted to shift and fly away.

"I assume any protections against vampires have been removed?" Asher asked flatly.

"It's safe for you to enter," Valerie called from inside.

That wasn't exactly an answer to his question.

Asher scowled, clearly hearing that too, but after a moment, he walked after her. Keeping me close, Ulysses followed, with Liam and Gideon falling in around us.

None of us burst into flame or turned to ash as we passed through the entryway. The air was cool in the dark space, and the minute the door shut behind us, the darkness became impenetrable, even to my night vision.

The gut-wrenching feeling of "get the hell away" faded like it'd never been.

Evelyn made a breathless sound of relief, and I couldn't stop myself from trembling. Along the floor, tiny gold lights came to life like pathway markers in a movie theater, casting us in the faintest of yellow glows and leading forward with no hint of what lay at their end.

"This way." Valerie started walking, Roland and Tammy following.

I glanced at the others. The GSS soldiers still stood nearby, the captain watching us as if he fully intended to stay put until we moved. A feeling of irritation passed through the link from the Sentinels, but without a word, Asher started after the archivists.

Thick carpet muffled our footsteps. Our breathing was the only sound. The chill made the hairs on the back of my neck rise, and my eyes twitched to the pitch-black space above our heads. Like the manor before it'd been destroyed, the hall gave the feeling of something watching us.

Demons didn't just protect the building, I realized.

I was pretty sure they'd built it.

Seconds turned to minutes in the chilly dark, and then suddenly, the darkness shifted. Blowing away like smoke on a breeze, the pitch-black shadows vanished like they'd never been.

"Gods..." Gideon murmured, wonder in his voice.

I blinked, looking around quickly. At our back, a plain metal door like you'd see leading to a utility tunnel was swinging shut as if we'd just come through it, even if I hadn't heard or seen a door before this moment. Metal shelves filled with books stood on either side of us, looking exactly like the library stacks back at my college, but that was where the similarity ended.

Holy shit, we'd landed in library heaven.

Through the gaps in the shelves, I could see aisle upon aisle of books that never seemed to end. Ahead of us, the carpeted path split, going left and right as a walkway around an open space easily a hundred yards across. The gallery stretched up to a shimmering stained-glass ceiling at least five stories above—and extended down who knew how many more. Row upon row of bookcases filled every level, stuffed with everything from books to scrolls to knickknacks. At seemingly random intervals, tables and leather chairs dotted the space between shelves, positioned to overlook the vast gallery as if providing comfortable reading spots. Gold lights shone down on it all, warm and buttery and practically inviting you to spend countless hours exploring everything in sight.

And God, every bit of my history-major self wanted to.

"Welcome to the Midwestern Annex," Valerie said.

"It is... impressive," Gideon admitted, his voice carefully controlled.

Tammy's tense expression flickered into a nervous but pleased smile. "You should see New York."

Gideon gave a small nod, his attention still on the stacks. "Indeed."

Ignoring them both, Valerie glanced at Roland. "Could you head to Level Archimedes and see about the charms I requested on the way here?"

My brow furrowed with confusion, but the older man just nodded to Tammy, then he started off to the right. The woman hurried after him.

"Protective spells," Valerie explained to us. "The defenses here are formidable, but rabids held us for quite some time. I am taking nothing for granted when it comes to Amalie and Urlfeige. They may have told their vampires to do something to keep tabs on us, but the charms should counteract that." She smiled at Evelyn and Brayden. "I requested extras for you both, just in case."

I wasn't sure whether to be worried about the two of them or impressed by Valerie's thoroughness.

But Evelyn only looked concerned. "What about Wren and these gentlemen?"

"Sadly, the charms are meant only for humans. But that's why we're here. To see if something in our records can be used to help them as well."

Looking barely mollified, Evelyn gave me a concerned glance. I tried for a smile, appreciating her attempt to help even if anything to do with the GSS and magic left me nervous.

"Captain," Valerie said. "If you'd be so kind as to escort this young man and his mother to the guest quarters on Level Agamemnon?"

The man nodded.

"And as for the five of you," she continued to us seamlessly. "We have alternative guest quarters available in that direction."

I couldn't stop the cold look that crossed my face. They *were* separating us.

"Actually," Brayden said before anyone else could speak. "If it's all the same to you, I'd rather stay near Wren."

He didn't take his eyes off Valerie, and I resisted the urge to hug him.

"Of course," the woman replied as if it made no difference to her. "If you'll follow me this way?" She took the pathway to the left along the edge of the open gallery, not looking back to see if we were coming too.

Brayden gave me a smile, but his eyes returned to the gallery and shelves too as he trailed after her.

We were both stunned by this place, I could tell.

"Come on," Asher said.

With soldiers behind us, we followed the archivist into the library.

When I was a kid, I'd gotten lost in a library once. My parents searched everywhere, through the kids' section, through the play area, and in all the public parts of the three-story building. I hadn't been in any of them. And when they were just about to call the cops in to help with the search, an old lady came downstairs and saw the commotion. She'd seen me, she told them, and when they hurried upstairs, I was right where she'd said.

Sound asleep in the city's historical archives, curled in an armchair next to a microfiche machine I hadn't been able to figure out how to operate.

I'd spent the afternoon there. I could spend *years* here. Everywhere I looked, there was more to read than I'd ever imagined existed.

Ghoul Operatives: Using the Dead as Spies in the Modern Age

Faerie Sexuality in the Twenty-First Century

Fire from Above: Dragon Contributions to Allied Efforts in World War II

My feet slowed as I stared at the titles. Dragons were a thing? And faeries?

God, my hands just itched to take the books down and flip them open. How many creatures were out there? And what the hell was the supernatural world's history like, anyway? I hadn't really thought about any of this when I was in the library at the manor weeks ago. I'd been too overwhelmed by the sheer fact vampires existed and that my sister and I were apparently half angel. And while I'd be kidding myself if I thought I wasn't still dog-paddling hard just to keep my head above water in this madness...

What if the answers to our problems really were in here somewhere?

I caught sight of Gideon watching me, and a blush heated my cheeks for no reason I could name. Maybe because he'd spotted me staring around like a kid at Disney World. Or because he would probably look down on me for *that* too.

I walked a little faster, and soon Valerie was leading us past a second metal door and down another corridor—this one with stone walls and an arched cathedral-like ceiling overhead, though thankfully the wall sconces lit it like a relatively ordinary hallway and not like something out of a... well, secret government installation.

Though, objectively, the thing looked like it belonged in a *castle*.

Nervousness prickled through me again. As amazing as the archives were, I suddenly hoped we wouldn't be here long. Nothing about this was safe for any of us.

The hallway turned and turned, following a winding path past unmarked wooden doors without another person to be seen. At long last, Valerie finally came to a stop. She looked at Brayden and gestured to a door to her left. "You and your mother can stay in this apartment. There are two bedrooms, so you should have plenty of space."

"And Wren?" Brayden asked immediately.

"Just down the hall," Valerie assured him. "You can see the

door from here." She pointed down the stone corridor and then turned to us. "Now, we'll need to split you up into separate apartments due to space." Her eyebrow arched. "Unless you all don't mind sharing beds?"

Well, that was blunt.

"Show us the rooms," Asher said.

Valerie smiled and headed down the hall. The soldiers stayed with us, standing to one side in silence as if waiting for us to move.

"You sure you're going to be okay?" Brayden asked me, his eyes flicking to them.

I nodded.

He didn't look totally convinced, but he nodded back all the same. Pulling down the brass latch, he pushed the door wide, revealing a dim apartment that looked like it could have been transplanted straight from any generic complex in America. White drywall, beige carpet, and what appeared to be a sofa and armchairs were all I could see, but nothing about them looked like they belonged in a castle or magical archive.

With a bracing breath, Brayden tossed me a tense grin and then headed inside.

"You take care of yourself, dear," Evelyn told me. Her gaze darted across all the Sentinels, and an *entirely* too knowing smile crossed her face.

A blush rushed into my cheeks all over again, but she was already following Brayden inside.

The door shut.

"I like them," Ulysses commented.

Gideon gave him an incredulous look. "The guy shot you."

"Yeah, well." Ulysses shrugged and started down the hall after Valerie.

The woman made no comment when we reached her, instead simply pushing the door aside and then stepping back while she waited for us to head in. All around, the soldiers took up positions by the opposite wall, watching us.

Asher held out a hand to stop me from coming any closer. "You first," he said to Valerie.

She lifted an eyebrow at him. "You do realize if we wanted you as prisoners, this would be an awful lot of trouble to go through."

None of us said a word.

Her lip twitched. With a slight bow of her head, she walked inside. Only then did Asher follow.

The air inside was slightly stale, like the place had been closed up for a while, but otherwise it looked identical to the apartment I'd seen down the hall. There was a kitchen, a living room, and even some paintings that were designed to look like windows, in deference to the fact that the building had none.

The pictures moved.

I blinked, walking closer while the guys spread out behind me, searching the place and confirming we could still leave the room. In brightly painted shades of late autumn daylight, abstract forms of people strolled along the edge of the Seine or ate at cafés with the Eiffel Tower nearby. The paint strokes shifted as they moved, carrying with the people or changing when they would turn or smile. There was no sound, but I could swear I smelled the myriad scents of flowers and bread and coffee and even salt on the air around the images.

Incredulous, I threw a glance over my shoulder at Valerie.

"The demons have a fondness for France," she explained.

"I assume you removed any surveillance implanted in these," Asher said before I could respond.

I took a step back, alarmed.

Valerie only smiled. "We've disabled it. We'll trust you if you trust us."

"Where *are* the demons?" I asked.

"Remotely located."

I waited for more of an explanation, but it never came.

"So it's just humans here?" Ulysses pressed.

"And now you." She stepped back through the doorway, one hand on the latch. "If you need anything, you only need to flag down one of the researchers. They'll find me, and I'll help take care of whatever it is you need. As I'm assuming blood will be involved in that, if you're able to give us a day or two, we should be able to bring in some bagged supplies for your needs."

"We'll be fine," Asher said neutrally.

She smiled. "Excellent. Oh, and I would appreciate it if you planned on meeting me later this evening to discuss what you know about Amalie and the creature known as Urlfeige."

There was a pause before Asher said, "A few of us will meet you."

Valerie nodded as though that's all she could've wanted. Without another word, she left the room, shutting the door behind her.

Liam moved immediately, opening it again and peering outside as if checking that we could still leave. When a moment passed and nothing changed, he leaned back in and closed the door behind him.

Are we trusting this? he signed.

Asher's brow rose and fell. "Until we hear back from Friday, I'm not sure we have a better option."

"Do you intend to be the one who meets with them later?" Gideon asked Asher.

He nodded. "Unless you want to?" he offered to Ulysses.

Ulysses shuddered. "Heh. No thanks. Pretty sure most of those soldiers would happily gut me right now, given the way they were looking at me."

With a grimace on his face, he began checking over the apartment like he was confirming no surveillance remained.

"You going to be okay here?" Asher asked me.

I nodded.

Echoing the motion, he glanced around again. "I'm going to check on their security—and make sure they were telling the truth about that surveillance, just in case." His eyes went to the others. "You all good?"

At Liam's nod, Asher headed for the door.

Silence hung over our group for a moment, and then Gideon cleared his throat. "If it's the same to all of you, I think I'll get started seeing what I can find about..." His attention twitched toward me and then away.

My stomach twisted. Everything we've been through, and he still could barely even look at me.

I turned, heading into one of the bedrooms and trying to ignore the sound of the door closing when he left. It didn't matter what he thought. We'd get through this and figure out everything else. Or something. But right now, we just needed to focus one step ahead.

The room around me was much like everywhere else in this place: already set up for someone to be here. The king-size bed was made with a fluffy white comforter and a mountain of pillows. A white wood dresser waited against one wall, a mirror reflecting the room and making it seem even bigger than it already was. Atop a chest of drawers made of that same white wood, an enormous television sat, so enormous I could probably lie atop it still have room to spare.

What kind of channels did they get in a magical archive?

I shook my head. Probably all of them, ever. But hopefully we wouldn't be here long enough for it to matter.

My eyes strayed back to the apartment's front door. Gideon wouldn't want me anywhere nearby. But screw him, really. If I could find something in those books to fix this myself—

"You okay?" Ulysses asked, leaning his head around the bedroom doorframe.

I hesitated. "Yeah."

He watched me for a moment and then stepped farther into the room. "Want to try to get some sleep?"

"Not really tired."

He hesitated. "Yeah, me either."

Something about his tone made me pause. "Are *you* okay?"

He shook his head dismissively. "Yeah, fine."

I wasn't buying it. I'd been so overwhelmed by the archives and the mess in my own head about Gideon that I hadn't noticed much else, but now his comment about the soldiers came back to me.

My heart ached for him. I walked over and took his hands. I couldn't erase the fact those people probably had been looking at him like that, and just telling him things were okay would sound hollow as hell. But maybe... "What was that word we settled on?"

His brow furrowed. "Word?"

"You know..." A grin tugged at my lips. "For when I want to fuck?"

Understanding took the place of his confusion, and he smiled as he laced his fingers through mine. "Pretty sure we never settled on one."

"Mm..." I stepped closer until I was only inches from him. "That's a shame."

"It is."

I spotted Liam in the living room, watching us both, and I hesitated. Ulysses had shared me with Asher before—and Liam had shared with Asher too, for that matter. But I wasn't sure how these two felt about sharing with each other.

Ulysses threw a look over his shoulder. "Our woman would like a distraction, Liam. Care to help me?"

Liam smiled, a deliciously wicked light coming into his eyes.

Guess that answered that question.

Turning, Liam crossed to the front door and locked it before walking back toward us.

"Let's get those off of you." Ulysses nodded toward my clothes.

Together, they moved in, Ulysses lifting my shirt while Liam pulled my jeans away, kissing lightly along my legs as he went. When I was naked between them, they stripped off their own clothes quickly before returning to kiss my lips, my neck, all while their hands ghosted over my skin, making me shiver with need and anticipation. I reached out to pull them closer, my body throbbing to have them in me now, but Ulysses stilled my hand.

He grinned. "How about we try something different, eh?"

Before I could ask, Liam shifted into shadows and smoke, wrapping around my waist and lifting me off the ground. I gasped, but I could feel the reassurance coming from him. He had me. He'd never let me fall.

But should I shift too? Was that what they had planned?

As if reading my expression, Ulysses said, "Stay like you are, baby."

Even though I was confused, I did like he asked, staying in human form and hanging suspended in Liam's grasp. And in only a moment, I figured out why. Liam was behind me, the touch of his shadow form playing over my ass, my back, and then encircling my ankles. Gently, he moved my legs apart while he did the same to my arms.

I was spread out and naked in front of Ulysses.

And goddamn was that hot.

Ulysses' eyes roamed over me. "You got her, Liam?"

I could feel his confirmation through our connection.

"You good?" he asked me.

I nodded, so wet I was dripping for him. "Take me, Ulysses. Liam. Please."

Ulysses smiled, stepping closer. Reaching down, he trailed

his fingers along my slit, gathering my juices. Still watching me, he stroked his cock, smearing my slick over himself.

I couldn't breathe.

"Now..." He grinned. "How about you have this side, Liam?"

Before I could do more than gasp, Liam spun me, and suddenly, his shadow form was at my front. I whimpered hungrily as his touch roamed over my body, all of him teasing across my skin like I was being held by a dark cloud.

One that was moving between my legs.

And then he thrust inside me.

I cried out, bucking in his grip. He was everywhere. Holding me wide, massaging my breasts, thrusting deep into me over and over.

Everywhere except...

A hand took my hips, holding me steady. Fingers teased around my ass, priming me, and I whimpered with need.

"That's right," Ulysses murmured. "That's our sexy, dirty girl."

Sweet God, that made me even hotter. Begging noises left me. "Please, oh pl—"

I cried out as he pushed into me. I was so full. So thoroughly possessed by them when they had me like this that I couldn't even think, only feel. Writhing and bucking between them, I moaned and pled for more as they fucked me, my body held fast and suspended in the air.

Liam's shadow form wrapped over my mouth, muffling my scream as I came.

Behind me, Ulysses moved faster, grunting as his orgasm took him. Shifting back, Liam pulled my legs around him and drove himself up into me until his cum rushed into me too.

I sagged against his shoulder, full and dripping from them both. Gently, Liam turned and carried me over to the bed while Ulysses pulled back the blankets. They lay down, nestling me between them.

"Damn." Ulysses wrapped an arm around me. "I think fucking that sexy ass of yours is my new favorite thing."

God, I never knew how much I loved hearing a man talk like that until now.

Liam turned my head toward him, claiming my mouth in a deep kiss. *Nothing like it,* he agreed when he finished.

I blushed. Never in my wildest dreams had I imagined this would be my life, and while yeah, okay, everything outside this tiny pocket of perfection was a mess, for this one moment none of that mattered. I had them. They had me.

And that was enough.

12

ASHER

Gideon left the apartment, but our connection made it pretty easy to tell that Ulysses, Liam, and Wren definitely hadn't.

Damn.

I adjusted my pants and shook my head to clear it as I reached the door to the main area of the archives. Last thing I needed were the archivists noticing *how* gods-damned turned on I was by whatever the hell they were up to back there.

But gods below, if I wasn't going to see if they wanted me to join them for a repeat performance later.

"Hold the door."

I glanced back to see Gideon striding toward me quickly, and even if I didn't know what my expression looked like, *his* was nothing but annoyed. Pushing past me, he strode out into the archives.

Resisting the urge to sigh, I followed, catching up to him after a moment. I'd kept my mouth shut for days, but the guy looked like he wouldn't have enough distance between him and that apartment if he was halfway to the moon.

"Whatever this is with her," I said in a low voice, "you need to get it figured out."

"I have no idea what you're talking about."

I didn't bother restraining a scoff, and his gaze cut to me, anger flaring before he smothered it back again.

Like I hadn't spent enough centuries with the man to read his expression anyway.

"She needs our help, Gideon."

"Which is exactly what I'm doing."

"By jetting out of there like your tail's on fire?"

"I am on my way to research how to undo Amalie's curse. Unless you think my time would be better spent giving her orgasms until our enemies succeed in killing her?"

My brow rose. He turned his face away, his jaw muscles jumping.

"You fed her more of your blood than Liam or me when she was unconscious," I said, still keeping my voice down. The gods only knew what eyes they'd have on us here, notwithstanding Valerie's promises that the surveillance in the apartment had been disabled. "I thought you were going to drain yourself trying to keep her alive. It's practically written all over you that you're worried sick about her—at least when she can't see you. But you've got that buried down to the point that even the link between us doesn't let on about it. And the minute she looks at you..." I gestured as if to encompass the fact we were here and she was back there.

He didn't respond.

"Is this really helping anything?"

"Yes."

"How?"

He turned back to me. "Because I believed she was the queen, and I treated her as such. And Amalie told me *exactly* how hurt Wren was by that."

Gods below.

"Sorting that out…" He shook his head. "She owes me nothing. Not forgiveness, not peace. I may never be able to make it up to her, and please know that I will still try. But she could have died a hundred times over this past week alone, and all my apologies are worthless if I put them ahead of saving her life." His voice hardened as he continued. "No matter what, I cannot let Wren die."

Grimly, I nodded, putting a hand to his arm in an effort to show him I understood. He nodded in return.

"You intend to gain access to their security?" he asked.

"Every piece of it."

"Good." He glanced around, scanning the shelves and the ceiling like I wasn't the only one who suspected they were watching us. "I trust nothing about this place, but the opportunity we have here…"

I made a noise of agreement. I didn't know how long we'd stay, and to some extent that depended on what the archivists did. But this was also the closest any of us had been to the GSS records and research in our lifetimes.

If I had my way, I'd know every detail of their operations before we left. Because Gideon wasn't wrong.

This was how we could help Wren—and the world too.

13

WREN

One week later

My eyes were burning. I wasn't sure when last I'd blinked.

But maybe it was worth it this time.

I straightened up in the overstuffed armchair and tugged my gaze from the heavy leather tome in my lap. I had no idea how long I'd been sitting here. If there was one oversight in the design of the archives, it was the lack of clocks. But if my stiff muscles were any indication, I guessed it had probably been hours.

I glanced to my left. Hours or not, he was still here.

"You could sit down, you know."

Liam just smiled. Leaning against one of the square pillars supporting the ceiling of whatever level we were on, he didn't look like he'd moved a muscle since I settled here with my latest find from the archives.

I didn't bother trying to press the issue. We'd had this nondiscussion for a week, first with him guarding my every step outside the apartment, and now with this. It wasn't that I minded his presence. God knew we all needed to be on guard here in the belly of the GSS beast, no matter how nonthreatening it currently seemed. But I hated the idea of him being uncomfortable.

I'm fine, he said, as if picking up on my own discomfort. *Find anything interesting?*

"Maybe."

He smiled. *Here or elsewhere?*

"Depends on whether they have the book this one just referenced."

He followed when I climbed to my feet and headed for the computer terminal that let me access the archive catalog. Finding anything on Tau or Urlfeige was almost impossible given the fact they'd lived so long ago; most records had decayed by the time anyone tried to dig for them. What little I'd located mostly existed in footnotes referencing older books that then referenced still older ones.

But that didn't stop me from trying.

I clicked the mouse to wake the machine up and then typed in the title I'd just seen. My stomach sank. It was here, which was great. But it was downstairs.

Way downstairs.

I bit my lip, clicking through a few more screens in the hope maybe another copy lurked somewhere else.

Nothing.

Dammit.

I closed my eyes. Over the past week, I'd roamed nearly everywhere. But I'd avoided the secure archives downstairs—and for only one reason.

Gideon.

He wouldn't want me down there. I didn't know much of what he'd been up to—the others wouldn't say or didn't know, and he'd pulled so far away from our connection that all I'd gotten were weird flashes of discomfort and irritation that left me confused. But the few times I actually had caught sight of him in the stacks, he turned away the moment he spotted me.

And no matter how much I tried to tell myself that shouldn't hurt, it always did. I'd never asked for this mess. I wasn't throwing myself at him. Hell, I'd gone out of *my* way to stay out of *his* way, and still, he'd rather pretend I was some sort of problem.

I didn't know how to fix it. I wasn't sure that would even be possible. It wasn't just on me, after all. If he still wanted to treat me like some pawn of Amalie's, that was on him.

But I had a book to find.

Exhaling sharply, I hit print and then grabbed the directions I needed from the machine below the computer.

Where are we headed? Liam asked.

"Basement archives."

He didn't comment, only nodded.

I strode toward the elevator. This would be fine. I'd just go down, grab the book, ignore the hell out of any snide comments or cold shoulders that guy tried to give me, and I'd figure out how to stop the *actual* villain in our lives. And as for what happened after, when we definitely all survived this and were one hundred percent entirely fine?

My fingers hesitated just shy of pressing the button for the bottom floor. The Sentinels were who they were. They wouldn't be separated; I didn't want to be apart from them, and Gideon didn't want anything to do with me.

And I had no clue where that left any of us.

Ignoring how I could see Liam watching me, I pushed the button and took another steadying breath as the elevator began to descend. One problem at a time. The archives made the chaos of St. Louis and Fort Briar and the whole damn world feel incredibly far away, but I had to stay focused. Stopping Urlfeige and Amalie was what was important.

Not some growly, eight-hundred-year-old vampire hottie who had *no* right to treat me the way he did.

The doors slid open. I definitely didn't hesitate because I worried he'd spotted me already. I was just... making sure the doors wouldn't close again.

Or something.

Gritting my teeth, I followed Liam out of the elevator onto the lowest level of the archives. Unlike the rest of the library, the floors here were black marble that glinted with silver flecks so pale, they could've been snow. The air was cool and dry, like an air conditioner set on overdrive. Glass walls separated the atrium from the bookcases, and panels with keypads affixed to the glass beside them served as the sliding doors to give entry only to authorized personnel. The light was dim here, and the whole place had the feeling of a mausoleum for books, as if this was where the oldest of the old were sent to their eternal rest.

I glanced across the signs glued to the glass divider walls and then headed for the sliding door to my left, typing in the code when I reached it. Some of the archivists had argued we shouldn't have access here—hell, some had argued we shouldn't be allowed *anywhere*—but after what Valerie, Tammy, and Roland had been through with the rabids, they'd made it clear they'd allow us the world if it meant stopping the rabids from taking anyone else.

Those three had surprised me, if I had to be honest. I was pretty sure they'd surprised the guys too. Anything we needed, we got. Questions about GSS troop movements? Valerie made damn sure the captain gave us answers for that. Help with an obscure section of text? Tammy stayed up all night translating it with me. Roland checked in every few days in case we needed more blood or other supplies, and between the three of them, they seemed on a mission to prove the GSS weren't what we believed.

The Sentinels didn't seem to know quite what to make of it.

I blinked against the even cooler air that rushed past me as the door slid back. As far as I could tell, no archivists were down here right now. Gideon was somewhere to my left, deeper in the stacks and hopefully nowhere near where I needed to be. Chances were, he was already aware I was here, but he'd made no move to head my direction—both a blessing and a confirmation he probably didn't want me around, just like I thought.

Whatever. I just needed the book, and then I'd get out of here.

Liam slipped past me, leading the way beyond the sliding door. It hissed closed at my back while I scanned the labels on the nearest bookshelves in the dim lighting. The archive itself was organized on a system the GSS had likely invented *just* to be confusing. The levels had random A names—everything from Agamemnon to Alice and Andromeda—while the book sections were arranged like someone put esoteric symbols and the Dewey decimal system in a blender.

Thankfully, the computers all had maps.

Eyeing the printout in my hand, I navigated through the tall black shelves, staying close to the center of the aisle. Leather-bound tomes rested on each shelf, not touching one another, with some wrapped in gold chains like they needed to be restrained. That the books down here were old was a given. But I could practically *feel* the age rolling off them, like the centuries radiated from their leather. The air seemed thick, not just with the scent of old paper and bindings, but with whispers just beyond my hearing, as if the old books were talking to each other in the shadows, telling stories of some forgotten time.

I fought the urge to linger, and maybe to strain to hear what they had to say. It seemed silly, thinking like that, but there was a magic to old books even in the supposedly "ordinary" world.

And this place was a thousand miles from ordinary.

Glancing back, Liam gave me a questioning look at how I'd slowed. Flashing a tight smile of apology, I started walking again, weaving a twisting path through the towering shelves. According to my map, this was the route to the book I needed, but unfortunately, every step was leading me closer to where I could tell Gideon was located too. A simmering sense of discomfort was coming from him, different from the weird flashes I'd gotten for the past week, and it was accompanied by something else so battened down, I couldn't hope to make sense of it.

What did he feel from me?

Dammit, that didn't matter. Screw him and *whatever* the hell was going on there. I had a book to find.

Resolutely, I rounded the corner and skimmed the shelves until I found the spot for the book I needed.

Except it was empty.

Swearing blurred through my head. If it was misplaced, I had no idea how anyone would ever find it in this place. If it'd been taken by an archivist, I'd just have to beg for it.

That didn't cover the third option.

Surely, I wasn't *that* unlucky...

Gideon started toward where I stood shielded by the bookcases.

Shit, shit, shit.

"Let's go." Not waiting to see if Liam followed, I started toward the door.

I didn't make it past the turn.

"Wren."

I bit back a curse. Gideon's voice was tight and measured, and I couldn't make heads or tails of what I picked up from him. Our connection wasn't nearly as strong as what I had with the other three—something I was honestly grateful for, and I had *no* doubt he felt the same.

Taking a calming breath, I turned to face him. "Yes?"

He stood at the opposite corner. In the dim lighting, his face appeared entirely closed off, and his powerful build seemed to take up so much of the space between the massive shelves. The cuts that had marred his face and arms were gone like they had never been, and he had a tooled-leather patch lashed over his missing eye, though I couldn't make out the design over the distance between us. He looked tired. Drained, somehow, and I suddenly wondered again what the hell he'd been up to this past week.

His gaze skipped between me and Liam. "What are you doing down here?"

I bit back a scoff. "Don't worry, I'm not staying."

I turned to leave. I'd get that book another time. After all, the guy had to sleep eventually.

"Stop."

Like hell.

But then Liam's hand took my arm. "Give him a chance," he whispered in my ear.

I closed my eyes, swearing inside. But I turned around.

Is it safe down here? Liam asked Gideon.

The other man nodded. "No one here but us, and I have spells in place to block them from spying on me."

Liam nodded. Without another word, he turned to leave.

I choked. "Wait, what are you—"

He threw a brief look back. *I'll be upstairs.* His gaze went between us. *Just talk it out already. Both of you.* His eyebrow arched at Gideon. *And stop wasting time. She deserves better. So get your big brain out of your ass and be that for her.*

I stared at him, at a loss. "Liam!"

He ignored my protest, disappearing around the corner.

Silence reigned.

Gritting my teeth, I made myself turn around. "Listen, I'm just looking for the book that was supposed to be—"

"I'm sorry."

My mouth snapped shut.

He shifted his weight, glancing after the direction Liam had gone and then away. "For everything. How I treated you. How I made you feel like a... like a bug."

I tensed. "Who told you that?"

His brow furrowed, his gaze dropping. "This wasn't how I planned on apologizing to—"

"Gideon."

He paused, saying nothing for such a long moment, I wasn't sure he'd go on.

And then he sighed. "Amalie did. She..." His focus was anywhere but on me as he carefully adjusted the position of a book nearby. "She brought it to my attention just *how* mistaken I had been for believing you were in any way influenced by the queen."

Horror spread through me. I could read between those careful lines. "What did she do to—"

"It doesn't matter." His eye flicked over to mine sharply. "What matters is that Liam is right. You deserve better. You always have. And I am sorry for never being that for you."

I faltered, not sure how to respond. "The... the hell it doesn't matter. Are you okay?"

He stared at me, and through the dim light, I saw the oddest look pass over his face—like wonder, pain, and irony all tangled together—and then his lips curled toward a smile like I was the most inexplicable thing he'd ever seen.

My heart twitched in response. I didn't think he'd ever smiled at me before. Not without a spiteful edge to it, anyway.

And damn if this didn't do strange things to my insides.

"Yes." He gave a small nod toward my chest. "Are you?"

I shifted my weight uncomfortably, looking away and

resisting the urge to rub at the mark on my skin. It was no larger or smaller, and over the past week, there'd been no more incidents like what happened at the apartment.

But that didn't stop some tiny part of me from worrying that starvation-level hunger might come back when I least expected it, maybe when I was near Brayden or some other innocent human. Which was why I was grateful Ulysses was sticking near Brayden and Liam was staying near me—to protect everyone from what I might do, just in case I was wrong about that hunger being gone.

But I wasn't sure if I should tell Gideon that. "I'm fine."

He hesitated again. "Good."

Silence hung for a moment. I bit my lip, wondering what to do now. This was good. Progress, and maybe now things could be more civil. But I had a lifetime of memories telling me about how things had once been between us.

We'd been different people. I knew that. But we'd also been a hell of a lot more than *civil.*

"Listen, um—"

"May I ask you a question?"

We both stopped, realizing we'd spoken at the same time.

"Apologies," he said. "You were saying?"

"No, that's okay. What?"

He hesitated and then walked closer, his movements careful like maybe he thought I'd bolt. "I've been delving deeper into the lore about Urlfeige, Amalie, and the magic they used in case I could reverse what's been done to you, and I may have an idea. But..." He grimaced faintly, not meeting my eyes. "It would require you to trust me. And I have hardly earned that."

My brow climbed again. I didn't know what to say. This was a different side to him than I'd seen thus far, and I didn't know what to make of it.

But if he'd really found something...

The others trusted him. In a past life, I'd died to save him.

And yeah, that wasn't now, in this life when he'd kind of been an asshole for weeks, but...

"What do you need me to do?" I asked.

A bit of tension left him like he'd been bracing himself for something, though I wasn't sure what. Me to refuse to listen to him, all because he was the one asking?

"It's a unique spell. It..." Again, he hesitated, though this time it looked caused more by unease than anything. "It draws on the empty realms."

"Uh..." I gave a nervous laugh. "Gideon, that's—"

"I know." He grimaced. "But I believe that place is the origin of the black mark on your skin—and what Urlfeige and Amalie drew upon when they attacked you as they did at the apartments. But I think I can block that. Perhaps remove it entirely."

My mouth moved. "How?"

He tilted his head back the way he'd come. "Will you trust me?"

I could feel the worry coming from him, stronger than any emotion I'd been able to pick up from him in ages. Maybe ever. And it wasn't aimed at me. No, I'd swear it was because, more than anything, he wanted to help.

I nodded. "Yeah, I will."

14

GIDEON

Wren's trust was a precious gift.

One I prayed she wouldn't end up dead for offering to me.

Trepidation churning inside me, I led the way back through the aisles until I reached the area I'd carved out for myself amid the tables and chairs at the heart of this portion of the archives. A collection of desk lamps drove back the shadowy twilight, casting a golden glow on the tables and surrounding shelves until the space was an oasis of light. Books covered most of the long wooden tables, though the ones at the center of the space were clear of every ancient tome, lined instead with my experiments.

A surprised noise came from behind me. I glanced back to find Wren staring at the rows of bowls and vials, each with a small tent of folded paper in front of it, a number written on every one.

"There's over a hundred. You've done all these—" She cut off when she spotted the sleeping bag I'd tossed into one corner, her eyes wide with incredulity. "You were sleeping down here?"

I gave a small shrug. "Finding the right combination and spell took time."

She blinked, her mouth moving for a moment. "Which one do we need?"

Another rope of tension melted from around my heart. She really was trusting me.

Gods, do not let me kill her.

Clearing my throat, I forced my attention to the matter at hand. Crossing to a nearby table, I picked up a book. "The combination of elements I found in here seems likeliest for producing the result we need."

She was staring at the title.

"What?"

"Nothing. Just... I was looking for that."

I hesitated. *Obscure* was an understatement for this book. "Why?"

"I've been researching, that's all."

"Researching?"

"All week. The situation with Urlfeige, the spell, the history of the supernatural world..." She drew her chin up like she was preparing to defend herself. "I wasn't going to pass this opportunity up."

Words escaped me. "You like history, then? And books?"

The defensiveness in her eyes grew. "I'm a history major at Claremont. Yeah, I like books."

I blinked. She studied history? How had none of the others ever mentioned that?

But then, such a detail wouldn't seem significant to them, assuming they'd even learned it. "And you've been researching."

"Look, I don't know why that's so shocking. My life is on the line, along with most of the damn world, so—"

"It's not shocking. It's..." I searched for a word. "Compelling."

Her eyebrow lifted skeptically. "Okay."

I floundered for an explanation that would not make her think I was patronizing her. "Books are everything to me. Windows into experiences beyond my own. Even with all the history I've seen, more happens in the world than I could ever hope to witness, and books provide the opportunity to learn about those things. So to find that you like reading and history as well is... pleasant."

She didn't speak for a moment, but the defensiveness was fading from her eyes, leaving something I couldn't quite interpret. "Pleasant."

I searched for another term. One that wouldn't make her uncomfortable.

Because by the gods, what I *wanted* to say was that it was sexy as hell.

She spoke before I could settle on a way to respond. "So what did you find?"

I glanced back down at the book I'd forgotten was in my hand. "A... a spell. This one." I gestured toward bowl number one-fifty-three nearby, only to narrowly avoid knocking over several others.

"Maybe I should take that?" Wren circled the table toward me.

Her hand brushed mine when she took the book, and I tensed, my mouth suddenly dry. Carefully, she drew the book back, not quite looking at me while she cradled it like a protective shield to her breasts.

Gods...

I pulled my gaze from the book's location, clearing my throat. "I believe this is the combination needed, and I've unearthed the wording of a spell that should assist in blocking that link to Amalie and Urlfeige as well."

She paused. "What do we need to do?"

"It's rather straightforward, actually. We burn the combination of ingredients, thereby simulating the smoke that we saw around Amalie, and then there is the wording I've found as well, which—when combined—should have most of the result we need."

"Most?"

I hesitated. "There is one other part. A balance, if you will. You happened upon it with Ulysses last week."

She tensed. "Gideon, are you saying I need to bite one of you?"

I turned to the experiments on the table, unable to make myself meet her gaze, not with what she might see there. "Yes."

She shifted her weight, taking her farther from me. "That's not—"

"It needn't be me," I interjected, not wishing to hear her attempt to let me off the hook. The gods knew I didn't need the confirmation I'd damaged matters between us beyond repair. "Liam is just upstairs, and I know he would be more than willing to assist."

She was quiet for a heartbeat. "Is there another way?"

Confusion brought my gaze back to her.

"Something that doesn't risk him," she said. "Or any of you."

"Wren, we—"

"I'm not forcing anyone. *Ever.* You need to understand that about me, okay? I know you don't want me to bite you, but the others don't deserve to be put in this position either, and if there's any chance this could hurt them, I won't—"

"I didn't say that." I blurted the words, taken aback by her vehemence.

She was silent.

"I..." Gods, how to say this without making things worse?

I was so gifted at making things worse.

"I would be *honored* to assist you. I simply thought you would be more comfortable if one of the others did instead."

Her distrustful expression had grown by the second. "You would?"

I nodded.

"But you... Back at the manor, you made it pretty clear how you felt about all of that."

Guilt twisted in my gut like a knife. "I lied."

Her brow climbed incredulously.

"I was not as... *repulsed* by the idea of you drinking from me as I let on that day. Quite the opposite. But because of my fear that you were Amalie, I chose to behave as reprehensibly as I did instead." I weighed my chances and then risked taking a step closer to her. "I know I haven't done much to deserve your trust or even your friendship, and I hope someday you may find it in your heart to forgive me. But please know I am more than willing to do whatever it takes to help you now—no matter what that might entail."

She stared up at me, her eyes searching my face as if I were a book she was trying to read. But then she stopped, her gaze catching on the intricate details of my eye patch.

"Wait, is that...?" Her hand rose toward it, and then she pulled back again, her fingertips resting on her beautiful lips as if restraining more words.

I nodded. When the archivists had offered to supply an eye patch, I'd been suspicious. The gods knew the demons on their payroll could place any manner of spells upon it. But I also had grown tired of the stares I received, and my own proficiency with research meant I'd been confident—and correct—in my ability to locate sufficient cleansing magics for it fairly quickly, just in case. So I'd agreed.

With one specific request as to the design tooled into the leather.

"A wren," I said.

She swallowed hard, staring at the tiny bird sheltered protectively by vines and branches. "Why would you..."

"Because..." My gaze dropped. "I failed to give your heart the protection it deserves. But there is nothing I wouldn't do to keep you safe. And even if I have broken things between us irreparably, I still wished to keep something of you with me... always."

She was silent, and at last I risked a glance up at her.

Her mouth was moving, though she didn't make a sound, and... oh gods, were those tears in her eyes?

Damn me. "I never meant it to upset you. Please, if you would rather I didn't—"

"No!" Her hand took mine.

I froze.

She hesitated for a moment and then adjusted her hold on my hand, squeezing gently. "No, I'm not. I'm just... Thank you. That's..." She laughed suddenly, blinking the tears away. "I don't know what to say."

Her smile emboldened me. I turned my hand, interlacing my fingers with hers. The mere touch of her skin made my heart pound, and when she hesitated only to set down the book in her arm, I found I couldn't breathe.

"So," she began, a touch of hesitancy in her voice. "If you weren't... repulsed, like you said." Her eyes rose to mine. "What were you?"

"Desirous."

Her lips parted. Carefully, I lifted my other hand, taking her cheek.

She didn't pull away. No, she was coming closer, her chin tilting up toward me, and I thanked every god I knew for a mercy I never thought to receive.

Her lips were sweeter than anything I'd ever tasted. Before I could examine the impulse, I was pulling her closer and plundering her mouth when her lips parted. Her body melded to mine like I'd been crafted to hold her in my arms, and nothing else existed but the soft feeling of her with me.

But she was here for a reason, and I couldn't get ahead of myself. Not when her very life was at stake.

Breaking away from her soft lips, I tilted my head to the side. "Please. Allow me to help you."

Her eyes searched my face once more, as if to be completely certain I spoke the truth. My heart ached. She'd been so resistant to the idea of being a vampire, right from the start. But I hadn't seen that for what it was. No, instead I'd put the weight of my fears on her and given her such doubt that even now she wouldn't take me up on my offer without once again making sure my consent was real.

But whatever she saw in my expression must have helped somehow. Her fangs slipped down, and she rose up on her tiptoes.

I groaned with pleasure when she bit down, putting one arm around her immediately to keep her close. Her hands slipped around me, one holding the back of my head while the other gripped my back. Arousal closed my eye, and my body ached to grab her, strip those interfering clothes from her, and show her all that I'd wanted to do since I first saw her.

But though my cock hardened and desire pounded through me in time to her gentle pulls on my vein, I couldn't let myself lose focus on why we were here.

With one hand I reached over, fumbling up a match from the supplies on the table and flicking it with my thumb to light it. Flames danced briefly in the bowl as the contents caught fire, and as smoke rose, I murmured the words I'd gathered for the spell.

Wren pulled away with a gasp, barely able to close the wound. Her eyes went wide, and then her head fell back.

I caught her. "Wren? Wren, speak to me. Tell me you're—"

A cold sensation shot through my core, as if a window had been opened in my soul straight to the Arctic. Oblivion waited beyond the opening, all of it so horrifying, the gods themselves would struggle to endure it. The endlessness was too much. Beyond comprehension. No life was meant to experience this place.

The empty realms.

Tensing, I fought to hold myself back from it inside my own mind, but already, I could feel how I was failing. The darkness wanted to consume us, destroy us. To even exist in this place was an abomination. Beyond reality, beyond life and light and time, nothing was meant to be.

Yet *something* lurked there.

Wren convulsed, her body spasming in my grasp. A wordless rasp escaped her, like nothing I'd ever heard.

But the hungry dark was coming.

And it had teeth.

Shapes slithered in the black abyss like eels with razor-sharp fangs, all of them drawing closer. These monsters had dwelled in the darkness since before the dawn of time, watching, waiting for their chance to end this ephemeral ghost called *life*.

They wanted us.

Her.

Panic shot through me, and with all my strength, I threw myself backward in mind as well as body, clutching Wren to me as I tried to flee from the endless abyss. Every incantation I knew to ward and protect us fell from my lips, the words tumbling over one another at frantic speed.

The dark vanished as I crashed down onto the marble tile of the archive floor. In my mind, the ice and the fanged monsters disappeared as if someone had slammed a door on them all.

Wren's body was limp in my arms.

I placed a hand to her cheek. She was cold as death. "Wren?"

Nothing.

Oh, gods, I'd made a mistake. Been too reckless, and now I'd hurt her just as she finally began to trust me.

I took a breath to call for Liam. Already I could feel him rushing back toward us. Had only a moment passed? It felt like eternity, and now—

Wren tensed again, inhaling sharply, and lurched forward. Blinking, she looked around, her eyes wild.

I shifted my grip to get a better look at her. "Speak to me, Wren. Are you all right?"

For a moment longer, she continued to blink. "Y-yeah. I think so." A whole-body shudder rolled through her. "God, that was... terrifying."

A breathless laugh escaped me at her dry tone, my reaction so spontaneous that it left me feeling mildly hysterical. But worry returned on its heels. "Those creatures. Did they touch you or harm you or...?"

"No. No, they..." She wetted her lips, shivering in my arms. "What were they?"

"Inhabitants of the empty realms, I assume."

She shuddered again, and then her brow flickered down. Glancing to her chest, she pulled aside the collar of her sweater.

And then froze.

"What is it?" Panic gripped me. "What's wrong?"

Her head shook. "Nothing. It... it's gone." Grinning, she looked up at me. "You did it."

If I had not already been on the ground, my relief would have taken my legs from beneath me. On the other end of the room, I felt Liam slow, as if he'd detected we were no longer in danger. Cautiously, the man retreated again, leaving us be.

"I don't feel anything from it anymore." Wren's happy expression became tinged by concern as she looked up at me. "Are *you* okay?"

"Euphoric now. I thought I'd killed you."

Sympathy filled her eyes, and my heart swelled at that gentle expression. All that she'd just been through, and she still cared that I'd worried.

I couldn't stop myself from taking her cheek, drawing her toward me, and when she didn't resist, the warm feeling inside me only grew.

Her lips met mine, and to kiss her was pure bliss. Finding heaven and home in one single instant. It was all I ever could have asked for. My desire for her burned inside me. If I lived for ten thousand years, I knew I would never get enough of her soft lips.

But after a moment, she pulled away, and swiftly, I worked to shove my disappointment down. If that was all she wanted, it would have to be enough. She'd just survived a curse, after all. I wouldn't press.

A hint of a hopeful smile tugged at her lips. "Could I ask…"

"Anything."

Her smile grew, but it was still a touch hesitant. And then her head tilted to the side, exposing her beautiful neck.

My breath stuttered. "You… you wish me to…"

"Please?" Her shoulder rose and fell. "It makes the connection stronger. Brings back… everything." Her smile dimmed slightly. "If you want that, I mean. I'm not saying you have to."

Oh, gods. What she was asking… *offering*…

Words were failing me all over again, and I cleared my throat, struggling to find my voice. "Are you certain you wish to share that with me?"

She nodded, still keeping her beautiful throat exposed to me.

There was no world in which I could ever say no.

15

WREN

Despite monsters and an endless abyss, despite magic and the horror of actually seeing the space beyond all of reality, in this moment, I felt more like myself than I had since we'd come to St. Louis. The curse was just *gone,* like Gideon had fully broken the connection to our enemies that Ulysses and I had started to close a week ago. My skin was healed, not a trace of darkness remaining. And I was simply *me* again.

With my Sentinel holding me in his arms and bending closer, his fangs slipping into place and making me wet as hell.

Could he hear my heart pounding? His scent surrounded me, stronger to my senses because I'd just fed. Leather and spice, a trace of the myriad herbs he must have been using in his experiments, along with something so unique and yet familiar, I felt like I'd know it anywhere even if I couldn't explain why. He drew me to him like I was the most precious treasure he'd ever found, and my core throbbed in anticipation of what I knew was coming.

His fangs sank into my neck.

I gasped, rocking toward him instinctively, and his grip

tightened, pulling me to him like he'd keep me as his forever. His mouth moved against my skin, swallowing me down, and in my mind, the connection between us flared to life like the sun *finally* rising.

A groan left him. His hand raked up through my hair, holding me close. My body burned with desire for him, and a moment later, he drew back, sealing the wound quickly before turning his attention to my mouth, plundering me, devouring me, kissing me like I was all he needed in the world. He moved me, and I barely noticed until my shoulders bumped up against the end of a bookcase.

He drew back, breathing hard, staring at me for a moment. I quivered at the heat in his gaze. The blatant need, so different from the closed-off way he'd looked at me for so long. Hunger pounded through the link between us, and there was no mistaking it.

But I wanted to hear him say the words. "What do you want?" I whispered.

His lips curled in a smile. "You." His gaze dropped, moving from my lips to my body and then back to my eyes with an intensity that made me ache with need. "Always you."

I smiled back. "Then what are you waiting for?"

The intensity of his desire and joy pounding through our link stole my breath. He came toward me. My clothes hit the floor, and his did too, and then he was lifting me. My back hit the cool wood of the bookcase again as he impaled me on his cock, and I moaned at the way he stretched me, my body rocking against him as I wordlessly begged for more.

He didn't make me wait. Gripping me hard, he thrust into me, as if every minute until now had been an unbearable tension inside him and he couldn't contain it any longer. Over and over, his cock hit deep inside, making my vision blur. My head fell back against the wood of the bookcase, and I dug my fingernails into his shoulders as pleasure built higher inside me. His beard scraped against my skin, a delicious counterpoint of sensation that made me shudder and quake inside. I couldn't even breathe for how hard he was taking me.

Gideon had always been so tightly controlled, so restrained. If I thought that'd carry over to how he'd be when he had me...

Goddamn, I'd been wrong.

My orgasm exploded through me, and I'd swear I blacked out for a moment from the intensity. He never stopped, though, thrusting and thrusting until finally, he roared as he came inside me.

I sagged against him as he shifted his hold on me, carrying me a short distance and then lifting me down from where I'd been wrapped around his hips. A thin layer of softness over hard floor met my back, and through dazed eyes, I glanced around.

A sleeping bag. He'd been staying down here, and now...

He lay down beside me, drawing a blanket over us as he pulled me close to him. Despite the intensity of the sex, he cradled me now with such gentleness that it stole my breath all over again. I felt treasured. Protected. Worshiped in an entirely different way than the sex we'd had moments ago, and when I nestled my cheek against the soft hair of his chest, he sighed, as if this moment was finally releasing a different kind of tension within him too.

"Mine," he whispered. His hand stroked my hair away from my face. "Ours."

I nodded. "Always."

16

ULYSSES

"Oh, you've got to be kidding me," Brayden muttered. On the screen, his character flopped to the ground and didn't move again.

I grinned. "Told you."

Brayden threw me a wry glance. "Okay, but in my defense, saying the game company programmed a cheat code just for you because you saved the CEO's life did seem a *little* like bullshit."

I chuckled as the booming voice of the narrator declared me the victor for the fifth time. "Want to try another—"

A shiver coursed over my skin, jarringly cold, but changing before I could do more than register the sensation. The ice vanished like a door slamming against a winter chill, turning into the sudden sensation of lights coming on inside.

Gideon.

And Wren.

Holy shit.

"Everything okay?" Brayden asked.

I shifted position slightly on the sofa, pulling my focus back to the video game on the massive television and not what was going on... six floors below? Seven? Damn, everything felt stronger now.

What the hell had they done?

I could tell what they were doing *now*.

"Yeah." I cleared my throat. "Fine. You want to switch games or should I keep kicking your ass for another—"

"Is it Wren?"

I looked over at him, alarmed.

Brayden gave a small shrug. "One of the archivists mentioned you all, um..." He seemed to search for words. "You have some kind of awareness of each other?"

I hesitated. "Something like that, yeah."

"Huh."

I couldn't read the tone. It wasn't cold or disinterested. It was just odd.

"That a problem?" I asked.

"What? No."

I wasn't sure I believed that. "So then there's nothing we should know about *you* and Wren...?"

He blanched. "Uh, no. Wren's my friend, but I'm not... She's not..." A look of consternation crossed his face.

"Because you like guys?"

He glanced over sharply.

"The GSS intern who brought dinner the other night. I noticed how you were checking him out."

He scoffed. "God, you..."

"Want to survive as long as we have"—I shrugged—"it pays to be observant."

"Well, I'm not into you, if that's the question."

I chuckled at his pointed tone. "Wasn't thinking that. But my friends and I *are* into Wren, and I just want to know that's not going to cause an issue here."

Especially given what was going on downstairs...

I made myself push the awareness of them to the back of

my mind. Gods, I'd never get enough of that woman, and if not for wanting her and Gideon to have time together too, I'd be down there in a heartbeat, helping him wring more orgasms from her sexy body until she was boneless from all the pleasure.

Brayden shook his head, absently twisting the small stone pendant he now wore around his neck. The GSS charm was meant to protect against Amalie and Urlfeige tracking him. I doubted he needed it—his mother had been the prisoner, not him—but he said he wore it out of solidarity, mostly to keep her from worrying.

"No issue here," he said. "And yeah, I like guys. And girls. And Wren's my best friend, and I care about her, but…" An odd look crossed his face. "It never felt like she and I were meant for each other like that."

I regarded him curiously.

"Anyway"—he looked down at the controller in his hand—"both she and Harper are just my friends."

I paused. "Harper."

He didn't look up. "Friends."

"Ah."

The silence stretched, and it wasn't like it was any of my business to break it. Brayden wasn't a bad guy, and if he had a crush on Wren's sister, well…

I clicked on another round of the game. The announcer's deep voice told us to get ready to fight.

"No cheat code this time, eh?" Brayden said. "Or can't you win without it?"

I scoffed. "Oh, now it's—"

The apartment door opened. At the expression on Asher's face, I hit pause. "What's wrong?"

His eyes swept the apartment as if checking no one else was here. "Security station spotted something on the monitors. Might be people out by the perimeter."

A chill rolled through me. The archivists said no one came near this place, and if the captain and his soldiers didn't recognize whoever this was...

Unless they were lying and this was a trap.

Fuck.

Brayden was already climbing to his feet. "Should we find Wren?"

Asher's eyes flicked to me briefly. He knew as well as I did what she and Gideon had been up to downstairs. And yeah, it felt like they'd finished, but...

"We can take care of that," Asher told Brayden.

The guy nodded.

"Go find your mom," I said to him. "Warn her." I tossed the controller aside and headed for the door with a nod to Asher. "Let's check this out."

17

WREN

The archives were so silent, I'd swear we were the only two people still within them. I could feel that Liam had returned upstairs a while ago, leaving me with Gideon as we lay on his makeshift bed. Asher was somewhere up there too, maybe with Ulysses still in the apartment.

My gaze slipped over to Gideon, my head turning slightly from where it rested on his massive bicep. "So..."

He glanced over at me. "So?"

I bit my lip. "What would you say about coming back upstairs and maybe, um..." In spite of myself, I could feel a blush rushing up my cheeks. How could I still be so shy around him, given what we'd just done?

But then, that was just the two of us. This...

"What do you wish to ask me?" he prompted gently, smiling.

I wetted my lips, bracing myself. "You told me once that sometimes you all, um... share." My eyes rose to his.

His smile broadened. "I did say that."

"So then...?"

He chuckled. "Would you like that?"

I nodded.

"Well." He shifted around and sat up, trailing a fingertip down between my breasts when the blanket fell away. "In that case, I suggest we return upstairs now so we can—"

An alarm blared through the room, shattering the stillness around us. "Please make your way to an evacuation exit. Please make your way to an evacuation exit. Please make your way to an evacuation—"

The voice cut off with a screech, like something had happened on the other end. Red lights flashed from emergency bulbs in the ceiling, blindingly bright.

And in the distance, I heard screams.

Gideon swore. Lunging to his feet, he snagged my clothing and tossed it to me before beginning to yank on his own.

My hands shook as I got dressed at high speed. The screams were getting closer. Gunfire undercut the sound. I could feel the Sentinels rushing toward us, unharmed for the moment.

But that didn't mean Brayden or his mom were safe.

Or that anybody else was either.

I shifted and flew as fast as I could for the exit.

"Wren!" Gideon shouted.

He shifted into shadow and smoke behind me.

I could feel his alarm radiating through our connection. Urlfeige had taken that power from him, but now that he'd fed from me and our connection was restored, it was back.

Not that he'd know that. And I didn't know how to explain in this form, so it was going to have to wait.

He raced up beside me. *I know you're worried for your friend. But Urlfeige is hunting you. We need to get you away from here more than anything else.*

His voice was in my mind as clearly as if he'd spoken the words aloud, and the shock of it made me falter. The Sentinels could talk in my mind when we were in this form?

Never mind what he'd just said. I wasn't leaving Brayden and Evelyn.

A crash shook the archives, sounding like it came from somewhere above. Up ahead, an enormous slab of steel suddenly began lowering over the glass wall separating this part of the archives from the elevators.

Go! Gideon yelled in my mind.

I shook off my shock and raced at the descending barrier. I knew about this. The captain had told us that in the event of an attack, the archives sealed shut, section upon section, for the protection of the priceless relics within. In moments, this level and the ones above it would each become an impenetrable box.

One we were about to be trapped inside.

Screams came from beyond the lowering metal slab, cutting off with a chilling finality. Howls and snarls followed them, sending more fear shooting through me. I couldn't see the attackers yet and couldn't feel anything but rage from my link to the Sentinels, but that didn't mean the rabids weren't possibly hurting Brayden and Evelyn right now.

And meanwhile, the massive barrier between us and the exit was closing.

We shot under the gate right before it slammed shut at our backs. More screams came from the levels above us, and the sound of gunfire too, echoing down the open gallery like a nightmare. I couldn't tell where it was concentrated, though.

Shadow and smoke came flying over the edge of the level above. In an instant, Gideon threw himself in front of me, and though he was still nothing but smoke and shadow himself, a slash of bright silver like moonlight and lightning moved with him as he struck at the creatures.

His knife. And the rabids shrieked, falling back.

Go! he shouted through our connection.

Not without you!

I had no idea how speaking like this worked, but the words left me all the same. And I could feel his irritation in response.

I didn't care. I wasn't losing him.

The energy of my sword surged inside me, not causing pain for the first time in a week. Relief filled me at that, even as I searched around fast, trying to figure out where to go. I could still hear screaming in the distance.

But the Sentinels were *that* way.

Come on! I yelled to Gideon before racing upward.

He slashed at another one of the creatures and then took off after me.

Level after level flashed past with steel barriers dented and dislodged on so many of them. Others hadn't closed at all. Rabids lunged at us, dying as our blades sliced into them. Bodies lay fallen in their own blood between the shelves, and I hated my relief that I didn't recognize them. But gunfire still rang out above us.

Two forms of shadow and smoke dove over the edge of a level far above, but this time, instant recognition made me want to sob with relief. Asher and Liam. They tore into the rabids trying to reach us.

This way! Asher called.

We raced upward and past the ledge of the level they'd come from.

Knife drawn, Ulysses was there. Brayden and Evelyn too, and my friend had his gun and machete in his hands. The GSS captain, half a dozen soldiers, and Roland were behind them, the archivist looking panicked even though soldiers surrounded him.

The moment I shifted back, Ulysses yanked me into his arms, hugging me tightly.

"What's happening?" I asked. "How did they find us?"

Brayden shook his head. "Not sure. Captain Evans says somebody messed with the defenses—"

An explosion reverberated through the building, making us stumble. Around us, books and historical artifacts quivered and tumbled from the shelves.

"Go!" Captain Evans ordered, pointing toward a path through the stacks to our left.

The Sentinels moved immediately to surround me while we all took off, leaping over fallen artifacts and gasping every time a bookcase teetered toward falling.

The red glare of an exit sign came into sight ahead.

Dead bodies were piled in the open doorway beneath it. Hunched over their victims, the rabids whirled, their faces smeared with blood. The nearest vampire grinned.

The Sentinels were moving immediately. Asher and Liam went right while Gideon went left, tearing into the rabids as Ulysses stayed between us and the vampires.

But the darkness through the doorway started to churn, radiating wrongness that made my skin crawl.

More rabids were coming.

"Fall back!" the captain shouted.

Ulysses grabbed my arm, pulling me with him as the other Sentinels moved to cover our retreat.

"Southern stairs!" A GSS soldier in the lead pointed. "That way!"

"Wait for us!" Valerie shouted.

I threw a look back over my shoulder to see Tammy and Valerie running through the aisles toward us, a handful of others with them.

A rabid lunged through the shelves to grab one of the archivists.

My sword was in my hand before I finished registering the thought. Whirling, I slashed through the air, striking the creature as it attempted to get a grip on the guy's neck. The rabid turned to ash, and the human stumbled away from me, staring.

"Go!" I shouted at him.

The guy staggered around me, running after the others.

"Come on." Ulysses grabbed my arm, bringing me with him. Behind me, Brayden slashed his machete at a rabid trying to cut us off by circling wide through more of the aisles.

Up ahead, the secondary exit came into view, thankfully free of any vampires.

A soldier caught himself on the wall, typing a rapid code into the keypad by the door. "When we get outside, head for the—"

A gunshot took the soldier through the head.

Horror made me whirl.

Roland pointed his gun at the rest of us. "Nobody move."

"Whatever you're doing," Gideon started, easing closer carefully. "It will not—"

"Don't." The white-haired man whipped his weapon over to point at him. "These are special issue. They'll kill you instantly."

Everyone froze.

"Roland," Valerie said slowly. "Where is your pendant?"

A pained look spasmed over the guy's face as he glanced swiftly down toward his chest and then back. "I-I don't know. It kept falling off."

My skin crawled at the crazed look in his eyes.

"I hear him." Roland's face twitched again. "In my head, all the time. He says he'll fix it. He'll make us like them"—his chin jerked toward the sound of howling rabids in the distance— "and then everything will be okay."

"You don't believe that." Tammy's voice shook. "Please, Roland. I know you don't."

His pained expression returned. "It'll be okay, Tams. Promise." He looked at me. "We just have to give him her." His gun swung toward me. "We just—"

A gunshot made every muscle in my body clench.

Roland lurched back. Blood soaked his shirt, turning the

white button-down red around the wound in his chest. His eyes rose to mine, such confusion and pain in them. His body spasmed, and his mouth moved, no sound coming out.

Light faded from his eyes as he slumped to the floor, his weapon falling limp from his grasp.

Shaking all over, I looked back.

Brayden lowered his gun, an anguished look on his face.

I couldn't speak, and I wasn't sure what there even was to say. Everything was so wrong.

In the distance, rabids howled.

"Come on." Ulysses pulled me with him.

With ruthless efficiency, the remaining soldiers grabbed Roland's body, yanking it out of the way, while the captain hurried to the front and finished typing in the code quickly. "Through the tunnel, fast. You"—the captain looked at Brayden —"with me."

I choked on a protesting sound. Yes, he'd just saved my life, but I didn't want my friend to be in any more danger than he was already.

But Brayden just gave a tight nod.

Sticking as close to him as I could, I followed the others through the doorway. In contrast to our first passage into this place, the tunnel was now as white as milk and brightly lit without a trace of shadows.

No chance rabids could hide here.

When we reached the door, the soldiers motioned all of us back, but Asher didn't move. "You're going to want us with you," he said to the captain.

A heartbeat passed before the man nodded. Counting down on his fingers, he paused and then yanked the door wide.

Shrieking shadows dove at them immediately.

Asher and Liam shot past, launching into the sky and tearing into the creatures while the soldiers opened fire on any that reached ground level. The bullets shredded into the rabids, courtesy of God knew what spellwork or technology.

"Run!" the captain shouted at us. "Trailers!"

Sword in hand, I tore after Ulysses and Gideon as they ran for the trailer homes.

"Take it down!" the captain yelled behind us.

I threw a glance over my shoulder to see one of the soldiers hit a sequence on a keypad by the door. The bar above the numbers went bright red, flashing faster and faster.

"Go! Go!" The remaining soldiers raced after us, firing at the rabids trying to follow.

A rumbling filled the air, and the ground beneath us shook. All around, the walls of the archives began to crumble in on themselves as if being sucked in toward a black hole at their center.

Horror filled me. People could still be in there.

But then, were any of them still alive? Or still human?

Explosions rocked the ground, coming from deep within the earth. We struggled to run faster as the gravel rolled and quaked beneath our feet.

And then it grew still.

"Transportation shed, that way!" The captain pointed.

We ran for the trailers. The closer we got, the blurrier the mobile homes became, until—when we were right on top of them—I could see something else inside.

Vehicles. Several dozen of them parked inside the spaces where, from a distance, it looked like only mobile homes stood.

"Hurry!" the captain ordered.

The soldiers and archivists dove through the translucent walls of the supposed mobile homes and climbed inside the vehicles. Brayden and his mom followed.

"Asher!" I cried. "Liam!"

The Sentinels swept down from the darkness above, shifting effortlessly back to human form. On either side of me,

Ulysses and Gideon kept their knives out, ready to slash at any rabid that came after us. Still surrounding us, the soldiers continued firing at the sky.

Quickly, I climbed into the vehicle as ash fell all around. The SUVs took off, leaving the archives sealed in the earth behind us.

18

ASHER

The sun was coming up, and we'd finally found shelter in a massive abandoned repair shop beside an equally abandoned gas station. Liam was checking the property, but it looked like we'd survived the escape with no sign of rabids following.

And none of that mattered *nearly* as much as the words that had just come from Gideon's mouth.

"You're sure?" I stared at him.

Standing in the shadows beside the open garage door, the other man nodded. "The damage to her chest is gone."

I glanced over my shoulder at where Wren sat deeper inside the enormous garage with Brayden and his mother. She knew we were talking about her. Every few moments, her eyes darted in our direction, but she'd made no move to leave her friend's side.

He'd just shot someone, and unlike Ulysses, this had been a human and now the man was dead. Brayden appeared to be holding up well, but I could see the tension in his body language.

This one would take a toll.

"So Urlfeige and Amalie can't reach her anymore?" Ulysses asked.

"That's my hope, yes."

Ulysses scoffed incredulously. "You realize this is the best news we've had in a fucking week. Hell, a *month*." He grinned. "So that's what you all were getting up to when, uh…"

Gideon straightened. "It required blood."

"Mm-hmm."

The other man's brow rose pointedly. "She also expressed interest in the rest of you joining us."

I went still and Ulysses did too. Yes, some of us had shared her before. But the four of us being with her, the strengthened connection pouring the intensity of it all through us?

Gods below…

Ulysses cleared his throat, his eyes flying to Wren and then back. "All at once?" he asked softly. "Really? She said that?"

Gideon nodded with a hint of a smile, probably for striking Ulysses off-balance.

"You're not hearing me!"

I looked back sharply at the gravel lot beyond the garage. About a dozen yards away, Valerie made a furious sound, her face red beneath her disheveled hair. The captain was there, giving her a look of patience on its last legs. They'd been arguing for the past ten minutes while the remainder of the archivists tended their wounded in the shadowed depths of the garage.

The humans were shaken, no matter how the soldiers tried to hide it, and that made them all dangerous.

"We need to head *north*," Valerie spat. "If there's anywhere they're going to be, it's near Chicago where we detected vampire movements!"

"So…" Ulysses let out a breath as Valerie and the captain continued arguing. "Setting aside *that* information about our sexy woman." A grin tugged at his lips, but he managed to bury it. "Now what?" He arched an eyebrow at the rest of us. "We stick with the bookworms?"

Gideon gave him a dry look, and Ulysses' lip twitched.

Nearby, Liam shifted back into human form and stepped out of the deeper shadows. To anyone who didn't know what they were looking at, it would appear he'd just been hiding there, rather than slipping around the property in shadow form, overhearing what he could from the humans and checking the perimeter.

They don't want us around, Liam signed. *Not now. Even the soldiers are muttering about leaving us behind.*

I wasn't surprised. They'd looked at Ulysses like he was a threat before this, to say nothing of how they'd watched Wren. And now, with what happened to Roland, a number of the soldiers were eyeing her when they thought we weren't watching. None of them would survive their mistake if they tried acting on the dark suspicion I saw in their gazes.

I shifted my weight, putting myself a little bit more between them and Wren.

"Any word from Friday or Barnaby?" Gideon asked me.

"Not yet." I'd lost count of the messages I'd left in the past week, but it'd easily entered the double digits for both of them. The demons' phones should have been accessible on the moon, let alone in Gateway City.

But that was when the world wasn't falling to pieces a little bit more each day.

I fought back a grimace as my insides churned. The things I'd seen on the GSS monitors... the destruction...

St. Louis was just the start. The human news networks still didn't openly show any sign of knowing what they were looking at, but in the past week alone, there'd been stories of world leaders suddenly becoming inaccessible and strange disappearances in everything from the tech sector to Hollywood.

Nothing in me could dismiss the reports as mere coincidences. Not with what I knew of Amalie from my own lifetime, let alone my memories of the past life when we'd last faced Urlfeige.

He was putting the pieces in place for a victory so sudden and swift, it wouldn't even require a war.

And against that... was us.

"We need to get her away from this," Gideon said. "*Far away.*"

"Fucking Siberia," Ulysses agreed.

My gaze slid toward Wren. Even with the curse broken, she was still a target for Urlfeige. Taking her to the other side of the world would at least buy us time to come up with a better way to keep her safe and actually stop this nightmare. It left me feeling sick, the fact that it would essentially mean abandoning everyone else—at least in the short term. But the problem was the same as it'd ever been.

If Urlfeige got his hands on Wren, curse or no curse, the world would be in far worse trouble than it was now.

I closed my eyes briefly, cursing inside. "Human travel routes are risky. But we might be able to—"

In my pocket, my phone buzzed. Drawing it out, I paused at the sight of the number and then lifted the cell to my ear quickly. "Barnaby? Are you okay?"

"We're fine," the old demon said calmly. "My apologies for the delay in responding to you. Frideswyd is settling a disagreement in that regard."

Something crashed in the distance on the other end.

"Ah, there we go. Settled."

A rustling followed. "Asher?"

"Friday, what happened? Are you all right?"

She scoffed. "Oh, just fine, dear. I'm so sorry it's taken us a few days to get back to you. The Consortium's communications team was... stubborn."

I glanced around. The other Sentinels were eyeing me

incredulously. But nearby, Valerie and the captain watched me from the corners of their eyes too, even as they continued arguing.

I turned away from the GSS, trusting the other Sentinels would guard my back. "And the Consortium itself?" I asked in a low voice.

The demon made a contemptuous noise. "It took a bit of work, but we've convinced them they no longer need to be so ridiculous about Wren. They're calling off the bounty hunters." She paused. "The ones who still respond to their messages, anyway."

"So the rest…"

"Hired away, from what I understand."

I grimaced. I hadn't really been able to make myself believe the *only* ones to switch sides were the mercenaries we'd already dealt with, but it would've been nice. "How many did they lose?"

"They're being rather closemouthed about exact figures."

"A lot, then."

"Sadly, I suspect yes. But that is part of why I asked Barnaby to call. The loss of their bounty hunters has unnerved them, I believe. They've become far more open to the idea that they've miscalculated and do not *have* to fight a war with you on top of the one they already face with Amalie and her companion. Instead, they would like to make you a proposal."

I was silent for a moment. "What is it?"

"Protection, to start. Safe passage away from this as well."

"And in exchange?"

"In exchange they don't die by our hands or yours, and Urlfeige doesn't gain control of our dear Wren to wipe out every one of their constituents." She chuckled lightly. "I know they annoy you boys, these bureaucrats. But us demons know how to handle politicians."

I blew out a breath. It was still insanely risky. The Consortium had put a *price* on Wren's head, for gods' sakes. And yes, maybe that was gone now, but it didn't change the fact we needed to get her as far away from this as we possibly could.

But rationally, strategically, was trusting the *Consortium* to help us with that the best move?

"What's to stop them from just trying to kill her?" I asked, the words making my stomach roil. "Remove the threat?"

She chuckled. "*Me*, dear. Barnaby too. And most importantly, there's what *you* boys would do to them if they touched a hair on her head. They're now well aware of the hornet's nest they kicked with their little bounty-hunter scheme."

Hornet's nest wasn't the half of it.

Scowling, I covered the phone and looked at the others. "Consortium pulled the bounty. They want to talk. Offered protection and safe passage if we'll meet them."

"Fuck no," Ulysses retorted immediately.

"Friday said this?" Gideon asked.

I nodded.

Ulysses scrubbed a hand over his face while Gideon looked away, thinking. Liam's gaze went to Wren, his face unreadable.

We need allies, Liam signed after a moment, turning back to us. *You saw the reports of what Urlfeige is doing. The disappearances. He's building an army. We need one too if we're going to protect Wren.*

"Yeah, but this is the *Consortium*," Ulysses countered. "We're seriously going to trust the bureaucratic assholes who put a price on Wren's head?"

From the phone, the thin sound of Friday's voice carried, trying to get my attention. I lifted the device to my ear.

"Put me on speakerphone, Asher."

From the exasperated look on his face, Ulysses must have guessed what she said.

"Just a sec," I told her. I glanced at the others. "She wants to talk to all of us."

Liam nodded for us to go on outside before heading toward Wren to stand guard over her. Eyeing the soldiers, we walked beyond the confines of the garage into the sunrise.

"Now, you listen to me, boys," Friday said the moment I clicked on the speakerphone. "That woman is the best thing that's happened to you in centuries. I know that. Everyone who sees you knows that. And I'm never going to risk you *or* her, so when I tell you I've got these silly children under control, you believe me."

I cast a wry glance at Ulysses and Gideon. "Silly children?"

"Putting a bounty on that woman's head or yours was the *definition* of silly. Their witches divined that Wren was involved in Urlfeige's plans—with no idea how!—and *that* was their solution. And after all hell broke loose in St. Louis, they were going to blame her. But Barnaby and I have explained the situation."

I wondered how many broken bones and bruised egos had been involved in the "explaining."

"We care about you boys," Friday said in a more serious tone. "Wren too—because she matters to you and because she's a sweet person. We're not going to let anything happen to you all if there's a damn thing we can do about it. So let's get Wren and the four of you somewhere safe, shall we?"

Gideon's mouth compressed into a grim line, but after a moment he nodded like he agreed. Nearby, I could tell Ulysses was swearing a blue streak in his head.

But finally he sighed. "Yeah."

I took the phone off speaker, lifting it to my ear again. No need to risk the GSS overhearing the rest of this. "Where do we meet you?" I asked Friday.

"Can you reach the travel plaza off Route 94?"

"Yes. Give us a few hours."

"Good. We'll see you there. Stay safe, dear."

I could hear the smile in her voice, and I chuckled in spite of myself. "You too."

Ulysses muttered another curse as I hung up. "This is insanity."

"It's also our only viable choice," Gideon replied. "Liam wasn't wrong."

I shook my head, tucking my phone away again. "Let's go tell him and Wren."

19

WREN

"You okay?" I asked Brayden softly.

Watching his mom help bandage a cut on one of the archivist's arms, he nodded. "Yeah."

He didn't sound it. Ever since we'd gotten to this little corner of the garage, he'd been sitting here with me, his eyes on the GSS and his face ashen.

I didn't know what to do for him. Roland was dead. And, yeah, there hadn't been any choice, really. Hell, Brayden had basically saved my life.

Didn't make it easier.

"I mean, it's not like I haven't shot someone before, right?" He glanced toward where Ulysses stood listening while Asher talked to someone on the phone.

"Ulysses didn't die."

Brayden was quiet. "Not quite what life was a few weeks ago, huh?"

I tried for a light tone. "Midterms and pop quizzes and wondering whether we'd pass math, oh my."

He looked away.

I didn't know what to say. He was right. This wasn't our

world.

It'd become it, though. Mine, anyway, and now he'd been dragged into it too.

Closing my eyes briefly, I shoved all that down somewhere deep inside and then reached over, putting my hand to his. "There wasn't anything else you could have done. He killed that soldier. He would've killed me."

Brayden nodded, but he still didn't seem like he believed it. "What now?"

I looked over at the Sentinels. Asher and the others were walking outside, while Liam was heading our way.

Taking a short breath, Brayden straightened. "I'll go—"

"It's okay. Stay."

He hesitated but didn't leave as Liam came up to us.

"What's going on?" I asked.

"Friday and Barnaby called."

Brayden gave me a questioning look.

"Some demons we know," I explained.

His brow twitched up, but he didn't say anything.

"They okay?" I asked Liam.

He nodded. "The others are talking with them now."

I sighed, wondering if that meant we'd be leaving soon.

Leaning against the wall, Liam kept the soldiers and archivists in view. Nearby, Brayden and I sat in silence, watching them all as time ticked by.

"Valerie asked if I was interested in joining them," Brayden said out of nowhere.

I looked over at him sharply.

"The GSS, I mean."

My mouth moved. "D-do you want to?"

He was silent for a moment. "I'm not sure." Discomfort flashed over his face at my wary expression. "It's just... I spent weeks convinced something was going on in Fort Briar, but no one would say what it was. But I kept digging. I even found my way onto the dark web. And what I learned…" His brow furrowed briefly. "It saved people's lives. It really did. When the vampires attacked, I got those spells up around the apartment building, and… people didn't die."

His head shook. "I'd never done anything like that before. Helped people like that. I was just the music geek, right? Chopin and Bach and Gault. Class weirdo. And now…" He drew a breath. "I don't know. It's not that I don't love that stuff. I do. It just feels like maybe this is part of who I am too. Like maybe I'm more than just that uptight kid who got his ass kicked in grade school."

"I liked that kid." My voice was small. "He was a good friend."

He looked over at me. "And so are you. But life… it can change you fast sometimes."

I nodded numbly. I knew that was true.

"I'll always be your friend, Wren. I want you to always be mine too. But maybe this is part of that. Maybe if I work with them, I can help you."

Brayden watched me, a question and yet certainty in his eyes like he needed to know I understood.

"They're…" I searched for the words. "They're not all good. Their director—"

"I know. I heard. But Valerie and Tammy have plans. Good ones. The GSS needs to change, and they know it. Maybe I can help with that."

Footsteps crunched on the gritty concrete floor near us, and I looked over to see the rest of the Sentinels coming our way.

"Everything all right?" Gideon asked, eyeing me and Brayden alike.

I floundered. No, but what could they do about it? "What's going on?"

"Friday and Barnaby are going to meet us a few hours from here." Asher paused. "The Consortium wants to help."

My brow climbed. "The people who set bounty hunters on us want to help now?"

Ulysses scoffed. "Yup."

"And you're trusting this?"

The guys looked uncomfortable.

"We need to get you as far from Urlfeige as we can," Asher said. "Planes and such are risky. The Consortium could help with that."

I looked away, shifting position on the ledge.

"Friday swears she and Barnaby will keep them in line."

"She can't stop Urlfeige, though," I said. "Neither of them can. And if the Consortium sells us out to him because they're scared or something..."

Asher grimaced. "We know. So we stick together, we take nothing for granted, and we get out of there as fast as possible once we have what we need. If anything looks suspect, we run like hell. Yeah?"

Nearby, the soldiers started gathering the archivists, directing them toward the door.

I didn't know what to say. "Okay, I guess."

The captain came up to us. "Our people are good to keep moving now, so we're heading out. But the, uh..."

"We're not staying," Asher said levelly when the man hesitated.

I didn't miss the hint of relief on the captain's face.

"We can spare a vehicle," the man said. "If you need it."

"Thanks."

The man nodded before throwing Brayden a brief glance. "And you?"

"Coming with you."

I could feel the pressure of the Sentinels' gazes on us, but none of them said anything.

The captain's nod was firmer this time. Without another word, he walked away.

Morning sunlight painted the gravel lot in pink and gold as we left the garage behind. Parked in the shadow of the abandoned gas station, the SUVs waited, and in silence, the archivists and the soldiers headed for them.

"You going to be okay?" Brayden asked me.

I nodded. "Please be safe." I bit my lip briefly. "Get through this alive."

He smiled. "You too. Or, you know..." He shrugged, looking for a moment like the guy I remembered from a lifetime and two months ago. "Whatever the right word is now."

My heart ached. On impulse, I moved toward him, and he grabbed me into a hug immediately. We broke apart a moment later, and he glanced at the soldiers as if slightly uncomfortable with the idea they may have seen that.

A grin pulled at my lips, though my heart still ached. "See you soon."

He nodded. With a gesture for his mother to go first, he accompanied her toward where the rest of the humans and the soldiers waited.

I watched him go. Together, they climbed into the GSS vehicles and a moment later, the engines rumbled to life.

"They'll be okay," Ulysses said.

I didn't respond. We both knew he couldn't guarantee that.

But it was somehow comforting to hear the reassurance anyway.

The SUVs pulled away, and as they turned and took off down the country road nearby, I sighed.

"Ready?" Asher asked me.

I watched the caravan disappear over a rise in the road. No? Yes? "As I'll ever be."

The sun was high in the sky by the time we pulled over on the strip of country road miles beyond the Missouri border. We'd traced a winding path along backroads for hours, avoiding checkpoints and towns alike. None of us wanted to explain ourselves to soldiers right now, and God forbid I saw a dormant and turned them rabid just by looking at them.

It'd made for a long morning.

"Time to walk," Ulysses grumbled as Asher turned off the engine.

I waited for him to open the door. I'd been sandwiched in the back seat between him and Liam for the past few hours, while Gideon and Asher took turns driving up front. Displeasure at this plan had radiated from Ulysses the whole time, and I couldn't blame him, even if our reasons weren't entirely the same.

The guys wanted to get me to the other side of the world, away from Urlfeige. They were determined to keep me safe, even if we ended up in Antarctica for the rest of our lives. But I wasn't about to just abandon everyone else.

No, we needed a way to stop Urlfeige and Amalie, and if the Consortium didn't have it, maybe they'd know who would.

Asher chucked the keys for the SUV into the trees near the road, and we walked away. The GSS could probably track the vehicle, especially given the amount of magic and technology that was probably in that thing. Better that the government have to replace the key than some human drive off with an SUV that, for all I knew, might explode if someone unauthorized was in it.

Picking our way carefully across the ditch to the side of the concrete, we headed away from the country road. A wire fence separated us from the field beyond, barely enough to keep out deer, let alone us. After checking it wasn't electrified, Gideon held it up for me and the others as we slipped past.

Overgrown grass swished around our legs as we hiked

across the field the guys said separated us from our destination. The sun beat down overhead, warm but not burning my skin like it had a few weeks ago, back before we'd fully woken the connection between us.

The memory ached. We'd come so far, the five of us. And now, if the Consortium betrayed us, or even if they just couldn't help...

Ulysses reached out, taking my hand and squeezing it. Gratitude spread through me, and as if picking up on the reaction, he pulled me to him. Looping his arm over my shoulders, he kept me close as we continued across the field, the others surrounding us protectively.

Warmth filled me in a strange mixture of joy and pain. This was us. Who we'd been for lifetimes, and who we'd be again forever if I had my way. So whatever happened, I wasn't going to lose these men. I didn't care what I had to do, what bargains I had to make with the Consortium.

We'd make it through this.

A line of trees divided the other end of the field from what lay beyond, and as we passed through it, another road came into sight. Cars whipped by, flying along past a decaying strip mall with most of its shops empty and a trailer park that was partially hidden behind another wall of trees. Metal signs on the roadside indicated we'd reached Route 94, while others showed our miles of distance from various small towns and St. Louis itself.

I swallowed nervously. We wouldn't exactly be inconspicuous walking along the road here.

"Anyone asks"—Asher glanced at me—"our car broke down, okay?"

Taking a steadying breath, I nodded.

We continued on, finally crossing to the other side of the road when we were opposite a large gas station at the intersection of another state highway. Semitrucks were pulling around to the spots for diesel behind the station, while a random assortment of cars and trucks sat closer by, some at the gas pumps and others parked in front of the building itself.

A middle-aged woman by a minivan gaped at us as we walked past, her eyes darting over everything from the way the guys were positioned around me to the black clothes and leather jackets we all wore.

Nope, not inconspicuous at all. We probably looked like a biker gang who forgot their bikes.

I made myself ignore any other odd looks we received as we continued up to the door of the station. The glass showed palm prints on the lower half where small children had pressed their hands to the door, and a bell chimed when Gideon pulled the door aside. Cold air rushed out at us, heavy with the mixed scents of cleaning solution, cherry cola, and the hotdogs turning in a roaster near the pop machine.

My gaze skipped around, but I couldn't see Friday or Barnaby anywhere. Confused, I turned to the guys.

"This way," Asher said.

Gideon gave a small nod to the cashier as we walked past, and the kid twitched his chin in acknowledgement, but I didn't miss how his eyes tracked us, a hint of surprise in his gaze. It looked like maybe he recognized the guys with me.

And he couldn't believe he was seeing them.

"What are we doing here?" I asked in a low voice as we continued past the kid and on toward the back of the convenience store part of the station. Nearby, a big guy who reeked of cigarette smoke glanced up at us briefly and then went back to his study of the potato chip rack.

Ulysses smiled at me. "You'll see."

The Sentinels paused at the opening to a short hall with restrooms to one side and an unmarked door next to the janitor closet at the back. Asher opened the fridge, taking out a bottle of water, while Gideon rifled through the magazines nearby.

I watched them, confused. Why were they stopping?

Potato chip guy wandered up front and paid for his snack. The door dinged when he left the store.

Turning immediately, Liam headed down the short hall while Asher stuck the bottle back in the fridge and Gideon abandoned the magazines.

Ulysses grinned at my questioning look. Bringing me with him, he followed the others to where Liam was opening the unmarked door next to the janitor closet.

"Took you all long enough."

A thrill went through me. "Friday?"

The old demon grinned at me. Her gray hair was tied back in a precise bun, but her maid outfit was understandably gone. Now she wore a black raincoat that hung down to her knees and black slacks with red flats beneath. She looked like she belonged in an artistic photo of New York City, complete with fancy stores and yellow taxis all around, not standing in a large supply closet with unmarked cardboard boxes all around. The bare bulbs overhead cast dull light down on the dingy concrete floor and did nothing to soften the look of the solid cinderblock wall at her back.

"Sorry for the delay," Asher said to her.

She chuckled. "Well, fair enough after keeping you waiting too, I suppose." She took a breath, smoothing her coat. "Let's get going, shall we? Barnaby is waiting on the other side to make sure they keep the vampire defenses down, at least here, but I'd rather not push things."

The guys glanced at each other. "They're still arguing about letting us in?" Asher asked. "I thought—"

"People are scared," Friday said. "The Consortium is trying to calm them, but some folks are prickly. That won't stop us from helping you."

I wasn't sure what to think, and the guys looked equally wary. But after a moment, Asher nodded. "Lead on."

Friday smiled. She turned and lifted a hand to the cinderblock wall.

Nothing happened.

"Play nice," she chided.

My brow climbed. Was she talking to the wall?

A shimmer like a heatwave suddenly rolled across the blocks, glistening like the rainbow reflection on an oil slick. Crackling light formed in the center and then spread out like it was peeling the shimmer back.

Leaving only darkness with the sense of a *whole* lot of space I couldn't see.

Floundering, I looked at the guys.

"Gateway," Ulysses said, like that explained something.

The light stopped retreating when the dark opening was large enough that it looked like a pitch-black cave mouth.

Friday smiled. Without another word, she disappeared into the opening, leaving us to follow.

"We'll be okay," Ulysses told me.

I nodded, trying to believe him. But it didn't stop me from flinching as Asher and Liam trailed her into the darkness and vanished. Instantly, I searched inside myself for the link to them—nearly melting with relief when I felt it a heartbeat later.

They seemed fine. And yeah, maybe that was a trick, but...

"Deep breath," Ulysses said.

I did as he said as I stepped forward into the dark.

"And if anything is in there with us," Gideon added behind me, "don't believe anything they say. The gateways haven't eaten anyone in centuries."

I turned toward him, alarmed, but the darkness was already closing in. The air was cold but with the strange feeling of wind moving around me, coming from everywhere at once, playing across my skin and tugging at my hair.

"*Mm, tasty...*"

My breath caught at the sibilant voice twisting around me. I couldn't see anything in the darkness, and only Ulysses' hand on my shoulder kept me from panicking.

"*Let's keep her.*"

"*Don't scare the girl...yet,*" a darker and smokier voice chided.

"*You'll destroy everything, you know,*" came another voice right at my ear, this one icy like the depths of outer space. "*Even if you save them, nothing will ever be the same.*"

I flinched, whirling toward the sound, but suddenly the darkness vanished and light returned, and I wasn't standing in a cinderblock room at all. An archway large enough for a subway train to pass through was there instead, trimmed in marble and set within a massive wall of brown, roughhewn stone. Darkness waited within the opening, still with the sense of more space inside than it should have possessed, while gold letters were affixed to the wall above it that read, Now Leaving Gateway City.

"What the hell was that?" I demanded.

"Guardians of the gate," Gideon said. "They have a twisted sense of humor."

Shivers crawled over my skin at the memory of what the last one had said. "Right."

Warily, I turned away from the dark portal.

And stared all over again.

"*What?*" I whispered.

Ulysses chuckled.

Trees stood ahead of us, but calling them *trees* felt like the understatement of the century. They were so massive, I felt like I was standing in some kind of fantasyland. The trunks were wide enough all five of us couldn't have stood in a circle and touched hands around them, while far overhead, birds flitted between branches wide enough to be sidewalks.

And people appeared to be using them that way.

Crisscrossing along the branches and all around the trunks

below, people hurried here and there across a floor that alternated between white marble tile and grass, like a ballroom and a forest had crashed into one another and now there was no discernible boundary where one began and the other ended. Flowering vines in a riot of colors wrapped the tree trunks and draped overhead, some of them supporting signs with city names and arrows on them, pointing in various directions. I recognized a few—Tokyo, London, Albuquerque—but others were unknown, ranging from random names like Maybell's Glen to words I couldn't hope to pronounce. But the branches served as paths just as much as anything on the ground, with more signs up so high among them, I couldn't make out the words.

"Excuse us."

I blinked, my attention dropping back to ground level just in time to see half a dozen people who *definitely* were security walking toward us. They each wore a gray uniform with a black sash across the chest. Silver emblems on their chests glinted in the light, a twisted combination of triangles and a tree shape. Nightsticks hung in holsters at their waists, and their expressions made clear they were bracing for us to be a threat.

"The Consortium sent us to collect you," said the man in the lead. His hand hovered by the nightstick on his hip. Strange symbols were carved in silver lettering into the length. I really doubted all it did was hit people.

The Sentinels shared a glance while Friday harrumphed.

"Thought we'd get lost, did they?" Ulysses commented.

To a person, the guards' expressions darkened with anger.

Friday drew herself up and stalked forward, striding past the guards as they pulled back to give her a wide berth.

Ulysses chuckled softly. Taking my hand, he started after her while the other Sentinels fell in around us protectively.

The guards' eyes tracked us as we passed, and when we

walked across the vast open space beneath the trees, other people stared too.

"Don't worry about them," Ulysses murmured, squeezing my hand.

"What *is* this place?" I whispered back, watching as people crossed a gold filigree bridge over a creek that wound along an ambling path through the room.

"Mephistopheles Station," Gideon answered. "One of the largest travel hubs in the western hemisphere, located underneath St. Louis."

"We're under *St. Louis*?" I gaped. "But we were miles from..."

I trailed off, trying to wrap my head around it.

Gideon gave me a pointed glance, though he softened it with a smile. "Thus the reason they call it Gateway City. The power down here is likely why the humans think St. Louis is a gate too."

Ulysses grinned as we started toward an archway up ahead. "Wait till you see the actual city."

I tried for a smile back, but I knew I had to look overwhelmed. I couldn't help it. If this was just the equivalent of their train station, what was the rest of the city going to be like?

We passed through another archway, and my jaw dropped.

The massive main room of the station was nothing compared to this. A vast cavern opened up ahead of us, wide enough that you couldn't make out where it ended and towering so high that the structures all along its walls looked the size of children's toys in the distance. Enormous columns of stone rose like pillars carved by giants, helping support the distant ceiling. Globes of light hovered at intervals along the distant stone roof, blazing bright like miniature suns. Everywhere I looked, there was color. Flowering trees grew on the ledges along the walls and traced crisscross patterns along the pathways up the cavern's sides. Vines climbed everything, overflowing with flowers and life. Birds darted through the open air, moving in unison and twisting through ever-shifting patterns, while little creatures scurried along the vines and over rooftops. Buildings of every size and shape spread along winding streets ahead of us.

And the *people*...

An open-air market lay up ahead, filled with booths in countless colors and people of every shade and body type I'd ever seen—and quite a few I hadn't. A man with pointed ears and a purplish tinge to his pale skin argued the price for a basket of apples with a gold-skinned woman who had a snake twisting around her shoulders. Two dark-skinned women who had to be twins packaged up a collection of corkscrew-shaped bottles for a pale woman wearing a shimmering red robe.

Wrapping his arm around my shoulders again, Ulysses smiled. "Welcome to Gateway City."

20

ASHER

Seeing the wonder on Wren's face almost made this trip into the lion's den worth it.

Except the lions might eat her.

I kept one eye to where Ulysses held her close as we walked through the open-air market that was a fixture outside the station, and I tried to tamp down the apprehension bubbling through me for her sake. I didn't want to take this experience from her, but gods below, they just had to lead us down the main thoroughfare, didn't they?

The thoroughfare with a few things obviously missing.

I doubted Wren noticed. She looked overwhelmed, and from what I could gather from our connection, she felt it too. But for all the myriad creatures around us, one kind was absent.

Vampires.

The magical suns overhead weren't deadly to them. They could have been out here as easily as any of the chimeras or harpies or shifters around us. But there wasn't a dormant in sight.

When I glanced back, Ulysses met my eyes with a dark look

before returning his attention to Wren, while Liam's hand clenched to keep from summoning his blade and Gideon's expression shared a lot in common with a thunderstorm. They'd noticed it too.

We followed Friday and the Consortium guards as they continued deeper into the market. Eyes of every shade tracked us as people turned to stare. We had a reputation. Stares happened on a good day. But these were different.

Even Wren noticed. "Why are they—"

A burly man spit at her, and she flinched back as it struck.

Our knives were in our hands instantly. Liam snarled with rage, lunging toward the man while the crowd recoiled.

"Liam!"

Wren's voice brought him up short, but he didn't take his eyes from the enormous guy who was absolutely going to get a beatdown if any of us got our hands on him.

Or die if Liam did.

Meanwhile, the Consortium guards did nothing.

A cold feeling settled in my core. Oh, this wasn't good. Yes, I trusted Friday and Barnaby. They'd saved our asses more than once over the centuries, even if they still felt like they owed us in spite of that. But what the fuck was going on here?

Friday walked back toward us, scanning the faces around us. "This woman and the Sentinels are under the protection of demons." Her eyes burned red with tendrils of smoke wafting up around them. "Do I make myself clear?"

A murmur ran through the crowd.

Wren stepped closer to Liam. For as much as she was trying to rein him in, I noted that her sword was also in her fist.

Good girl.

"Don't, okay?" She put her other hand to Liam's arm. "I'm fine."

A low, rasping growl came from Liam. The burly man

flinched back in spite of the bravado still clinging to his expression.

Oh, now he was scared? Big man, *spitting* at a woman half his gods-damned size...

"I'm *okay*," Wren emphasized. "Let's go."

Jaw muscles jumping, Liam followed as she urged him away. But his knife didn't disappear, and neither did mine or the other Sentinels'. Little shit like what that man had done was all it could take to start a riot, and if any of these fuckers thought they'd hurt Wren...

The crowd pulled back farther, alarm and fear clear on their faces. We'd tried to make it clear enough over the centuries that no one should mess with us or our kind. And now the vampires were... what? Missing?

Gods below, the Consortium had a lot to answer for.

"Wren!" a familiar voice cried.

Immediately, we pulled in defensively around her.

Ollie rushed from the crowd, paying no attention to anyone as she barreled toward us. "You're here!"

Wren smiled, relief radiating from her. "It's okay." She pushed at Gideon's shoulder, trying to get past.

"Friend of hers," I told him.

Cautiously, Gideon eased aside.

My eyes slid to the rest of the crowd, daring any of them to try taking advantage of the slight distraction. Meanwhile, Ollie slowed, a wary look on her face as she seemed to catch on to the tension all around.

Wren drew her into a hug. "You remember Asher and Liam, yeah?"

Everything in the woman's expression said hell yes, she remembered us, and she wasn't sure how to feel about that.

"This is Ulysses and Gideon." Wren nodded to each of us. "And that's Friday." She smiled. "This is my friend Ollie."

"Hey." The young woman twitched her chin at us in

cautious greeting, though she blanched a bit at the sight of Friday's red eyes.

"Is Emma here?" Wren continued.

Ollie nodded.

I returned my attention to the crowd as the two of them caught each other up. We were reaching the far end of the market now, and as we rounded a corner, the buildings fell away into a broad, open square.

And at its heart stood the Consortium headquarters.

Massive didn't come close to describing the damn thing. Humans tended to make the centers of their government near coasts, where their settlements had first begun in whatever territory they currently occupied. But supernaturals gravitated toward power, and so while Gateway was technically in the center of the United States, far from coasts or waterways besides the Mississippi River, it was also the heart of a fair amount of the power in this region.

And the Consortium wanted everyone to know it.

"Wow," Wren murmured, cutting off her conversation with Ollie as she spotted the building. Constructed like a cross between a Mayan temple and a federal building in DC, the thing towered over the square and took up more space than a football stadium. The walls and enormous stairway in front were built of dark-gray stone without a single seam or crack, as if it was all one solid piece drawn from the earth. The staircase extended nearly the width of the building, funneling us toward the columns arrayed at the front and the broad door at the center.

The guards leading the way paused. "You will wait here," they said to Ollie as if there was no alternative.

But she didn't look inclined to argue. "Emma and I are staying with our families over on Court Street, if you want to come find us later."

Wren nodded with a shaky smile.

"You've *got* this," Ollie continued. Her eyes darted to the building. "Whatever it is."

A hint of a smile tugged at my lips in spite of everything. Wren had good friends, and I was grateful for that. She deserved for the people around her to be supportive of her.

Especially when the world was in danger of going to hell.

Leaving Ollie at the base of the steps, we continued toward the main doors, Friday and the guards ahead of us. Every step was short and yet broad, making the climb awkward—which was likely the point. Everything about the Consortium was designed to leave people uncomfortable and overwhelmed.

Just another example of these damned bureaucrats trying to assert their power.

The door towered dozens of feet above us, carved of dark wood with the shapes of all manner of supernatural creatures on its surface. Each figure had its face upturned toward the people at the center, and rays of light made of carved wood extended down from them as if they were gods.

Nothing like putting your ego front and center...

Wren shifted her shoulders and glanced at us. Ulysses tightened his arm around her.

The doors opened of their own accord, bringing a massive room into view. The floor was gray marble veined in glistening white. The ceiling above was so high it could be barely seen in the shadows, while the space around us was eerily quiet. People moved in the distance, not glancing our way, their steps nearly silent.

We continued through the massive hall until we reached the doors on the other side. Like the ones at the entrance, these were huge, but whereas those were carved with figures staring up in worship at the Consortium, these were plated with glistening metal that looked like silver and was probably enchanted beyond belief.

The guards stopped several yards shy of the doors. "The Sentinels may enter," the one on the left said. "The girl stays."

Ulysses snorted. "Not happening."

The man turned, giving Ulysses a furious look. "You should stay as well, you—"

"If either of them stay," I cut in sharply, "we stay. Understand?"

The guard opened his mouth to argue.

"The Consortium demanded their presence." Friday arched an eyebrow. "If the boys refuse to go any farther without Wren or Ulysses, what are you going to do? Tell the Consortium you knew better than them, so you kept the Sentinels out?"

A sour look twisted the man's face while his companion ground his teeth together, glaring at us.

The first man turned away. "This way."

Of their own accord, the massive silver doors began to swing open.

I glanced at Ulysses. Any trace of humor was gone from his expression, and a dark, haunted look tinged his gaze.

"You're with us," I said to him.

His eyes flicked to me.

Wren took his hand, keeping his arm tight around her, and she nodded. "Screw them."

Affection for her touched his gaze, and after a moment, he echoed the nod. "Well, then. Let's go fuck up some bureaucrats."

21

ULYSSES

I shouldn't have come.

Cavernous darkness surrounded us as we passed the silver doors, the space beyond eerily silent but for the sounds of our footsteps. Cool air brushed over us like things were moving past, yet nothing was there. Columns of black marble rose to a ceiling at least a hundred feet above our heads, and when we came closer to the center of the room, I could see a large round opening at the apex of the roof. An idiot would think that opening was a way out. Anyone who knew the Consortium would know it was probably a trap.

They liked traps. Politicians always did.

I kept my face as blank as possible. I was a liability to the others right now, what with Amalie and Urlfeige having gone all Manchurian Candidate on my mind. It wasn't like I believed those two still had a chance in hell of controlling me. Not really. But my sheer presence would remind the Consortium of just how bad things were out there, when—on their own—the other Sentinels might not have.

Not to mention the fact that even on a good day I wanted to

tell those bureaucrats exactly where they could shove their policies and their slow-as-molasses debates. If they tried to fuck with Wren when she and the whole damned world were at stake...

Brilliant lights flared to life around the open ring in the roof, glaring down onto the floor at the center of the room. A golden light rose from behind a high wall on the opposite side of the chamber, illuminating the members of the Consortium, most of them seated in their ornate chairs like a parliament of administrative gods.

Except the chair for the vampire representative, Mathias, was empty.

My jaw clenched.

"That's far enough," the dragon shifter said, his eyes glowing like they were lit by fire. Mordecai could have been any age from his late thirties to a thousand, and we wouldn't be able to tell the difference. His human form didn't fully disguise his dragon nature, though. Gold scales showed on his cheekbones and temple, and his hands steepled in front of him were tipped by dark claws.

Asher and Liam stopped, and the rest of us did too. We stayed silent, waiting to see what the bureaucrats would do.

"You are here for transport away from the conflict," the witch said. Gray-haired with enough jewels and pendants hanging from her neck that she probably clattered like a Yahtzee cup when she moved, Theodora held herself with all the arrogance of someone who thought they ruled the gods-damned planet. "A conflict that has gripped the world thanks to you all. Is that true?"

Oh, fuck them.

"We are here to stop a war," Asher responded, but I could hear the anger carefully restrained in his voice.

"And how do you propose to do that when your kind are determined to initiate it?" the centaur demanded, stomping a hoof as he shifted his weight between the chairs occupied by the wraith and the fae representatives.

The fae grinned like we'd walked into the middle of some great joke and his pointy-eared ass was just waiting to deliver the punchline. He appeared to be about Wren's age, which was totally a lie. For centuries, we'd known him as Elchorr, but the gods alone knew his real name. A fae would never share it.

"Our *kind* are imprisoned," Gideon replied in a measured tone. "Held inside their own minds by the force that is intent upon initiating a full-scale war. We seek your help to prevent this situation from becoming any worse."

"We were told you could help us," Wren said before the Consortium members could comment.

As one, their eyes turned to her.

"We are considering it," retorted a petite woman who gripped the sides of her chair like she was keeping herself from bolting. She was five one if she was an inch, and her eyes were large enough she could have passed as an anime character without even trying. Rabbit shifter, I wagered, though like the centaur, I hadn't seen her before. Chances were, she was the representative of the non-predator shifter species, but anyone with a brain knew that didn't make her any less dangerous. Predator or not, she might let fear drive her, and fear was behind most of the horrible shit we'd seen over the centuries.

I ground my teeth, wishing there was even *one* of these bastards I could trust.

"Where are the vampires?" Asher asked like he'd read my mind. "Mathias and the dormants who live here?"

"Given the situation," Mordecai said, regarding us over his clawed and steepled fingertips, "Mathias chose to take Gateway's resident vampires to a safer location until the threat subsides."

"They're okay, though?" Wren asked.

The worry in her voice was so real, and I loved her for it.

She didn't even know those people, but she was concerned for their welfare.

It shouldn't have surprised me. It didn't, exactly. It just made me want to keep her with us always, if only so we could create a world where she wouldn't have to worry for anyone again.

The dragon shifter eyed her like he saw something valuable in her compassion too.

Alarms went off in my head, and I moved ever so slightly closer to her, letting my body language do the talking because my mouth would probably get us killed. But Wren was ours, not some bauble for a dragon to acquire.

Mordecai's eyes narrowed at me.

"Yes," Theodora answered her, ignoring us. "But now we need to know what you're willing to do to keep them that way."

The alarms in my head went berserk. My eyes darted across all of them, searching for some hint of just what the fuck that was supposed to mean.

"We are attempting to leave the country." Asher's voice was careful, but the tension I could feel coming from him rivaled a tight rope. "And given what you know of me and my fellow Sentinels, that alone should make clear what we're willing to do to stop this from worsening."

"Yes," the witch replied. "We know you'd stay and fight if not for the fact you each possess a tie to this young vampire woman. But that is, in essence, the crux of the issue."

"Okay, enough dancing," I snapped. "What the fuck are you getting at?"

Eyes ranging from black to gold and every color in between all locked on me, and I could read the affront in all of them.

Yeah, we never did well here, and it was usually my fault.

Theodora turned from me dismissively. "Are *you*"— she leaned forward, staring down directly at Wren—"willing to do whatever it would take? Will you make any sacrifice that is required?"

Oh, fuck no.

Gideon and I moved closer to Wren's side while Liam stepped in front of her as if to keep them from snatching her away from us this instant.

"What are you asking, excellencies?" Gideon asked, his words respectful and his tone only barely so.

"She is the reason the vampires are in danger."

I barely bit back a curse. Of course the witches knew that. Eden wouldn't have told them—I trusted her that much—but divination spells weren't exactly rocket science to that group.

Theodora looked down her nose at us from her position high above. "The enemy is using something inside this young woman to exercise his influence upon the world. At first, we thought her a willing party, but the demons have made clear that is not the case. But the matter still stands that her connection to the vampires puts us all in danger. The enemy we face is drawing on the empty realms themselves. Reality itself could crumble if he is not stopped. All the worlds beyond this one could come crashing in upon us. But you..." She leaned forward, studying Wren. "You've touched that darkness." Her eyes went to me. "Because of him."

Pain and shame quivered through me, but I kept from showing any of it on my face. Gideon had told us what happened in the archives with him and Wren, how he'd undone the curse Amalie and Urlfeige had placed on her, and obviously the Consortium had no clue about that. But before he saved her life, Wren had used our connection to reach me despite everything Urlfeige had done, and that bastard used the empty realms for his power.

So yeah, she'd probably been exposed to them.

Just to save me.

"Breaking his connection to that dark space is beyond our power," Theodora continued. "Beyond anyone's, even your demon friends, which is how he and his puppet Amalie had the strength to destroy their home. But that does not leave us without a plan. So I ask again, what will you do to stop this enemy from destroying the vampires and the rest of the world?"

I fought the urge to push Wren entirely behind me. "We'll get her the fuck out of here, that's what."

"Silence," Mordecai said. "The girl must answer."

Swallowing hard, she lifted her chin. "Whatever it takes."

Liam looked back at her in horror while Gideon closed his eye like he was cursing inside. Asher's hand trembled like he wanted to summon his blade all over again.

And I couldn't fucking move. "Wren..."

Her gaze went to me, every inch of her my beautiful, stubborn woman.

"Well." The interest in the dragon shifter's eyes hadn't faded. "In that case..." Mordecai smiled. "In conjunction with the Grand Coven, the Consortium has come to a decision on a method to stop this burgeoning war and potentially secure the vampires' safety at the same time."

"We break the girl's connection to them all," the witch said. "Every last vampire on earth—including the Sentinels."

Shock reverberated through the link between us like we'd all just been electrocuted.

"What?" Gideon demanded. "You *cannot*—"

"You didn't see this coming?" the fae chimed in for the first time, amusement thick on his voice. "Her link is the key. Break that, stop the bad guy in his tracks. Duh?"

"If we eliminate your connection to all the vampires," Theodora said, "he cannot use you to take control of them any longer."

Gideon scoffed. "And if that gives him unlimited power over them all instead?" His carefully calm tone was gone, replaced with so much incredulity, the Consortium might as well have sprouted extra heads.

"Exactly," Asher ground out. "What if she's the only thing holding him back?"

The witch pursed her lips briefly. "If that were the case, Fort Briar and St. Louis would not be the epicenters of this destruction. The rest of the world would have fallen with only those locations safe. And the enemy would never have been able to touch one of your own." She gave me a pointed look.

I felt sick.

"The key to this situation rests with her," Theodora continued. "The vampire queen, if you will."

"She's not the damn *queen*," I snarled.

Mordecai arched an eyebrow. "She is more their nexus than Amalie ever was, and even with Amalie returned to the world, our enemy still requires this young woman to complete his plans. All the vampire world could rise or fall because of what she is. What else would you consider her?"

"What—" Wren started before I could tell the dragon where to shove that damn title. "What happens to the Sentinels?"

I looked at her sharply. "*Hell* no. We're not considering this."

She didn't take her eyes from the Consortium. "What happens?"

The fae representative scoffed. "Well, they didn't exactly need you around for the past few centuries, did they? Stands to reason they'll be fine."

Fine, my ass. I was going to gut that fairy bastard.

"And if it kills her?" Asher demanded.

Theodora bobbed her head slightly. "That is a concern. We cannot ascertain what would become of her if that connection was broken, only that it stands the best chance of saving the rest of the vampires from destruction." Her gaze returned to Wren. "This is why we asked: what are you willing to sacrifice to save the world?"

"This is your grand plan?" Gideon snapped. "You stopped the bounty hunters only to ask her here to *sacrifice* herself?"

"We are protecting the entire world," Mordecai replied. "Not just one vampire. What is your goal?"

I couldn't find enough curse words to encompass what I wanted to say to that asshole. To all of them. And the other Sentinels looked the same.

Wren only dropped her gaze to the floor.

"If you agree"—Theodora rose to her feet and smoothed her velvet skirt with both hands—"we will begin preparations for the spell."

"No," Gideon responded immediately. "We will find another solution."

"It is not your decision, vampire."

"And it cannot be the only way! You—"

"I'll do it."

My eyes snapped back to Wren. I couldn't even think clearly enough to speak.

She didn't take her gaze from the Consortium.

And all those bastards had the audacity to look relieved, like they'd worried their strong-arm bullshit wouldn't work.

"Thank you," Mordecai said.

Wren didn't respond.

I wanted to gut them *all* for this.

"In the interim," the dragon shifter continued, "we've had a space prepared for you all away from the city—for security's sake. The guards will lead you there."

Wren gave a tense nod and then hesitated, not quite looking toward the four of us. Without a word, she turned and walked toward the door.

I stared at the others, my mouth moving, but I couldn't think what the hell to say. And here wasn't the place for it anyway. These Consortium bastards would try to argue like their opinion mattered. Like they got a vote on whether Wren lived or fucking died.

We never should have come here.

Gideon glared up at all of them, while Liam didn't wait and took off after Wren immediately, like maybe the guards would try to steal her away the moment she had any distance from us.

I met Asher's eyes. Mister Responsibility and I often disagreed, but right now, it was like looking in a fucking mirror. Like hell she'd be forced into *this*. We wouldn't lose her *or* the connection we shared with her.

There'd be another answer.

He made a slight motion of agreement like he'd damn well read my mind. Together, we started after our woman.

The one nobody was going to take from us, now or ever.

22

WREN

I didn't make it far before the Sentinels were coming after me, and honestly, it wasn't a surprise. They would want to argue this. To debate when there was nothing to say. It wasn't like we had another plan, and if this was the best anyone had come up with...

My insides were cold. I could tell my body was shaking. I didn't want to lose my connection to the Sentinels. God help me, I didn't want any of this. But even without that link, we could still be together.

Maybe.

If I didn't die, anyway.

I hugged my arms to my middle. I wasn't an idiot. Sacrificing my link to the vampires wouldn't actually *end* Urlfeige. But it'd stop him from wreaking any more hell on the ones still free, and wasn't that worth something?

My heart ached while my treacherous memory played back the faces of the vampires I'd seen over the past few days. So many of them looked like they might've been regular folks before they went rabid. Normal clothes. Actual haircuts and not just the shaggy mess of monsters who couldn't care about anything but their next meal. They'd probably had lives before Urlfeige.

Before me.

Every passing day meant more people were being turned or taken over. More were losing their lives as food to the vampire horde. Who was I if I could stop that, and instead I did nothing?

The princess had been right. Here she and I were again, and we were doomed. And maybe we always had been. Maybe this was where our paths were always going to lead. But now, when faced with what it would take to end this, I knew I was going to make the same decision.

Stop him, no matter the cost.

I kept walking, trailing the guards while they led me past the stone buildings of the city and toward a sloping road that led upward along one wall. I could feel the guys' eyes on me. I could feel the tension of everything they wanted to say.

I didn't look back.

At the top of the slope far from the other structures, the guards stopped at what looked like a small two-story building half-sunk into the stone cavern wall. Without a word, the guard unlocked the door and then handed me a key, stepping back to make room for me to enter. I heard one of the Sentinels make a protesting noise, but I didn't stop, walking inside and only then realizing that maybe there could've been a booby trap.

But why bother? Unless they worked for Urlfeige, but even then...

I pushed the thoughts aside before they could start to spiral. There wasn't any point in speculating.

Everything in me felt so cold, I couldn't even summon up worry anymore.

Despite being tucked into a wall of the cavern, the room around me still had white plaster across the walls and ceiling. But it hardly looked like a house. The furniture was stiff and gray, barely more than a collection of geometric shapes without a hint of softness, like someone had been given a general description of what a home should have inside without ever having been told why. The floor was cold, bare stone. There were only windows at the front, letting in the sole light in the room.

Maybe this was where they housed people they didn't really want in town.

Outside, I heard Asher speaking. "...defenses around this place too."

"Of course, dear." Friday paused. "It'll be okay."

No one responded.

The crunch of gravel moved away from the house, and a second passed before more footsteps approached the door. The Sentinels. I could feel them through the connection between us, and didn't that just hurt? This could be the final day that ever existed. Maybe the final day *I* existed.

The door shut. A tingle ran through the air, coursing past me in a wave. At the corners of my eyes, the walls seemed to shimmer, while all around me, soft pillows, blankets, and a luxurious carpet materialized in the utilitarian house, taking away every hard edge. In spite of everything, a pained smile pulled at my lips. Friday, always taking care of us.

But no one behind me said a word.

The silence pressed down on me, and despite how numb I felt inside, discomfort grew with every moment, as if the quiet was driving the air from the room. Even if I technically didn't need to breathe, I still felt like I was suffocating.

I made myself turn around.

The Sentinels were watching me.

"Where's Friday?" I asked, my voice calm no matter how my muscles felt like they could crack at any moment.

"Going to find Barnaby and make arrangements regarding where we go from here," Gideon answered.

I nodded.

Nobody else spoke.

I swallowed hard. "I'm sorry."

Asher shook his head, his expression as if there was no way in hell he would accept any alternative from the universe than what he chose because it was not open for debate. "This can't end like last time."

"I don't want it to."

"Then don't do this," Liam replied, his voice rough.

"At what cost? More people dying? Urlfeige winning?" Fear ached in me at the possibility. That, yet again, no matter *what* we tried, somehow he would still win. "I don't want this, okay? I swear. I want..."

I faltered, my eyes going across all of them as pressure built in me from all the words I desperately needed to say.

"I want you. All of you. Us, together for..." My throat closed up, tears burning my eyes as the numbness cracked under the sheer weight of their presence. My heart was a ball of pain. I wanted everything. A life with them. A family with them, if such a thing were possible. But I didn't know how that could happen unless we stopped this monster from our pasts. "For as long as we all want to be..."

Asher came toward me. "And we can't lose you."

He brushed my hair back, and I leaned into his touch, everything in me aching. The others drew closer, putting their hands on my shoulders, brushing the tears from my cheeks.

"Be with me," I whispered. "All of you. Please."

"You only ever have to ask, baby," Ulysses whispered back.

They shared a quick glance, and Asher nodded at whatever passed unspoken between them all. Taking my hand, he pulled me to him. His touch roamed over my body for a moment before slipping beneath my shirt and drawing it off me. Somehow, just the way he was watching me and the anticipation building in the air combined to make my blood heat up, thawing the horrible cold inside my bones. He slid my jeans and underwear away too, his eyes trained on me the entire time, and my lips parted, need washing away my pain.

A slight smile lifted the corner of his mouth, cockeyed and confident. I was naked between them all, and their attention felt like fire on my bare skin.

Like lightning, Asher stripped off his clothes and brought me down to the soft carpet. I gasped, pinned beneath him, while the others stood back, watching me with their gazes full of dark desire.

Asher's hand took my cheek, drawing my focus back to him. He moved between my legs, his cock at my entrance. "Do you remember," he whispered, "the very first time you fed from me? How I made you come? How we didn't get the chance for more?"

I nodded.

"Do you know what I wanted to do to you that day?"

My mouth moved, wordless, and he smiled.

He thrust his cock into me. "Did you know how I wanted to make you mine and ours that very afternoon?" He drove himself into me again.

I moaned and rocked beneath him, whimpering with need.

He chuckled, and then we were moving again as he rolled me on top of him. I straightened, seated on his length. The others were naked around us now. Someone had closed the curtains and locked the door as well, sealing us inside. Lamps that I'd swear hadn't been there before Friday's magic created them now burned with golden light, like we were inside a beautifully furnished cave.

Like the ancient past and the incredible present had combined, and now here we were, just as we'd been thousands of years ago.

Asher rocked his hips up beneath me, thrusting over and over. I braced myself against him as his hands slid over my body, one embracing my breast and squeezing my nipple while the other moved down to massage my clit in time to his motions.

Tension built inside me as pleasure shot from my nipple to my cunt and back again to my brain with ever-increasing force. Inarticulate begging noises escaped my lips. I felt on display, the others circling us, watching, and it was exhilarating. Asher was supporting me now, more than my hands on his body, because everything in me was drawing down to the intense motions of his fingers and his thrusting cock.

He grinned again, his face tense as if he was holding back from coming. "Do you know," he murmured, "how fucking beautiful you looked that day, falling apart when I touched you for the first time?"

I cried out his name as I came, and a moment later, his hot cum shot into me. My muscles clenched around him, drawing out everything I could from the orgasm ricocheting around my body.

"Masterpiece," he said as I began to relax.

I grinned, breathless. "You too."

He smiled, but then his gaze flashed beyond me. Before I could even glance over my shoulder, hands caught me, drawing me up and away from him.

"That hot pussy of yours isn't done being filled yet, baby." Ulysses hoisted me away from the ground. My legs wrapped around him on instinct, and I gasped as he slammed his cock into me. "Asher got you warmed up nice and good, but this night is just getting started." He grinned devilishly. "It's about time we all showed you just how many ways we know to make you come."

He lifted me up and took my nipple in his mouth, sinking his fangs into it only long enough to get a taste of my blood before sealing the wound. His teeth nicked his lip as he shifted me around, driving his cock back into me, and then he was kissing me, the mingled taste of his blood and mine on his tongue.

My muscles spasmed at the surge of arousal that roared through me. My God, how the hell was that *this* hot? But the connection between us was like a live wire, and the link to the other Sentinels was too, fueling everything like kerosene. My veins burned, and my body rocked on his cock in desperate reflex.

And it didn't stop. My hips jerked against his, driving him deeper into me over and over without any conscious thought of my own. I felt possessed, utterly out of control with pure need to have him and the desire pounding through me from all sides. I couldn't have stopped fucking him now if I'd tried.

I loved it.

"That's it, baby," Ulysses urged. "Let us see you fall apart around my cock."

My head dropped back and my vision blurred out as I came hard, the orgasm made even stronger by the arousal of the other Sentinels. With every passing second, whatever barriers separated us in my mind were falling, until I couldn't even think, just give in to the need to have them all and let them have me.

Ulysses gripped me harder, grunting as he found his own release. I could feel his cum dripping down my legs as more hands took me, lifting me again, and next thing I knew, Gideon was inside me as I straddled his lap on the sofa. But I wasn't facing him. Instead, he'd positioned me toward the others in the room, my body supported by his grip. Ulysses sat in a chair nearby, his gaze trained on me. Arms crossed and smiling, Asher leaned against the wall, still gloriously naked as he watched me too.

"Would you like to claim her luscious mouth, Liam?" Gideon asked.

Heat darkened Liam's eyes. He advanced on me, pure

predator, and a thrill shot through my veins as if I were his prey. Taking my chin, he opened my mouth as he smiled down at me.

He eased his length in, and I made a noise urging him on, breathing through my nose as I tried to relax my throat and take more of him.

"That's it, sexy," Ulysses urged. "You like him fucking your mouth, don't you?"

God, that man and his filthy words.

One of Gideon's hands stole around me, slipping down to tease at my clit while his other supported me. Liam reached out, bracing my shoulder too while he thrust into my mouth. Tears seeped from my eyes as I tried not to choke, but I wouldn't have stopped him for all the world. Gideon rocked beneath me, hitting me so deep, while I tasted the salt of Liam's precum and the others watched me get filled.

I felt dirty and beautiful all at once, and I reveled in it as my orgasm hit all over again.

Gideon groaned as my body clenched around him, milking his cock as he erupted in me. A heartbeat later, Liam came, and I swallowed him down, licking my lips on impulse when he drew back.

The heat in Liam's eyes scorched me.

"Tease," Ulysses murmured.

I grinned.

Gideon hefted me up from his lap only to lay me down on the thick carpet. "I think perhaps one more... at least."

He moved my arms, holding them together by my wrists above my head. My heart raced. Glancing up at the others with a wicked smile hovering around his lips, he let his fangs slip into place. His brow twitched up above his eye patch.

The other three moved in, grinning, too, around their fangs.

My swollen pussy throbbed, begging for more. They crouched down around me, Asher and Ulysses each taking one of my legs, drawing them apart. Gripping my ankles, they bent over my inner thighs.

I was splayed out before them all, pinned to the carpet. Liam sank onto his haunches, ghosting his hands along the length of my body before flicking my clit just once, enough to make me buck in their grasp. Seeming satisfied, he leaned down over my left breast, teasing my nipple with his tongue while Gideon twisted his head toward my neck.

My eyes flashed around at them. I knew what was coming, what *had* to be coming, but the anticipation was enough to make pleading noises leave my throat.

"Greedy girl," Ulysses teased.

I opened my mouth to respond.

They struck as one.

I screamed, my back and hips arching off the ground as their pleasure and mine hit me like a freight train, sending an orgasm ripping through me, wiping away the world. And I was only this moment, only this feeling of ecstasy. I was theirs, now and forever.

Just the way it was always meant to be.

The sheer weightlessness of my orgasm gradually receded, but it couldn't take the smile from my face. Even if the ecstasy was fading, all their love and desire still poured through our link.

And I knew they could feel the same from me.

The men sealed the wounds and released my limbs. I was limp and boneless, exhaustion pulling at me while I lay there between them. But as Asher lifted me up to carry me toward the bedroom, he chuckled. "Don't go to sleep until you get a drink from us too, beautiful."

In all my lives, I didn't think I'd ever been this happy.

23

ASHER

Wren was here with us. We'd fucked her, fed from her, and made sure to feed her in return until she passed out from the pleasure of it all. Now we lay in a tangle of limbs and bodies around her while Liam stood guard at the doorway, all of us sated in a way so deep, it defied words.

It was everything I could have hoped for.

And yet... it wasn't, because who would only hope for one time? Who would want to taste ecstasy and then give it up for the rest of eternity? I didn't want *only* what we'd just shared. I wanted her forever.

I only had to look at my fellow Sentinels to know we all did.

And she might die again. Today, tomorrow. However long it took for this mad plan of the Consortium's to take place. But even if she survived what they planned, we'd still never feel this close again.

I wrapped my arms tighter around her, trying desperately not to relive the memory of the time, centuries upon centuries ago, when I held her close and it *also* hadn't been enough. Of her body crumbling away right before my eyes, taking her from us. And the thought it would happen again?

Hell didn't come close.

Her eyes opened, and swiftly, I tried to shove my concerns aside, instead giving her a smile I hoped hid my concerns.

"Are you okay?" she asked as if picking up something from me anyway.

"Yeah," I answered, working to focus on this moment rather than the fears crowding my mind. "How about you?"

An impish look crossed her face. "Ready for more."

This time my smile was genuine, and I reached over, touching her cheek. She rested against my hand, and at the slight motion, Ulysses glanced over.

He grinned and slid an arm around her, cuddling her more tightly against him. Nearby, Gideon hoisted himself up on one elbow, smiling too, while Liam mirrored the expression from his guard position near the window. But when they all looked at me, I could tell they knew what had been going through my mind. Gods below, it must have been going through theirs as well.

"So, in *that* case..." Wren strayed her fingertips down my side, making my skin pebble. "Now what?"

I exhaled, wanting nothing more than to kiss her and start all over again. But the Consortium guards could return at any moment, summoning her away from us—maybe forever.

"Now we come up with a better solution," Gideon said.

Wren looked over at him. "Better than...?"

"Than losing you," Ulysses filled in.

Pain filled her eyes. "I don't want to lose any of you either."

"Then we need a better plan," I said. "A more effective solution than the—"

"Than what?" Wren pushed up onto one elbow. "Letting countless more people die?" She made an incredulous sound. "The whole world could be screwed because of me, guys. That's the deal, right? That's why we've hidden and run and done everything like we have so far..." The pain in her eyes deepened. "And why all those people in St. Louis died while I was unconscious. Because of what could happen if Urlfeige and Amalie get their hands on me."

"Wren," I started. "That's not your fault."

"It is if I don't do something to stop it. Not taking action *is* an action." An anguished look flashed over her face. "We finally have a chance to make sure he can't use me to hurt anyone else. Are we really going to pass that up?"

I felt sick. I wanted to grab her and take her to the nearest transport portal and get us to the moon, if only to keep her safe.

But she wasn't wrong. All those days and nights of hearing the screams, the begging, the explosions, and knowing we could have helped but that it would have cost us Wren and then the world... The shame and pain of that still burned. We'd done it all to protect her, and now...

Gods, it killed me, but she wasn't wrong.

"Guys, I want to be with you. All of you. And if I make it through this, I hope we still can, connection or no connection. But I can't let the world die for it."

"What if there was another way?" Gideon asked.

My gaze went to him, questioning.

"How?" Wren asked.

He paused, glancing between all of us as if gauging how we might respond to his next words. "We serve as a buffer."

"Uh, still not following," Ulysses said.

Gideon's head bobbed thoughtfully. "Rather than unleash the spell on Wren and take the Consortium's word that this is the only option... We modify it. We see if there's a way to sever that connection to the dormants that Urlfeige has used through her, but the four of us form a buffer against any blowback of the spell. We stay connected to her, and we keep her from dying by taking the brunt of that and dispersing it between us, thereby weakening the impact. We've done it before, with Amalie. She used us that way centuries ago to regain her defense against the sun." His brow rose and fell. "Only this time it's *our* choice."

I exhaled, nodding already, and I could see the agreement on the others' faces.

Except for Wren.

"No." She appeared flabbergasted. "That could kill you all too."

I took her hand. "You're assuming their plan won't anyway."

Anguish filled her expression.

Ulysses shifted around, giving her a wry look still filled with love. "Come on. If you think for one *second* that we're going to protect ourselves while we risk you..." He arched an eyebrow at her.

"You're the heart of us, Wren," Gideon told her. "Our center."

Liam nodded. *Whatever it takes, we stand or fall with you.*

"And," I added, "if this means we can use our connection to protect and help you..." I smiled. "Maybe there's a reason we've always been called your Sentinels."

Her eyes flashed over all of us, her mouth moving. "That was just... just something people said. It wasn't—"

"Sometimes coincidence is prophecy," Gideon interrupted kindly. "And sometimes, it's just useful. Either way, we shouldn't waste this. Not if we can use it to help you."

Ulysses reached over, squeezing her hand, silent encouragement in his eyes.

Wren was quiet, but for the first time in longer than I could remember, I suddenly felt something in my chest that remarkably resembled hope.

"What we do?" she asked softly.

Gideon drew a breath. "We find the Consortium witch, and we make sure she understands this is not negotiable. We are not throwing you into this situation as some sacrifice. Not now or ever."

I nodded, and the others did as well, though a nervous look still flickered over Wren's face.

"And then what?" she pressed, still not looking at us.

Ulysses scoffed lightly. "Then we live happily ever after, yeah?"

A smile tugged at her lips, even if it was still tinged by worry and pain.

Someone knocked at the front door.

Around the room, tension rolled through us in a cold wave. Likely it was the guards and the Consortium, come to tell us it was time to try their version of the spell, given that someone wanting to cause trouble probably wouldn't knock.

But gods, I wanted more time.

I climbed to my feet and started tugging on clothing, grim resolve settling in me like a shield around that fragile hope. We weren't going to do their plans their way, no matter what the Consortium or the witches tried to argue. No, we'd make it to the future Ulysses described. Come hell or what-the-fuck-ever, we'd all get as close to happily ever after as we damn well could.

Or die trying.

24

AMALIE

St. Louis was all but ours, and the slayers were on the run with the downfall of their archives. Yes, the little bitch had *somehow* thwarted my spell to drain her—at least for the moment—but I couldn't help but smile as I strode across the marble tile of the shopping mall. Hundreds of vampires now filled the space—everyone from schoolteachers to city leaders. Anyone who hadn't run far or fast enough now assembled here for the final days of our assault on this region.

A fitting entourage for my father.

"Ah, Amalie." He turned, letting the drained corpse in his hands fall to the floor. A vampire scurried forward to drag the body away. "How goes our search?"

I made myself hold on to my smile, for all that I was sick of being asked about the girl. My Sentinels? Yes, them I cared about. Some paltry thief?

Gods, the girl couldn't die fast enough.

"We'll have the slayers soon. They won't run far, given that everything they care about is here. Our attack, their archives... It's only a matter of time."

He nodded but said nothing, turning away.

I took a step forward. "If you would allow me to try again. Whatever they did to the curse may not have removed it full—"

A strange coldness suddenly raced through my connection to the empty realms and to him, as if thin slivers of ice were threading through my veins.

His attention snapped to the north, his blood-red eyes going wide.

I waited, feeling quickly for my connection to him and the empty realms, not because I was afraid it had been damaged. Of course that couldn't be the case. But... "What is this?"

His eyes stared past the wall as if it wasn't even there. "The supernatural city. They've chosen to interfere after all. They're crafting a spell to shatter her connection to us." His lip curled with a snarl. "To everything."

I was silent. We didn't need her—alive, anyway. But the power she clung to like the little thief she was still mattered.

And now some petty magic user thought they could interfere with that?

My fingers clenched into fists, smoke twisting under my skin. "Then let me destroy them."

He turned toward me, considering. I trembled with the urge to crush everything around us, if only to show him I could.

Slowly, he walked closer, coming to a stop in front of me. His expression was like stone as his hand took my chin. "Indeed." He smiled. "My perfect weapon."

Pride swelled inside me like the sun. "What should we do to them?"

His smile turned cruel. "Unleash the hordes. It's time to show those fools what happens when you interfere with the creation of a perfect world."

25

WREN

The guards outside didn't appear thrilled to see us, even if they'd been the ones knocking on the door. Four of them flanked the entrance while a fifth stood in front of it, his cold expression making it obvious he would just as soon have seen us locked up.

"The witches will see you now." The guy stepped away from the door, one hand on the nightstick at his belt and his body language making clear he expected us to file past them all.

Ulysses chuckled. "Oh, we'll follow you. After all, we haven't been here in a while. Directions might've changed."

Nothing in Ulysses' voice indicated that he thought that was possible, and from the irritation on the guard's face, he obviously heard that too.

But without another option, the guy turned and started down the slope away from the house. With a curt gesture over his shoulder, he motioned for his soldiers to follow.

Asher shook his head, and Gideon grumbled something under his breath about whether the guards thought we were stupid. Looking like icy death, Liam moved to keep himself between us and the soldiers, his hand splayed as if ready to snatch his knife from the ether at a moment's notice.

Drawing in closer to me, Ulysses put a hand to my back. "Stay between us, okay?" he murmured.

I nodded. A tingle rushed over my skin as I passed the door. Friday's defenses, though the demon herself was nowhere to be seen.

I let out a breath, trying to appear calm and not at all worried that somehow, this new plan would backfire. Or maybe just not work at all. There was no way in hell I could accept either option now that there was even a *chance* I could stay connected to the Sentinels through all of this.

God, I wanted that more than anything.

With Ulysses staying close by and the others beside and ahead of me, I descended the slope toward the city. In the time that we'd been in the house, no one seemed to have become any calmer about us being in town. As we walked through the streets, people still turned and stared, their eyes tracking us. Some retreated, slamming the doors or hastily closing shutters over their windows. Every single one of them looked at us like we might go mad and kill them all at any moment.

How were vampires ever supposed to come back from this? The supernatural world hated and feared us all now. And if Urlfeige was defeated, would it even make a difference?

My eyes slid upward. High above, I could see the cavern ceiling, balls of light hanging there like miniature suns. It was so bizarre to think there was a whole world above us that had no idea this city was here. That somewhere beyond that ceiling, there were streets and cars and houses and whole lives.

Assuming we stopped this, anyway.

We came around a corner, and a broad gate waited at the end of the road. The guards stepped away, gesturing for us to continue onward while their expressions made clear they had no intention of continuing.

Ulysses shook his head, his amused expression failing to fully hide his tension.

The road was still as we walked toward the gate, with no windows or doors slamming or even any sign of life at all. When we reached it, the gate opened all on its own, and warily, I followed the others in. The walls on either side looked like they were just crafted of thick logs, but the hairs on my arms stood on end as I passed them.

Another kind of magical protection, I guessed.

But as empty as the road had been outside, the courtyard within the walls was full of people.

And most of them were watching us.

My eyes tracked across them, and I clasped my hands tightly to keep my sword from appearing. To say they were a wide assortment felt like it barely scratched the surface. Every gender and none; every shape, size, and skin tone. There were animals near them too, but not like a barnyard or zoo. One woman had a snake twisting around her waist and up to her neck. A man had a monkey seated on his shoulder, the creature still as a statue as its gaze tracked us. Another person had butterflies dancing around their short-cropped hair. The witches eyed us, but unlike the people outside, their expressions were far more weighing, and infinitely less fearful. Like they were waiting for a predator to attack so they could put the creature down, with no doubt they'd be the ones to win. And each animal was the same. Whether wolves or birds or bunny rabbits, they studied us with an intensity that was far too calm, too still.

Shivering, I pulled my attention to the building ahead. The structure was massive. Easily four stories high and made of dark wood, it was shaped like a house transplanted out of medieval Germany but blown up to epic proportions. It didn't have the same "get the hell away from here" energy radiating from it as the manor or the archives, but it did make my eyes ache when I looked at it, like it was something from a dream where the dimensions were weird and not quite real. And the closer we got, the more my focus drew inward involuntarily, as if my mind could only make sense of what was in front of me.

Because trying to take it all in would drive me insane.

At the dark wooden door, Asher knocked briefly and then stepped back again. Beside the entry, a lantern flickered, the flame inside spitting sparks. I tensed, feeling for some reason like the thing was watching us.

The door swung open. A young witch stood in the entryway, her blond hair plaited in pigtails and a splattering of freckles across her cheeks. Her eyes were an eerie shade of gray without a trace of color, and her expression was solemn as she studied us all.

"This way." She turned and started down the long, dark hall without waiting to see if we would follow.

Ulysses gave me an encouraging smile while the others led the way inside.

It was like walking back in time.

Sconces lined the walls, their waxy candles casting everything in alternating pools of golden light and shadow. The wood floor creaked under our feet, and the air was cool like a cave. As we passed rooms on either side of the hall, I half expected to see cauldrons of boiling green liquid with old crones stirring them.

But that was where the illusion of age ended.

In the room to my left, several people were doing spells that made the objects in their hands glow, while another witch studied them and typed something into a tablet. In another room, a woman was reading from an iPad as she gave instructions to a man threading twigs into a broomstick. In a third room, a woman was filming herself on her phone while, out of view and in the corner, a little girl was moving her hands in a way that made the air sparkle.

At the end of the dark hall, the young witch opened a door without a word. The Consortium witch who the guys told me was called Theodora was inside, seated behind a dark desk and framed by a large window that was blurred in such a way that I couldn't see what was outside. At the base of the desk, the black cat eyed us briefly and then turned its back and sauntered out of sight behind the desk.

"Ah, you're just in time." The witch set her pen down in precise alignment with the middle of the leather-bound journal she'd been writing inside. Just like when I'd seen her at the Consortium, she had an air like she already knew exactly where every piece would move on a chessboard.

She opened a wooden box nearby and drew out a teardrop-shaped vial barely larger than a nail polish bottle. The liquid inside gleamed with light, making the purple glass glisten. "Our spellworkers just dropped this off." She extended it to me, and when I made no move to take it, she gave me a pointed look. "Reneging on our deal would be unwise."

"We are not," Gideon replied. "But we have alterations."

"Nonnegotiable ones," Ulysses added.

Her brow climbed with amused curiosity, but she didn't say a word.

"We are not going to use the spell as you have proposed it," Gideon stated. "We have another solution."

As he relayed our plan to her, a considering look crept into her eyes, and once he finished speaking, there was only silence.

"Will it work?" I asked at last.

"It could." She was back to watching us all as if something amused her, but in a way that she hadn't anticipated.

I wasn't sure what to make of the expression.

Briefly, she looked down at something behind her desk. A heartbeat later, the cat appeared, walking past us and heading out the door.

"Just a moment," Theodora said.

I glanced at the others, not sure what was going on. Seconds crept past, and then the cat returned, leading a tall person with straight dark hair brushing their cheekbones. They didn't look quite masculine or feminine, but instead neither, both, or something else entirely. They wore a long black coat with a stiff collar up around their neck, and their vivid blue-green gaze reminded me of a cat, unblinking and somehow staring straight through me. Their eyes skimmed us before turning to the witch at the desk.

"We're changing the spell, Marin," the witch told them.

In brief terms, Theodora relayed our plan. "I want you to gather the spellworkers for this project again, and tell them we are going to attempt what—"

A rumble went through the wood slats beneath my feet. Screams came from beyond the walls.

Theodora spun, slashing a hand through the air over her window. The blurred glass cleared instantly, giving us a view of the courtyard and the city past its walls.

"Goddess," Marin whispered behind us, aghast.

A crack was breaking across the cavern ceiling, widening with every second.

And rabids were pouring through it.

"The defenses around this building," Asher started. "How—"

I gasped as one of the suns suddenly shuddered and began to fall from the roof. Like a glowing rock, it plummeted toward the city, growing larger as the distance between us and it closed with every second.

"Get away from the window!" Gideon shouted.

Hands grabbed me. Liam. He yanked me to the side as the miniature sun struck and a blinding explosion shook the city. Glass shattered. Liam wrapped himself around me like a shield.

I struggled to break free of his grasp as the blast wave faded, and my eyes went wide when I saw the slices across his cheek and arms. Bits of glass peppered his jacket, sunk deep into the leather with blood seeping around them. "Liam, you—"

He shook his head as if to cut off my words, already looking around for the next threat. Asher, Gideon, and Ulysses were nearby, cuts on their skin too, though it looked like they might have managed to take shelter behind the desk. Shimmering shells of light were fading around both Marin and Theodora, broken glass at their feet but with none inside the spheres.

Force fields. Convenient.

The floor shook again, snapping me back to the moment. Oh my God, the city was under attack.

I pushed to my feet. The other suns hadn't fallen yet, but rabids were still pouring through the break in the cavern ceiling, sweeping down on the people below like ghosts from a nightmare. Screams carried through the air, and howls too, and everywhere I looked, fires were breaking out in the city.

Just like St. Louis. Or Fort Briar.

And my friends were in this... again.

My sword materialized in my fist.

"You must get out of here." Theodora glared at me and the Sentinels alike. "If he gets his hands on her"—she jerked her head at me—"every city Gateway can reach will be in danger."

Liam grabbed my arm, starting for the door.

"What about the spell?" I asked, pulling free.

The witch scoffed. "No time for adjustments." She shoved the vial into my free hand. "Drink it now."

Horror and a whole lot of *hell no* radiated through my connection to the Sentinels. "We'll find another way," Gideon snapped.

"With what time?" The air crackled as the witch glared at us.

Knives appeared in the Sentinels' hands.

"We will *find* another *way*." Gideon bit off the words.

For a heartbeat, no one moved. The screams outside were the only sound.

And they were getting louder.

"Fine," Theodora relented. The electricity in the air vanished like it'd never been. "But get her the hell out of this city." The witch crossed to her desk, yanking open a drawer and pulling out a large gold token. She tossed it to Asher. "Consortium clearance. It will activate whatever gate you can reach."

Asher nodded. "Thank you."

"Go!"

"Follow me," Marin ordered. Turning, they took off, their long black coat waving like a flag behind them from the speed at which they moved. They sliced a hand through the air as we raced after them, and a glowing trail of green light followed. The dark halls around us warped, and even though to my eyes they still looked as if they twisted and turned, same as before, somehow what lay in front of us was always straight ahead.

"What the hell is this?" Ulysses called.

"Shortcut."

A doorway flashed into view, flying open of its own accord, and then suddenly we were outside in a different part of the courtyard than where we'd arrived. Bushes clustered along the log wall surrounding the compound, and there wasn't a single person or animal to be seen. But the smell of smoke and the sound of screams came from the other side of the wall.

"There." Marin pointed at a patch where two bushes didn't quite butt up against one another. The log wall shimmered, and a door appeared. "Beyond that is Quarrel Street. Follow it left and you'll reach Mephistopheles Station."

Asher nodded and headed for the door.

"Stay alive," Marin said to me as I passed, their bright blue-green eyes worried.

I didn't know how to respond. "I'll try."

Their lips compressed. Without another word, they spun and raced back into the massive house.

At the wall, Asher paused, his knife still in his fist. Jerking his chin at Ulysses and Liam, he waited until they'd taken up positions on either side of me with Gideon ahead before he carefully pushed open the door.

My fingers tightened around my sword, my heart pounding in my chest. This was insane. Yes, running made sense. Getting to where Urlfeige couldn't find me made sense.

But leaving Ollie, Emma, their families, and the whole damn city, and just hoping they survived the attack? That was awful. How was I supposed to live with myself if I abandoned them? "Guys, we…"

"Wren, come on." Ulysses took my arm, pulling me with them as Asher slipped past the door.

Knots in my stomach, I followed them outside. "Please, we can't—"

Chaos reigned.

People were running for their lives, their arms full of whatever they could carry. Belongings lay scattered in the street, dropped and left behind by their owners. A child cried in its mother's arms as a family ran past, and somewhere, I heard a little girl screaming for her mommy.

My feet rooted themselves to the stone sidewalk. "We can't abandon them."

Asher's eyes were anguished when he looked back at me.

"We *can't*," I begged. "Not again. Not like St. Louis. Please."

"Protecting you protects the world," Gideon said, his gaze snapping around, searching for threats. "We have to—"

"No! Please. We—"

"Would you truly ask me to leave you, Wren?" Asher cut in. "To save them?"

My mouth moved. What was he saying? "I—"

Shrieking rabids whipped around the corner like smoke come to life. As a unit, the mass of darkness pulled up short.

Somehow, I just knew they were staring at us.

"Go!" Gideon shouted.

We shifted form and took off, racing away as the rabids howled in our wake.

26

ULYSSES

I f we survived this, a cute little cottage in fucking Antarctica was my new life goal.

I slashed through a rabid who tried to catch up to us as we flew along Quarrel Street. There were at least two dozen in that tangle of shadow and smoke, and while I wanted to be happy that at least they weren't attacking the civilians we were flying past, that still meant they were on our tail.

And the gods only knew how long it'd be until one of them split off to go tell Amalie and Urlfeige *right* where we were.

I snarled as one tried to make a break for it like the bastard had read my mind. Twisting in midair, Liam darted after him, the energy of his blade tearing through the vampire. Veering around, he slashed at the others chasing us.

Liam! Wren cried.

Keep going! he shouted back.

Cursing blurred through my mind. We had to get the fuck away from this mess and regain human form. Weapon fire was coming from somewhere to our left, getting closer with every moment. The Consortium's security force had defenses against vampires—against damn near everything, probably—and that didn't even bring into it the other creatures in this city who could kick ass. None of them would be able to tell the difference between us and the rabids if they spotted any of us in shadow form.

We need to shift back, I snapped at the others over the connection between us.

Station's two hundred yards ahead, Asher replied. *Cut right and shift in—*

Rabids rushed over the top of a building ahead like a black tidal wave.

Evade! Gideon shouted.

I grabbed at Wren in shadow form and whipped us both to the side, veering into a gap between two buildings. The rabids who'd been chasing us shot after us both.

A blast of fire ripped down the other end of the alley, heading straight at us.

Wren screamed, yanking us both back and upward as several rabids shot past beneath us. The fire caught the creatures, sending them howling to their deaths, while overhead, a gold dragon beat his wings and whipped his head around, aiming for another blast.

Mordecai. Had to be. There weren't any other gold dragon shifters in the city, far as I knew.

And now the bastard was about to kill us.

Stay close to the building! I told Wren as we fled the alley and darted into the open street.

She did as I said, gluing herself to the stone wall. But we were now back where we'd been. The wave of rabids was flooding along the road to my left, while any who slipped past Liam were howling and shrieking on the right, heading our way.

And that damn dragon was overhead, still searching for a target.

Gods, we were fucked.

Galloping hooves carried from somewhere beyond the turn, and then a dozen centaurs with flamethrowers charged into the intersection ahead. Aiming at the rabids, they opened literal fire, sending torrents of flame spewing out to catch the vampires in midair. Rabids screamed, plummeting onto buildings and the street alike, setting everything around them on fire when they fell.

This is insane! Wren cried.

I couldn't agree more. Also, we were now cut off from the station by a bunch of centaurs wielding a fucking inferno.

We have to get off the street, I sent to the others.

Asher raced toward us, shifting to human form when he reached our side. In the street, Liam was still fighting off rabids, while Gideon was near him in human form again, slashing at attacking vampires while keeping an eye to the dragon in the sky. Maybe he hoped Mordecai would recognize him and not barbecue our asses.

"Head right," Asher ordered. "Stay clear of the market in case the—"

Tentacles of black smoke erupted from beyond the turn, slamming into the centaurs, knocking them down like bowling pins. Their skin began to crackle and lose color, turning to ash as they screamed with pain. Frantically, they tried to flee, only for their legs to crumble into dust beneath them.

Oh, *fuck...*

Amalie strode down the street after the tentacles. Smoke tumbled and churned around the bottom of her black skirt, rolling out into the street where it became the thick cords grabbing any who tried to flee. Rabids flooded the sky around her, still pouring from the crack in the cavern ceiling. They raced at Mordecai, who banked hard and unleashed a blast of fire at them. But he couldn't hit them all, and I watched in horror as the rabids slammed into him, driving him into the ground with a crash that shook the stones beneath me.

Ignoring it all, Amalie scanned the street. Her blood-red lips curled into a smile at the sight of us.

The deadly smoke turned. For a moment it hovered like an amorphous attack dog awaiting its master's command.

"Go!" Asher shouted.

We took off.

In an instant, the smoke raged toward us like an oncoming tsunami, charging down the street and mounting higher and higher until it towered above the buildings. Flooding around and above us, it cut off any hope of retreat, trapping us inside a shell of deadly darkness.

Skidding to a stop, I grabbed Wren, holding her close as the other Sentinels slashed at the smoke, leaving burning trails of light through the darkness like they'd cut a living being.

But it didn't fall back. Instead, the entire wall of clouds shook like it was laughing at us.

Shifting to human form, I spun, searching for any openings. Something. A gods-damned sewer grate would be peachy right now.

No way we were going out like this.

Amalie strode through the smoke, grinning. "It's over."

"Fuck you," I spat.

"That's coming, pet."

Wren shifted back to human form between us and Amalie. Pure rage poured off our woman so strongly, I was amazed the air wasn't on fire. In her fist, she gripped her sword, white radiance shining from it like moonlight gone supernova.

Amalie smirked. "Pretty little toothpick. He's looking forward to destroying that for you."

"You're not coming near them," Wren snarled. "You or that old bastard."

Amalie's brow arched. "Is that so?" She made a sharp gesture.

The walls of smoke flooded toward us.

27

WREN

Smoke hit us like battering rams from all sides, and in an instant, the ground was gone. Pain nearly blinded me, but I wasn't dying. My body wasn't disintegrating.

And I could still feel the Sentinels, even if I couldn't see them. They were hurting too, and it made my body shake from rage. In my fist, my sword blazed, but the light couldn't extend far. Swirling clouds of black smoke surrounded me, carrying me but not burning where they touched me. I had the feeling that we were moving upward—and damn fast.

Worry started to gnaw its way through my anger. Was she taking us toward that crack in the cavern ceiling? Was she going to hurl us into the walls to crush us?

Or, really, was she going to do that just to *me*? Because I'd seen the way she looked at the Sentinels. I didn't need her in my head to know what she planned for them.

I'd kill her before I let her touch those men again, let alone force them to do *anything*.

"Wren!" Ulysses' voice carried through the smoke, muffled and distant.

"I'm here!"

Relief carried through the connection.

"Follow my voice if you can move," Asher called.

I twisted in the smoke, trying to do as he said. I could feel them straining toward me. God only knew where the hell we were, but if we could just find each other in this swirling mess, maybe—

The smoke's grip on me vanished.

I screamed as I plummeted. My sword vanished, and frantically, I tried to shift.

The ground hit hard.

Groaning involuntarily, I pushed up from the hard surface beneath me, my whole body feeling broken. Bright white light glared down on me, making me blink in an effort to get my eyes to focus. I wasn't dead, though. I hurt like hell, but I wasn't dead.

Where was I?

Colors and the white glare resolved. In spite of everything, my brow climbed with my surprise.

A *shopping mall*?

One from hell, anyway.

Rising to my feet and summoning my sword, I scanned the area quickly. White marble tile flecked with gold stretched out around me, and the walls were mostly glass with everything from shoe shops to clothing boutiques inside. But bloody palm prints showed where the rabids had trapped people against the glass, and red smears on the tile made clear where they'd dragged their victims away. The whole space was eerily silent, but the stench of death hung heavy on the motionless air, mingling nauseatingly with the remnants of the perfumes and scented candles from the shops all around. Meanwhile, ficus trees with white lights strung amid their green leaves stood around the open area where I'd been dumped, shimmering brightly in surreal contrast to the destruction.

And to the massive fountain of blood in the middle of it all.

Shivers rolled through me as I spun, clutching the hilt of my sword. I could feel the Sentinels. I couldn't see them, but they were somewhere to my right and angry as hell.

I started toward the department store beyond the fountain.

Footsteps broke the quiet and brought me up short. From the wreckage of a clothing shop, a man strolled out, casually wiping his bloodied hands clean with a shirt he must have plucked from one of the racks, given the tags still hanging from the fabric. The twist of his lips spoke of amusement, none of it good. He wore a suit, the black fabric somehow absorbing the light and not letting any of it back, and when they turned to me, his eyes were red like blood without a single trace of white or iris.

My insides quaked. I didn't need to wonder who he was. Everything in me knew.

Urlfeige.

"You don't look a thing like her," he commented. "I would have expected something of my bloodline to survive her reincarnation."

I lifted the sword.

He chuckled. "Ah, now you do."

Tossing the bloodstained shirt aside, he strolled toward me. I retreated, keeping the blade between us as I backed toward the direction where I could feel the Sentinels. They were coming this way. I just had to buy time.

For what, though? I had one play. Maybe. If it had survived everything else.

Never taking my eyes from him, I dropped my free hand to my pocket. The vial with the witches' spell was still intact.

"I am going to kill you," he said, seemingly ignoring me. "Again. You understand that, don't you? All these centuries, and your own self betrayed you."

A dark laugh came from behind me.

I threw a quick glance over my shoulder. Amalie stood there, grinning.

And the Sentinels were there too. A sphere of wispy black smoke surrounded them, enough to stop them from breaking free though not enough to keep me from seeing them trapped inside. Gags of more black smoke wrapped their mouths and bound their wrists.

They were still fighting to reach me, though. Yanking at their restraints, they tried to breach the walls only to be turned back when it burned them so badly I wanted to sob at their pain.

My heart racing, I drew myself up, determined not to show fear as I attempted to keep both Amalie and Urlfeige in view. "So what is this, then?"

"The end," Urlfeige replied, smiling. His teeth were too white, his mouth dark and red like it was full of blood. "After millennia of rebellion against the way things always were meant to be, yet again you find yourself here. But this time"—he glanced over at Amalie—"even your own reincarnation has understood the truth."

Amalie preened at his words, and for a heartbeat, I couldn't help but stare. Dear God, she didn't see it, did she? He wasn't looking at her like she was his prized daughter. He wasn't even talking about her that way.

He was talking to me. I was Tauluria to him.

What did that make Amalie?

The answer came to me like Tau was whispering in my ear. A tool, same as any of us. Same as *everything* had been since that fateful day when he'd let the empty realms take him and turn him into the first vampire out of some horrific belief it would let him protect his people. But whatever he'd been before—a king, a father—now he was a soulless monster who only saw weapons for his endless quest to turn the world into a kingdom no one would ever overthrow.

One with himself at the top, the immortal ruler of a vampire hell filled with predators and prey, neither of whom had asked for their lives to be taken away.

"He's just using you," I said to Amalie.

She gave me a withering look.

"He doesn't care about you. Just listen! He's talking like you don't even matter!"

Amalie scoffed. "I'm the only one of us who matters."

Ignoring her, Urlfeige strode toward me.

I retreated and yanked the vial from my pocket. "Stop!"

In the smoky sphere, the Sentinels shouted at me. Their words were muffled, but I could feel how they were begging me not to do this.

Urlfeige paused, his brow twitching up. "And what is that, hmm? Some weapon to thwart me? As if I haven't had millennia to prepare for whatever you might try."

I wedged my thumb against the lid of the vial. "It's not for you. It's for me. And if you come any closer, I'll use it."

He smiled and glanced at Amalie.

Like lightning, a tentacle of black smoke cracked out from her, striking my hand. Pain scorched through me, and the vial was ripped away, carried back to her by the smoke.

She smirked as she tucked the glass container into her skirts. "As if I needed any more proof you were pathetic."

I started toward the Sentinels.

"Uh-uh." Smoke rolled out from her, surrounding me like a fence, cutting me off.

"Now," Urlfeige said. "As I was saying, this is the end. You may have briefly stolen your lover's mind back from what he should have been." He nodded toward Ulysses. "But that is only temporary. I am the first. Of all the vampires, I am the most pure. I am what our kind were meant to be. Your foolish corruption cannot mask that truth forever." He walked toward me. "Surrender. See the truth of a world made safe at last."

I gripped my sword tightly. "Go to hell."

He smiled. "Hell was our past. Surely you remember that? Hell was what our people suffered before I found the answer to protect us all. So here's my counteroffer."

The shell of smoke crushed inward around the Sentinels.

Their pain hit me like a punch to my gut. My sword vanished as I doubled over, my vision swimming as the connection between us all screamed with their agony.

The smoke pulled back again.

My body felt like it had been electrocuted, but it was nothing compared to the Sentinels' pain. Shaking all over, I looked for them, and relief made me want to sob for the sheer fact they were still alive.

"Surrender," Urlfeige ordered.

I turned back to him. With his hands clasped calmly before him, he regarded me with a patient expression.

My heart ached. I couldn't do that. I knew what would happen if I gave him what he wanted—and how we'd all die anyway. But what the Sentinels were suffering now...

A strange sense of comfort filtered through the connection. I looked back at them.

As one, they were watching me, a calm sort of resolution in their gazes. Liam lifted his bound hands, fingerspelling what they couldn't say.

See each other again.

Tears burned in my eyes. My head shook. I couldn't lose them.

But the men climbed to their feet, strong and brave and so goddamn unbroken, no matter what anyone tried.

Amalie's eyes flashed between us, settling at last on me with hate burning bright in her gaze. "You little..."

She stalked toward me.

I had my sword between us in an instant, the glowing blade pointing straight at her. "You'll never touch them again."

Rage and contempt twisted her face. Her hands came up, black shadows and mist twisting around them.

Urlfeige made an impatient noise. "Enough of this."

The shell of smoke crushed down on the Sentinels, and the interior of the prison flared bright like electricity filled it. Pain roared through our connection as the energy drove them back to the ground.

And it didn't stop. Magic burned over them, slicing like knives while their backs arched, pain nearly bending them in half.

"Stop!" I cried. "You're killing them!"

He ignored me, watching the Sentinels with a smile.

Amalie's brow twitched down.

I lunged into the smoke, no matter how it burned me. I had to stop him from doing this. "Dammit, don't! Please!"

He turned his smile on me. "You need to be taught a lesson."

The connection shuddered like dying wood on the verge of breaking. I screamed, fighting smoke that burned my skin and gripped my legs like mud, resisting my every step. My sword slashed, but I couldn't cut through it fast enough.

The Sentinels thrashed like they were having seizures. Their life forces were fading from my mind like dying sunsets.

"Father..." Amalie started.

He ignored her.

"This wasn't the plan."

"Nonsense. When this is done, I will make you new toys."

"*What?*"

Tears streamed down my face. I couldn't let this happen. I couldn't lose them. Not now or ever.

Urlfeige studied me. "You see the foolishness of hanging on to this connection you forged? How much easier would it be to surrender to me and—"

A bolt of black smoke struck him.

"The Sentinels are *mine*," Amalie ground out. "Not hers. Not yours. *I* am the one who breaks them, no other."

Urlfeige stared at her. "You dare attack me?"

He turned back toward the cage of smoke around the Sentinels, and the air crackled with the energy building inside it.

"No!" Amalie charged at him.

His hand flung out. A spear of dark magic lanced through the air, striking her in the center of her chest.

Her eyes flew wide, and she stumbled back. The smoke around me vanished as ink-black poison spread across her chest, rushing over her shoulders and out along her arms.

It was the spell she'd used on me, I realized. The one to drain me of what he needed to control all the dormant vampires. But the spell had been his power, not hers, all along.

And without the Sentinels and Friday to save her, the destruction was moving at lightning speed.

"You..." Her hands grasped at the spear, yanking on it, but it only made her fingers begin to turn to ash. Horrified, she stared at her disintegrating hands and then looked up at him. "Why would you..."

He scoffed, returning his attention to the Sentinels, who were trying to climb to their feet again.

Amalie's gaze turned to me, pain so clear on her face, but an almost childlike confusion in her expression too. "But I'm what he always wanted me to be."

The black ink climbed up her throat, and she cried out as she crashed to her knees. Smoke erupted from her chest around the spear, rushing back toward Urlfeige.

Draining her.

"Now, daughter," Urlfeige said to me, ignoring Amalie as the power poured into him. "What will it be? The destruction of your pets or your surrender?"

A ragged sound left Amalie. The spell was climbing up

across her face now. Her body was beginning to crumble like her hands. But her lips curled back into a savage smile at Urlfeige. "As *my* pets would say," she rasped. "Fuck you, Father."

I could read her expression, and I dove for shelter as suddenly her body exploded into a blast wave of magic. Crashing to the tile behind a planter, I cringed in on myself as the power scorched through the air, setting the ficus above me ablaze and turning the shop windows into nothing but ballistic shards of glass.

The magic faded. The crackle of burning wood became the only sound.

I pulled my head from the shelter of my arms.

On the floor beside me, the tiny magic vial glinted.

I blinked. Of all the places for it to land...

My hand shook as I picked it up. Unsteadily, I sat up and peered over the edge of the planter, afraid of what I'd find.

Amalie was gone, only scorch marks remaining where she'd been. The shell of smoke around the Sentinels had disappeared too.

I stared at where they lay, fumbling after the connection in my mind. They were alive. I could still feel them.

A sob escaped me. Their pain pulsed through the connection between us, but the agony was fading. With a grunt of effort, Asher pushed away from the ground, Liam doing the same, while Ulysses helped Gideon upright.

Their eyes found my own. I couldn't tell whose relief was whose, theirs or mine, it was so strong. Together, they hurried toward me.

But where was Urlfeige?

I climbed to my feet too, looking around. I couldn't see him.

Had she destroyed him?

A shuddering breath left me. Nothing but burning trees and

smoldering shops surrounded us. Destruction she would have loved, sure, but had Amalie actually—

Urlfeige was directly in front of me when I turned back.

His hand wrapped my throat, driving me backward until I slammed into the wall. The Sentinels shouted, running to reach me, but at a sharp gesture from Urlfeige, a wall of magic roared up, cutting both of us off from the men.

Burns scored Urlfeige's face, the wounds charred and dripping blood, and his red gaze locked on me. "Very well. If you won't submit, daughter... I'll burn it out of you."

He released my throat and stepped back, his arms lifting. The air hummed like I was standing in a power station on overload, and the energy made the hairs on my arms rise.

"I only needed your magic. Never your life."

Beyond the shimmering wall, I could see the Sentinels fighting to reach me, their blades slashing at the shield but not damaging it enough to let them through.

Urlfeige chuckled at my expression. "Say your goodbyes, daughter."

The magic in the air grew stronger, and horror gripped me. I was out of time. Out of options. He'd had thousands upon thousands of years to prepare for this.

And I only had one move left.

Cold resolution rose inside me. "Like Amalie said..." Meeting his blood-red gaze, I took the vial from my pocket. "Fuck you."

I ripped off the lid and swallowed the contents whole.

28

WREN

I was breaking…

Glass shards. Eggshells. Fragments of life so delicate, they'd never survive the light of day. All of it shattered.

All of it was me. Alone on a terrain of black rock and even darker sky, I stood. The ground was arid and cracked like a desert that hadn't seen the sun in a thousand years. There was no moon. No stars.

There was only the hungry dark and the breaking.

"What are you doing?"

I knew that voice. Father. No, Urlfeige…

It didn't matter.

I wrapped my arms around my middle, huddling against the darkness. I'd never survive this. I couldn't. There was so much more to the connection than I'd ever imagined, and now…

A rumble carried through the shattering wastelands of my mind, and fear spiked through me. He was coming.

"You little fool."

Terror built higher. This shouldn't be happening. He'd

never reached Tau in her mind. Not like this. And I'd burned him out when he tried with me.

But I'd made a mistake. I'd missed something when I trusted the witches. Something vital. Deep inside, I suddenly *knew* I had, and yet whatever it was slipped like smoke between my fingers, as fleeting as a dream you couldn't remember upon waking. I couldn't grasp it.

"You thought to shatter your strength to spare them? As if mere magic could change what you are down to your very core?" He laughed. "Your paltry spell won't save anyone. Fracturing that link only gives me an opening into your mind... and damns you."

The darkness drew down like a predator who'd cornered its tiny prey.

"All that is vampire in you is because of me."

Dark magic rushed at me from all sides, and there was nowhere to hide. Pouring into me, through me, it blasted away the terrain beneath my feet until only *it* was left. Fangs and blood-soaked teeth. A heart that only beat to tell me how long until I needed to feed again. Breath that only existed to detect the scent of my prey.

And everything I'd been was nothing in the face of that. A single spark already dying under the crushing emptiness that had to win in the end.

Because it already had. It *always* had.

For protection...

Confusion flickered in me. What?

"And what else is there?" His voice rang in my mind. "An angelic power you gave up for nothing? A twisted former incarnation who tried to drag some of that power back? A *human* whose only purpose was to die?"

His voice drew in closer. "Perhaps you'd prefer death."

Fangs that fell from my mouth. Crushing hunger. A body decaying because it was already dead.

I screamed.

"Half angel. Half vampire. Now... nothing."

Because we were never safe...

My vision swirled, the darkness striating enough to give me a glimpse of his face. My father... no, not that... but...

Memories filtered back, fragmented like torn pieces of snapshots. Ulysses. I'd seen him inside what Urlfeige tried to do. I'd felt him, deep inside, past all the darkness and clinging to life. Even in the shadows, even surrounded by endless darkness, truth persisted. *Life* persisted.

A world for us all...

But I couldn't feel anyone anymore. The spell had shattered my connections to the others for the safety of everyone.

Safety of everyone...

Except... one. The original.

The one who'd just invaded my mind, building more of a connection between us than ever before.

Through the striated darkness, I looked out at the monster that was Urlfeige, pieces falling into place inside my mind. Amalie wasn't the only one who'd misunderstood everything. But then, she'd never listened to Tauluria. She'd never really paid attention to the princess's memories or even sought to restore all of what we'd truly been in that past life.

Warrior princess. The first of our *own* kind.

And the daughter of Urlfeige as he'd once been, before the blood and the death. A man who'd given up his humanity millennia ago, all in a desperate attempt to save the ones he loved.

A tiny quiver moved through me, like the world's thinnest guitar string resonating a single note, one filled with longing and pain and so much need it had once carried past the barriers of reality itself into the depths of the empty realms. And it wasn't from me. No, it was from him, and without even questioning, I strained toward the sound, following a connection *he'd* forged between us the moment he thought he'd take my mind.

Darkness rushed around me. Through me, burning everything in me away just as it had burned everything of the man Urlfeige had been, once upon a time.

Everything except for one *true* thing, deep in his core.

The oh-so-human need that started all this.

A tiny star shone ahead of me, growing closer and closer.

The darkness fell away.

I stood in a white space, everything utterly colorless. Shapes around me suggested stone slabs covered the floor. Pieces of pillars hovered in midair, holding up a ceiling that didn't seem to be there. A sconce hung where there should have been a wall, but only endlessness remained.

And at its center was a throne.

The old man seated on it lifted his head. His hair was gray and gnarled. His face was weathered and pitted with age.

The ancient human king down at the heart of it all.

Urlfeige narrowed his bleary eyes at me, confusion in his gaze. "Who are you?"

A shuddering breath left me. I barely remembered the answer to that question. But then his confusion faltered.

"Tauluria?" Joy suffused his face. "Oh, my Tau."

The old king tried to stand, but his legs gave out beneath him. Regret touched his expression. "So hard to..."

His gaze strayed around, and where it touched, walls and tapestries shimmered into being while scenes played out across surfaces like ghosts. His gray hair changed, becoming dark, and his wrinkles faded, returning the face I'd seen in Tau's lifetime. The man who had been her father before he left to find someone to help him protect his kingdom.

Like a memory.

All of it was. But I wasn't Tau, and when I looked at the

walls, images shifted and moved for me of the world *I* remembered. The Sentinels. My family. Friends.

And towns burning.

Urlfeige made a pained noise, turning away, and the walls vanished, taking all the images with them. His gray hair and aged face returned. "What are you doing here? You didn't go with me when I..." His brow furrowed. "When I went out to find..." The confusion faded, shifting into anger, and his younger, dark-haired self returned. "I'm going to stop them. All the bastards attacking our home. I'll make this world safe for us, Tau. I promise."

An ache moved through me. In my past life, this was all Tau had ever wanted, really. Beyond her anger. Beyond her hatred of the man who'd taken her life not once but twice was a simple longing she'd never been able to fulfill.

The desire to speak and maybe, just *maybe,* have her father hear her.

I stepped closer. "But you're not saving anyone."

"No. No, I..." His face flickered between old and younger. "I am. I know I am. We're all going to be safe now. Forever."

"But that's not what you did. Or what you're doing."

The younger man's brow drew down again. "No. I—"

I reached up, taking his hand on the armrest of his throne as the old man returned. "You wanted to keep us safe. To make a world where no one could hurt us."

Urlfeige nodded fervently. "I will. I—"

"You didn't."

He stared at me, rheumy eyes searching mine.

"You saw those memories," I said. "My memories."

His head shook. "War. I will stop that for you. For us. No one will ever—"

"Look again."

He froze.

"Please." I swallowed hard. "For your daughter. For every-

one's daughters and sons and the whole damn world. Please..."
His own words came back to me from the life I'd left behind in
the ruins of a shopping mall. "See the truth of the world you
thought you were making safe."

Fear flickered through his eyes, though his gaze never left
mine.

"Please," I whispered. "For her."

Trembling, his hand lifted and took my cheek.

Images flared to life all around us, vibrant with color and
overwhelming with sound. The dormants in Fort Briar,
pleading for him to stop and retreating from me while their
minds were taken. Ulysses and his agony and shame at what
he'd been forced to do. The rabids who'd once been dormants,
now turned into blood-soaked monsters.

Crying out, the king recoiled from me, his hand falling from
my cheek.

"Those are the people you made. The vampires. And that's
what you're doing to them. *That's* your world."

Urlfeige's head shook. "No, we... I... I'm making everything
better than it..."

Tremulous hope filled me at the confused horror in his
eyes. "Look again."

His gaze flashed up to mine, baffled.

I reached out, catching his hand. "Look. Again." I put his
palm to my cheek. "See what you're taking."

Color and sound surged into being. Images from my
memory played across the walls again. The dormants I'd met,
back before he stole their minds. My town before rabids
destroyed it.

And the Sentinels with their kind smiles and promises of a
life beyond this nightmare.

His hand fell away again, and for a long moment, he only
stared at the walls as the images gradually faded. "You're not
my Tauluria."

I hesitated.

"But you..." His brow twitched down. "You gave it all up. Both of you. You had to sacrifice everything... because of me."

An ache throbbed inside me all over again, and he turned back as if picking up on it somehow. Grief touched his eyes. "You're not her."

I shook my head.

"But you were," he continued, his voice growing stronger. "And maybe that's enough."

Confusion rose in me, but I had no chance to ask. A rumble carried through the floor, and I froze, fear spiking in me. Through the hovering pillars, cracks spread. Chunks of white stone fell from the nonexistent ceiling.

But he only smiled as light began to radiate from him.

"If any remnant of my daughter remains in you, tell her I'm sorry." The blinding light grew, engulfing me, pouring into me until I felt like it filled everything inside. "And that she was right."

The bright world exploded out into the darkness.

***

I opened my eyes.

In the destroyed shopping mall, Urlfeige still stood in front of me, his blood-red eyes locked on me and his arms outstretched. His shield of magic hovered in the air around us, separating me from the Sentinels who were slashing at the defense and shouting my name.

But horror and confusion filled Urlfeige's face. "What..." His head shook as his skin began to glow. "The empty realms. The link." His red eyes widened, blood leaking down his cheeks like tears. "What have you done?"

I let the vial fall. "Reminded you of that truth you're so fond of talking about."

He lunged toward me only to stagger to a stop as the glow from his skin became brighter. The horror in his expression grew. His body started to shake. "No..."

Throwing his head back, he howled as his body erupted into light that exploded like a supernova. The blast buffeted me, pressing me back against the wall again, but none of it hurt.

And when I lowered my arm, blinking against the glare, nothing of him remained.

Air left me, shaky and raw, like I'd found myself on the other side of a threshold I'd never been sure I would make it across. Millenia ago, I'd died trying to destroy him, and it hadn't worked. But this was different. I felt it. I *knew* it.

This time, Urlfeige was really, truly gone.

"Wren!"

Hands grabbed me. Asher, with Ulysses right there too, and Gideon and Liam right behind. They tugged me to them, hugging me so tightly it was a good thing I didn't really need to breathe.

Except... they weren't in my mind like they had been.

I straightened, looking around at them all. I couldn't feel them, not like I had. Maybe a whisper? I didn't exactly feel alone in my own mind like I'd been for all the years before I met them.

But it wasn't the same. Not even close, and that ached.

God, how that ached.

"We'll figure it out," Asher promised like he was reading my expression. "The important thing is, you're alive."

"But—"

"We don't need that to be with you, baby," Ulysses said, cupping my cheek like he couldn't believe I was really here.

"And surely, the answer is in a book *somewhere*," Gideon promised with a smile.

Liam nodded. *We have time. That's all that matters.*

I trembled. I wanted to believe them, but I felt so strange.

Like I'd missed something... a detail I should have known...

My brow furrowed. What had he said?

You thought to shatter your strength to spare them? As if mere magic could change what you are down to your very core?

But I'd felt the spell shatter everything. The magic inside me cracked and flew apart.

Except... then there'd been Urlfeige. One last connection, formed when he barreled into my mind to destroy me.

The old man's smiling face floated back up in my mind's eye.

And maybe that's enough.

The strangely-alone-but-not feeling flickered through me again.

I stepped back from the Sentinels.

"What is it?" Asher asked, worry tinging his eyes.

I shook my head. But this time, I didn't let grief keep me away from that strange sense in my mind. Closing my eyes, I stretched toward it instead.

Lights glimmered on the horizon of my mind. But not like the glow of the Sentinels.

Stars. Thousands of them.

Vampires.

My eyes flew open. Oh my God.

It wasn't possible. I'd never felt whatever it was in me that Urlfeige had used to turn the dormants rabid. That power that let Tauluria create dormants—entirely by accident—wasn't under my control.

But it'd still been inside me. Urlfeige had still connected to it.

And maybe that's enough.

I looked back at the Sentinels. We'd recreated the bond between us, even when I didn't believe for one second that I was really a vampire. We'd strengthened it despite Urlfeige trying to take the guys' powers from them. I'd given up so much millennia ago as Tauluria—my protection from the sun, my weapon and defenses—but we'd gotten it all back again because, at our cores, we were who we were, and the Sentinels had always been a part of me, same as I was a part of them.

And now...

"Bite me," I whispered.

Alarm showed on the face of every man around me.

"Wren," Asher protested, "you just survived—"

"Please."

The men shared a wary look.

Ulysses stepped forward. "If you're sure?"

I nodded. He lifted my wrist to his lips, his fangs slipping down. A short gasp left me as his teeth sank into my arm.

And light spread through my mind.

"Holy shit," he whispered, pulling back.

I grinned. Nothing broke us. Not witches' magic. Not vampires from centuries and millennia ago. The bond was a choice.

And nothing could take away who we were at our core.

Extending my wrists to the others, I closed my eyes, reveling in the flood of my connection to them returning when they bit down, and with my whole heart and soul, I willed it to grow stronger. To be like it'd been.

For us to be us.

And for all the vampires to be free.

The Sentinels were staring at me when I opened my eyes again.

"How is this possible?" Asher asked.

"Magic can't change who we are at our heart." My gaze skirted across the tiles while in my mind, I could feel all the others out there. Back now. Not rabid, and it brought tears to my eyes. "And I think Urlfeige gave me the other part of the ability he was using to connect to the vampires. His half. The one that let him turn them rabid... so I could stop that."

Baffled looks met my words.

They only faded slightly when I finished trying to explain.

"So..." Ulysses started. "Urlfeige... I mean, the *original* Urlfeige guy, from way back when, was... what?"

"Down inside his mind, like you were in your own, only not as a prisoner. Just... lost. But once that fragment of Urlfeige understood what was *actually* happening, he broke the connection to the empty realms." I hesitated. "Theodora said no one could, but I don't think anyone thought *he* would. And that's what destroyed him." I bit my lip briefly. "But he intended it to. And for me to have a way to help the others as well."

"So what does that mean for you?" Asher asked.

My mouth moved, searching for an answer.

"Queen," Gideon murmured.

My head shook immediately. "No. No way."

"Protector, then," Asher amended. "But not alone."

Liam reached out, taking my hand and squeezing it encouragingly, his love flowing to me through the bond between us.

I didn't know what to say.

"Well," Ulysses said, a grin hovering around his lips. "Regardless. What do you all say we get out of here? Malls give me the creeps."

I laughed.

EPILOGUE
WREN

Three weeks later

"I'm *fine*, I swear."

Seated behind her large desk in her office, Doctor Sissoko met my protest with a smile. "The Consortium just wants to make sure the queen is—"

Her smile broadened when I made a furious noise at the title. Clicking her pen off and tucking it into a drawer with her notebook, she said, "How about we're doing these weekly checkups for your guys' peace of mind then?"

I rose from the chair on the other side of her desk, debating whether to tell her the Sentinels had checked me over a number of times in the past few weeks. *Thoroughly.*

"See you next Monday, then?" she asked.

My exasperated look returned. Her brow rose.

"Okay, fine," I relented.

She smiled.

I managed a smile in response as I headed for the office

door. It wasn't her fault, I knew. And honestly, I didn't mind the chance to make sure *she* was okay. Yes, I had an awareness of being connected to the vampires now, and I was still getting used to that. Yes, it let me know she and the others who'd been turned at the sight of me were still alive, still okay—as much as they could be after all they'd been through. And no, that connection wasn't the same as with the Sentinels. Something in me suspected it never would be, given that what the guys and I shared stretched back for lifetimes. But a psychic link wasn't the same as actually *talking* to the vampires. Listening to them. Making sure they were recovering all right from everything they'd been through.

Ulysses told me my concern for them was a sign I was a good queen. I told him he was full of shit.

It always made him laugh.

I stepped into the hall, and a gray-haired woman slammed to a halt at the sight of me. Blanching, she bobbed her head and squeaked out, "Ma'am," before scurrying away.

"How many times do I have to tell them..."

Doctor Sissoko chuckled. "Considering we all have you to thank for the fact even the *rabids* aren't rabid anymore, let alone any of us? I'd say it's going to take a few more." She grinned as Asher and Liam rose from the chairs in the waiting room.

"Next week, then?" Asher asked.

I glared. "Bite me."

His brow rose. Pulling me close to his side, he whispered in my ear, "Yes, please."

Heat rushed up my cheeks at the dark promise in his voice, along with a fair amount of embarrassment at the fact we stood in the middle of the makeshift clinic. My eyes skirted around, but all the nurses and staff were suddenly looking elsewhere.

I murmured a goodbye to the doctor and then retreated down the hall, Asher and Liam at my side. "So what now?" I asked, trying for a light tone despite how my cheeks still felt like they were burning. The dormants wouldn't pick up anything from me—we'd tested that *right* away—but that didn't mean they wouldn't notice how uncomfortable I looked and think they needed to do something to help. "Consortium want to interrogate us again? GSS have another meeting for us to attend?"

Asher chuckled. "No, we thought maybe we'd head home for a bit first."

A breath of relief left me. *Home.* I loved that word and what it meant for us all now. Not to mention it seemed like an eternity since we'd had a moment's peace. If we weren't meeting with Mordecai, Theodora, and the rest of the Consortium amid the rebuilding of Gateway City to discuss—aka argue about—how to handle vampires returning to supernatural society after everything that had happened, we were having those same discussions with the GSS about all the dormants and newly turned vampires who needed a pathway to return to their regular lives.

When it came to the human world, there were only so many options available. Most of the vampires who'd been dormants before all this were relocating under new identities to wait out the next few decades until maybe, *hopefully*, the rumor mill surrounding the events of St. Louis and Fort Briar died down. The ones who'd been turned in the attacks were either trying to find ways to go back to their lives—with a lot of help from other vampires—or were moving away too. Meanwhile, the former rabids were a divided lot, some of the older ones seeming almost scared to enter modern society, while others were like wide-eyed children with their desire to explore all they'd missed of "normal" life as vampires. A number of dormants had formed support groups to help them, though the guys and I still stopped by to make sure they were doing okay too.

It was a whole new world for us, even if lots of humanity

still believed everything that happened was all a hoax—and we were happy to let it stay that way.

But the countless meetings and arguments were only part of what took up our time. The vampires and the Consortium alike seemed determined to make sure I wasn't going to turn into a megalomaniacal lunatic—or fall victim to one—which meant countless checkups by the doctor or examinations by Theodora's protégé, Marin. The solemn witch had taken some getting used to, but they were gradually warming up to me and vice versa. I was pretty sure I'd even seen them crack a smile the other day. And true, I still wished Eden could have been the one to determine if there were any lingering aftereffects of the witches' spell, but the woman would only say she was sorry, she couldn't come, and that was all. It worried me, but then, she'd also finally promised that—if she really needed help—she'd call.

Sunlight glared in my eyes as we left behind the double layers of security doors that separated the outside world from the interior of the brick building that currently housed the clinic. The underground complex was unsalvageable, but a week ago, ground had been broken on a new installation about thirty miles outside Fort Briar.

Everywhere, people were rebuilding. In the case of St. Louis and my hometown, the reconstruction was taking place with the help of mysteriously generous federal grant programs that came with the stipulation—and a hefty dose of threat—that no one discussed vampires or what had actually happened there.

Most people actually seemed to be going along with it, if not for the money, then because the truth would only make them look insane. Some folks still wanted to spread the real story, though, and warn the world that vampires were real. The Sentinels told me that, in years past, the GSS would have simply made sure those people were locked up in institutions, never to see the light of day again. But Valerie and Tammy were making good on their promises to create a different GSS than had come before. With Brayden's help, they'd formulated a plan to replenish the ranks of the GSS with the survivors, giving those people a way to protect humanity and maybe see a different side of the supernatural world than the violent introduction they'd had.

After lots of counseling, anyway.

Asher swung a leg over his motorcycle and waited for me to climb on behind him while Liam got on his own bike. They'd promised to teach me how to ride as soon as we all had a spare moment—so, probably sometime next century at this rate—but in the meantime, I found I loved wrapping my arms around one of the guys and riding this way too.

The town flew past as the guys drove along, heading for the manor's new location about twenty miles outside the Fort Briar city limits. There'd been a little bit of debate about moving elsewhere, but not much. The guys—Ulysses especially—wanted me to be able see my parents and sister whenever I wished.

And Mom, Dad, and Harper were back in Fort Briar now. They seemed to be settling in okay, all things considered. Some of Mom's cops had survived after all, albeit barely in a few cases, and gradually the police department was trying to rebuild. Dad was helping in between his own work hours, filling in for office staff and generally keeping Mom's spirits up, and Harper was doing the same.

My sister and I hadn't discussed much of what'd changed about us both, but from what Friday told me, Harper might be the only angel—or even *half* angel—left on earth, though the demon had been vague on details as to why. I'd tried to talk to Harper about it, to support her however I could, but she didn't seem to want to think about that. Instead, she'd thrown herself back into "normal" life like she was determined that the only supernatural things in her world would be me, the guys, and

Friday and Barnaby. These days, if she wasn't helping Mom with the police department, she was volunteering with her sorority and making plans to head back to college when it started up again next year.

I understood it. *God*, I understood it, considering how I'd been when people first told me I was a vampire.

I just hated the idea of her being alone.

I'd be with her at school, though. Gideon insisted I finish out my degree, vampire "queen" or not. I'd argued—God knew we all had a lot to do—but not for long. Truth be told, I sort of missed the normalcy of college, too, even if it'd be weird going back after all this.

At least Ollie and Emma would be returning. Brayden too, though I suspected he planned to keep working with the GSS as well. I was under no illusions that any of us were the same people we had been a few months and an eternity ago when we'd all hung out at a bonfire party by the river. We knew what was out there now.

But I hoped we'd be okay.

The rumble of the motorcycles cut off as we finally pulled into the vast grassy lot around the manor. The old farmhouse look was gone, replaced by the decaying exterior of a rotting bungalow, complete with a broken swing lying in pieces beneath rusting chains dangling from the sagging porch roof. An even smaller bungalow waited about fifty yards off, stained with mold and nearly swallowed by bushes—home to the demons now "to give the boys and I privacy"—though I knew from visiting the spacious house inside that every inch of its rotting exterior was just as much of an illusion as the manor's was. While we walked away from the bikes, a black cat disappeared through a gap in the crisscross fencing around the base of the smaller house. I'd asked Friday once if the animals were real and, if they were, what they'd find under houses that sort of didn't exist.

The demon only smiled and hadn't said a word.

"Oh, by the way, your parents asked if we could stop by for a visit this evening," Asher commented while we climbed the steps to the rotting wood door.

"They asked you? Why didn't they call me?"

He shrugged.

My eyes narrowed. He was keeping his emotions tamped down, which wasn't exactly odd these past few weeks. All the guys were trying to give me space to adjust to having the whole vampire world floating around like stars in the sky inside my mind. "Did my parents say what's going on? Why do they want to see us?"

He didn't respond, pushing open the door.

"Asher." I followed him inside, the decaying interior of the bungalow vanishing as I did.

And I stopped. "What the..."

A multitude of flowers filled the wide hallway. Garlands in every color of the rainbow draped across the ceiling, while arrangements spilled over the edges of vases on the walls. Petals were scattered across the polished wood floor until they formed a multicolor carpet as thick as the dark-blue runner beneath my feet.

I turned to Asher and Liam. "What is this?"

The two men were watching me, something almost worried in their eyes, but at whatever they saw in my face, they seemed reassured. *This way,* Liam signed.

They led me to the study. Gideon and Ulysses were inside, standing by the bright flames of the fireplace like they'd been waiting for us, and they flashed tense grins as Asher and Liam walked over to join them.

I looked between them all. "Guys, seriously."

We wanted to give you a surprise, Liam signed.

"And depending on how it goes," Asher added, that worry creeping back like maybe he didn't know how I was going to react, "your parents wanted us to come by later to celebrate... or whatever you need."

My brow twitched down. "Okay..."

The Sentinels glanced at each other, and then on some unspoken signal, Ulysses stepped forward. His hands were behind his back.

"Guys, what—"

They each got down on one knee, and my words dried up as Ulysses pulled a small box from behind his back.

"We were trying to figure out where to do this," Asher said. "Here or elsewhere. But we thought perhaps it'd be nice to make some good memories at home."

"Better ones than how we first met," Gideon added with a hint of chagrin.

Ulysses nodded insistently.

I shook my head, tears in my eyes. "No, this is... great. Perfect."

God, I couldn't find words.

"Plus, we never know what's going to happen next," Ulysses added. "So none of us want to wait any longer."

A choked laugh left me, but it dried up as he opened the box, revealing the ring inside. A diamond glistened in the center, flanked on either side by rubies, one for each of the Sentinels.

"A ring is not really a vampire custom," Gideon explained. "But we thought you'd appreciate the human one."

My mouth moved. "I..."

"When vampires promise themselves to each other," Asher said, "it's for eternity. It's through anything, *for* anything. To be a family."

"Or have them... if they can," Ulysses added, and my heart swelled at the hope in his tight voice.

I nodded fervently, trying to communicate how someday I wanted that too.

"So we're asking you to be that with us, Wren," Asher said. "To marry us and be ours through good and bad and everything in between."

Ulysses held up the ring box. "Forever."

"Forever," Gideon echoed.

Liam nodded. *Forever*.

"So what do you say?" Ulysses asked.

I stared at them, these men who'd come into my life so impossibly, who'd been more amazing than I ever could have imagined, and who meant the world to me. Now and...

I smiled. "Forever."

***

Not ready to say goodbye to Wren and the Sentinels? Join my mailing list at sierrarowan.com for an exclusive bonus scene of Wren and guys' first Christmas!

Want more reverse harem vampire romance? When Snow White narrowly escaped death at the hands of her evil vampire stepmother, she never imagined meeting seven sexy men who'd do anything to keep her safe. But can any of them survive the curse that's coming for her? Of Snow So White is coming soon!

Eden's and Harper's stories are on their way! Subscribe now to be the first to hear about these new series!

ABOUT THE AUTHOR

Sierra Rowan is the author of action-packed reverse harem paranormal romance and urban fantasy novels. They love to write stories filled with steam, heart, and adventure where a happily-ever-after is guaranteed, even if it takes a few magical battles and car chases to get there.

Get updates about all of Sierra's books at sierrarowan.com.

- amazon.com/author/sierrarowan
- bookbub.com/authors/sierra-rowan
- goodreads.com/sierrarowan
- facebook.com/authorsierrarowan
- twitter.com/SierraRowanBook
- instagram.com/authorsierrarowan
- tiktok.com/@sierrarowanbooks